W9-BAK-091

VOLUME II/SPRING 1985

EDITORS IN CHIEF

Jerry Pournelle   Jim Baen

MANAGING EDITOR   SENIOR EDITOR

John F. Carr   Elizabeth Mitchell

ART EDITOR

Terri Czeczko

BAEN
science fiction
BOOKS

FAR FRONTIERS
Summer 1985

This is in part a work of fiction. All the characters and events
portrayed in this book are fictional, and any resemblance to
real people or incidents is purely coincidental.

A Baen Book

Baen Enterprises
8-10 W. 36th Street
New York, N.Y. 10018

First printing, April 1985

ISBN: 0-671-55954-0

Cover art by Michael Carroll. Interior art by Janet Aulisio,
Vincent DiFate, Arthur George, Val Lakey Lindahn, Judy
Mitchell, and J.K. Potter

Printed in the United States of America

Distributed by
SIMON & SCHUSTER
MASS MERCHANDISE SALES COMPANY
1230 Avenue of the Americas
New York, N.Y. 10020

CONTENTS

FICTION

Novellas

Short Stories

SPECULATIVE FACT

BOOK REVIEWS

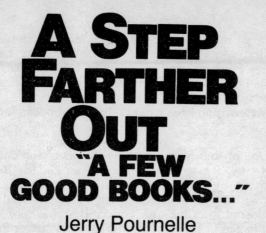

A STEP FARTHER OUT
"A FEW GOOD BOOKS..."

Jerry Pournelle

I used to do this column monthly. Friends and colleagues asked how I found enough to write about, and I would just smile. So much was happening in the world; the problem was to be sufficiently selective. After *Destinies* vanished, I still did a bi-monthly column for *Analog*.

The column—*this* column—is only quarterly now, but it's not quite so easy. I understand why. I already do two computer columns each month (one each for *Byte* and *Popular Computing*). My contract with McGraw-Hill forbids me to write a computer column for any competing magazine, even one I edit; and since a great deal of the time I used to spend mucking about with general science is now spent playing with small computers, I have less non-computer information to work from. Meanwhile, I am Chairman of the Citizen's Advisory Council on National Space Policy, so that what time I have left from computers tends to be devoted to space. Willy-nilly, my horizons have been narrowed.

I intend to remedy that. Now that *Footfall* and some of my other work is finished, I should have time to return to the life of a scientific dilettante. (Dilettante and bard; Poul Anderson once called science fiction writers "bards of the sciences," an idea I liked so much that now my license plate reads "SCI BARD.")

Meanwhile, I have read a few good books lately.

Open or Shut?

One of the most influential books of the decade is *Godel, Escher, Bach: An Eternal Golden Braid*. Written by Douglas Hofstadter, a previously unknown assistant professor (not even tenured!) of philosophy at Indiana University, the book was published in 1979; it instantly won a Pulitzer Prize, was acclaimed by most of the scientific establishment, and moved Hofstadter into the intellectual limelight. It also caught the imagination of a large part of the student population, particularly those in computer sciences.

Anyone wishing to understand the intellectuals of the next generation had better read that book several times over. You may not care for it—if you are over forty years old, you probably won't—and if you've been brought up on linear thinking you'll have problems understanding it; but it's worth your effort and then some. Hofstadter doesn't settle many questions, but he has a fresh approach to some of the most perplexing problems of human intellectual history. What can we know? And how can we be sure that what we "know" is true?

Among other issues, he addresses the central matters of computer science: in particular the problem of "Artificial Intelligence" and "can machines have free will? For that matter, do we?"

What Godel (a mathematician), Escher (a very unusual artist), and Bach (a musician) have in common besides a lot of talent is a regard for, and use of, *recursion*. In computer science, a recursive program is one that calls itself as a subroutine. This is not only possible, but in computer languages like LISP (the favorite programming language of the artificial intelligence community) recursion is both common and indispensable.

One of John von Neumann's chief contributions to computer history was the notion of the "stored program": the computer program could be put into the machine's memory in exactly the same way that data could be kept there; indeed, program items could be manipulated like data. John McCarthy's LISP computer language carries this even further: a LISP program is pretty well indistinguishable from the data it operates on, so that LISP programs can not only be recursive, but can recursively modify themselves with little difficulty.

Kurt Godel's model of a rotating universe allowed an even more interesting form of recursion: in theory, a traveler could follow a path through time and space which returned to the exact starting point—in both time and space. This disturbs some theorists, although practical application is likely to be difficult. To take advantage of a Godel path we would first need to find the proper path in the real universe, and secondly construct a vehicle. Following a Godel path involves no logical contradictions, but it has not been shown to be actually possible.

In the world of mathematics Godel is best known for his Theorem: in any self-consistent theory of numbers, there will be propositions which can be neither proved nor disproved without going outside the theory. In other words—there are no closed mathematical systems. If you want to know who shaves the Spanish barber (who by definition shaves all and only those who do not shave themselves) you'll just have to follow him around and see.

Hofstadter tackles all this and more. His book is not only influential, it deserves to be.

Recursion and Life

There have been numerous studies of the rather profound implications of recursion. One of the most interesting—and readable—is *The Recursive Universe* (Wm. Morrow & Co., 1984) by William Poundstone. Poundstone's book is a lot easier to read than Hofstadter's; it won't be as influential, and those who like it won't like it as much as Hofstadter's fans adore *his* book; but it tackles questions no less profound.

Is the universe closed? Not merely "closed" in the physical sense. If the universe is closed in the physical sense, then eventually all the stars and planets and other matter will stop flying apart and come back together, and we will, presumably, have another Big Bang to begin the whole mess all over again. That's important enough; but still less important than philosophical closure.

Can we understand the universe?

Can we, from some number of first principles, deduce everything else? Recognizing that the burden of actual calculation may be too great, is it possible, *in principle*, to describe mathematically everything that can and will happen?

After all, although physics is still a bit messy, the number of special constructs is diminishing, while the scope of physics theory has expanded to include the *very* early (10^{-43} seconds after the Big Bang) universe, the formation of galaxies, and other such matters in addition to particle mechanics. We have Grand Unified Theories (GUTs) which combine all the forces except gravity; as well as the "standard model" of quantum mechanics.

The standard model will explain all known experiments. True, it is messy. It has some 19 parameters which must be put in by hand, so to speak. It doesn't explain why, for example, the number 10^{40} keeps cropping up, or why the electron masses what it does, or why the speed of light is what it is, or why the universal constant of gravitation is what we observe it to be, or why gravity is so much weaker than the electro-magnetic force. It doesn't even relate those basic quantities to any other quantities. Still in all, the "standard model" will account for an amazing lot of experimental results.

Moreover, some GUTs *do* seem to explain fundamental relationships, with cosmological theory. Calculations about what might have happened in incredibly short times after the Big Bang affect physical observations in big colliding-beam physical laboratories, and observations in those labs have led to predictions of observations on the astronomical scale. These are exciting times for physicists.

Poundstone's book attempts to look at these matters without getting bogged down in mathematical details. In particular, he asks: do we have any everyday experiences that will lead us to believe that the universe, in all its profound complexity, might actually be simple in structure? Do we have evidence that the universe might be philosophically closed?

He believes we do; and he uses the fascinating Game of Life (by Richard Conway) as his example. Life is a game of very simple rules; yet if we simulate it on a small computer, we can generate highly complex, and entirely unexpected, results;

the game is recursive, and recursion produces almost unimaginable complexities.

By analogy, cannot the universe be the same?

After all: if you begin to calculate the value of pi, you will never stop. The number is infinite and non-repeating. It appears to be indistinguishable from a random number, except, of course, that it is not random. It is a unique number, and if you follow the proper procedures you will get one sequence and no other—yet you can transmit that infinitely long number in the single statement, "the ratio of the circumference of a circle to the diameter." Isn't this a violation of some kind of conservation law? If we can consider physics to be a form of information theory—and Poundstone does— then how can all that information be contained in so small a statement?

Poundstone is an MIT graduate. Claude Shannon, who first developed information theory, and John von Neumann are both closely associated with MIT. It isn't surprising that Poundstone has been greatly influenced by them.

Among his other contributions von Neumann investigated self-reproducing patterns. Can machines, in theory at least, make themselves; or does this involve a logical contradiction? Von Neumann examined this through computer programs; rather than building actual machines, he simulated machines through patterns of cells which can assume different states. Each state corresponds, more or less, to a component of a machine. The state of each cell depends on the initial condition of the cell, and the states of its four orthogonal neighbors.

In a logical model universe in which each cell can assume 29 different states, you can set up a starting pattern that, after much time and complex growth, reproduces itself. It is not small and hardly simple; but it is possible. There is no logical contradiction in the concept of a machine that reproduces itself.

New Health

So far so good. Poundstone doesn't consider all the implications of self-replication; let's look at a couple.

Imagine that we build a self-replicating machine and send it into space. Things might be more complex than that; for example, we might send forth a robot which builds a factory; the factory in turn builds more robots. (One might think of human beings as "factory" stages for the manufacture of spermatozoa and ovae.) We, in turn, harvest either robots or factories, depending on what we need.

If our self-replicating machine went to the Moon, or an asteroid, or Mars, then after a few generations we would have a nearly infinite return on our investment. The wealth created by the robots would be *new* wealth, generated by a capital investment, but hardly fitting the Marxist view of "surplus value" derived from exploitation of labor. How such wealth should be distributed—who "should" have it—need not be explored here.

Self-replicating machines are logically possible. Can they actually be made?

A few years ago NASA held a symposium on that subject. Experts in robotics and manufacturing worked for a long and stimulating weekend. Alas, although there were intriguing ideas, there were no practical approaches.

None save one. I was a participant in that symposium, and it was obvious to me that we could build one space-located self replicating facility within this decade: we could send a colony of humans to the Moon. A human colony would have a self replication time of about 20 years. It would require heavy investment at first, but it ought to be self sufficient within a generation; after which all the wealth it created would be "new," wealth created from previously untappable sources.

Of course the colonists would be humans, not robots; and would therefore have their own theories as to the ownership of that wealth, just as the colonists of the New World had views different from those of the kings of Spain and England. On the other hand, they would be able to generate so much wealth—well over 90% of the resources, such as metals, easily available to mankind are not here on Earth—that they can spare some. Perhaps one day we will see the outer space equivalent of the Marshall Plan under which the United States helped rebuild Europe. The Moon sends foreign aid to New York City. . . .

Are We Alone?

If it is theoretically possible to build self-replicating machines; and it is in practice possible to build self-replicating space colonies; then these achievements are possible not only for humans, but for any other intelligent species in the galaxy.

If it's that easy to do, someone will have done it. No one has; for if they had, they'd be here. Therefore, we're alone. Frank Tipler of Tulane seriously proposes this answer to Enrico Fermi's profound question: "Where are they?" They don't exist, says Tipler; for if they did, we'd already know.

Neither Tipler nor Godel are discussed in Poundstone's book. It's still a good one.

Down With Darwin

Tipler thinks we're alone in the universe. On the other hand, Sir Fred Hoyle believes the probability of evolution of life is so low that it wouldn't happen in the galaxy in hundreds of billions of years. The galaxy isn't hundreds of billions of year old, yet we're here. How could that happen?

In *Evolution From Space* (Simon and Schuster, 1982) Sir Fred Hoyle and Chandra Wickramasinghe argue that we—indeed all life—have been planted here by purposefully sent payloads of spores from outer space. The spores contain genetic "programs" and are capable of modifying existing organisms—not just bacteria, but people. (There's a section on noses and their effect on inhalation of spore-laden raindrops.)

They examine such evidence as the startling fact that sweet peas and certain varieties of beans can produce hemoglobin, despite any evolutionary benefit the peas and beans can gain from this; and end with the more startling conclusion that God exists. Now true enough, their God has little to do with the oriental monarch portrayed in the Old Testament and, far from creating the universe, appears to be the Universe Itself; but since the probability that life evolved by chance is insignificantly small, *something more than chance* is needed in explanation.

Adrian Berry (author of the excellent books *The Iron Sun* and *The Super-intelligent Computer*) is not shy of saying that Sir Fred has gone stark staring mad; and he is not entirely alone in this view. Hoyle's thesis is certainly revolutionary.

However, Hoyle is not entirely alone in his views. John Gribbin in *Spacewarps* (Delacorte, 1983) takes Hoyle quite seriously, although he doesn't agree. Moreover, Hoyle isn't the first to present this thesis. In his book Hoyle examines the "panspermia" theory of Arrhenius (Nobel prize winner for the theory of ions and ionization), who first concluded that life originated in one part of the galaxy and was carried in spore form by light pressure from star to star.

Hoyle also asks embarrassing questions about Darwin's theory. They are not questions likely to comfort Biblical literalists; but a universe that has room for a universal Creator is an entirely different place from one made of accidental encounters between quarks.

If life has been created and dispersed through the universe by a Creator—could not that Creator be an agent of an even greater Creator? The traditional Catholic view of the Universe is that it was made by Christ. ("And without Him nothing was made that was made," says the beginning of the Gospel of John.) I do not argue the point, but it is intriguing to think what C. S. Lewis might have made of it.

Watchmakers

If we take all the parts of a watch and put them in a bag, how long must we shake the bag before the parts fall randomly together to become a watch? If we put fifty million monkeys at typewriters, how long must they type before they produce *Hamlet*? Indeed, given *any* random process, how long will it take for *Hamlet* to emerge by chance? However you calculate it, the number will be very large compared to the age of the universe.

Hamlet could not have arisen by chance. All very well, and indeed we know it did not: *Hamlet* was written by William Shakespeare. Of course we are no better off with that explanation. A random Shakespeare is even less likely than a random *Hamlet*! If finding a watch implies the existence of a watchmaker, what does finding a watchmaker imply?

To attack this question, Poundstone studies recursive games such as Life. If something as complex as Life can be generated from simple axioms, while at the same time there is no logical contradiction in self-replicating systems, then perhaps the universe can be philosophically closed. Watches may imply watchmakers, but watchmakers imply nothing more than biophysical laws; complex laws, surely, but nothing in principle beyond the understanding of humans—or at least of humans plus computers.

After all, we can *enhance* our intelligence by computers, and we know they are our creatures. We could even teach them to sing hymns and require them to teach the hymns to their descendants. "It is Man who hath made us, and not we ourselves. . . ."

Poundstone's book includes source code for computer programs that will play the game of Life. It's a good read.

Einstein vs. Bohr

There are other views of philosophical closure.

In *Quantum Theory and the Schism in Physics* (Rowman and Littlefield, 1982)—a very readable book, despite the formidable title—Sir Karl Popper tells us that in 1932 John von Neumann "gave a mathematical proof purporting to establish once and for all the final, the end-of-the-road character of quantum mechanics: he proved that all those were mistaken, who, like Einstein, thought there may be a layer of physical reality deeper than the one represented by quantum mechanics.

"In order to make the proof quite general, von Neumann introduced a concept that became very famous: the concept of 'hidden variables.' A hidden variable was anything to be taken into account in atomic theory (in the sense in which atomic theory included the nucleus as a matter of course) that was not taken into account by quantum mechanics. Von Neumann proved (or so we were told) that such hidden variables could not exist in quantum mechanics; or, according to a slightly different interpretation, he proved that the existence of hidden variables contradicted quantum mechanics.

"Now it so happened that in the same year in which von Neumann's book was published, two new particles were discovered: the neutron and the positron.

"Were these not (previously) hidden variables? And if not, what would have been?"

Popper, in his *Logic of Scientific Discovery*, argues—some would say demonstrates conclusively—that the essence of science is "falsifiability." A statement which cannot be falsified cannot be scientific; under the rules of scientific truth and discovery, it cannot be true—or indeed, have any meaning at all.

Popper also argues that science is open; that something can come from nothing; that the future is not contained in the past. There is genuine indeterminism in physics, biology, and history. Mind is not "mere" matter, and thoughts are not predetermined; hence his dedication to "the open society" in an "open universe."

In *Quantum Theory and the Schism in Physics*, which is the third volume of his *Postscript to the Logic of Scientific Discovery*, Popper reviews the nearly forgotten Einstein/Bohr controversy; and concludes that it was not really settled at all. The question was, had physics reached the end of the road with quantum mechanics? Was quantum mechanics "complete," and at least in principle the end of the road in physics?

Heisenberg and Bohr claimed that it was; Einstein rejected the view, at first because he could not accept a probabilistic theory as final. According to Popper Einstein later gave up that reasoning in 1950; but he always believed that "there must be a further, deeper level." Physical theory was not "complete."

The argument was never settled. Popper says it is nearly forgotten today. Few ever dared criticize Bohr (although Murray Gell-Mann, who first named the quarks, has said that "Bohr brainwashed a whole generation of theorists"). Instead of a final confrontation between Bohr's "completist" physics and Einstein's "open" universe, there was a subtle transformation of what quantum theory was all about. The term "quantum mechanics" was applied to quantum electrodynamics, field theory, and even the study of quarks—which were certainly entirely unsuspected in the year of von Neumann's proof.

For Popper and his intellectual descendants the universe is philosophically open. We can never understand everything, nor is any theory ever complete. It is a conclusion that Godel would have accepted.

Where Is the Antimatter?

A final observational problem: there appears to be too much matter and too little anti-matter in this universe of ours. Of course "too little" is a subjective thing; if there were plenty of antimatter we wouldn't exist, since matter and antimatter mutually annihilate each other when they get together; but there's too little for the theorists.

Why should nature prefer matter to antimatter? Yet it seems that this universe does.

The cosmologists think they see an answer to that. When the universe formed from the Big Bang more happened than is at first obvious. The universe underwent a "phase change," analogous to the change of state when liquids freeze. Frozen liquids are not, in general, one single great crystal. The change of state began in several places at once, and those places were out of phase with each other, so that when the crystallizations met the crystal structure didn't match.

This was much discussed at the 1984 New York meeting of the American Association for the Advancement of Science. Most there concluded that the "phase change" universe could be real. If so, we live in one of a series of universes, each existing in its own spacetime, each independent of the other, isolated from the other by the very structure of reality (as we understand it at present).

There is no way one of these universal bubbles could influence another. They are completely cut off . . .

Comes The Revolution

Gribbin (*Spacewarps*) quotes Edinburgh astronomer Victor Clube as saying that we stand on the brink of revolutionary new theories in astronomy. The physicists meanwhile look forward to new observations that will confirm or deny the Grand Unified Theory that eluded Einstein. Certainly there was a genuine sense of excitement in the physics panels at the 1984 AAAS meeting in New York. Something is about to happen.

Cosmology is at last contributing to astronomical theory and making predictions that can be confirmed in high-energy laboratories. We have "inflationary" theories of the Big Bang. These produce "phase changes," and a possible infinity of universes. We have GUTs and standard theories. Meanwhile the tools of science are also taking a quantum leap forward.

We not only have larger and better computers; we have *more* computers, enough so that nearly every physicist and graduate student has access to more computing power than was available to *anyone* twenty years ago. We have space observation systems, such as the Infra-Red Astronomical Satellite (IRAS), with others, like the Large Space Telescope, due within a few years.

Mankind stands at a peculiar threshold. Within our lifetimes, indeed within a few years, we will have the ability to make it trivially easy to make our presence unambiguously known across much of the galaxy. If we can do that, so could any other civilization that reaches our level; yet our level of science seems inevitable to any intelligent society.

If we have learned so much in a hundred years, what more must we learn in the next thousand? Yet it seems inevitable that if there are other civilizations at all, some must be not thousands, but millions of years older than we. Fermi asked, "Where are they?" and the question seems more and more profound as we examine it.

The next step in physics promises to integrate particle theory, astrophysics, astronomy, and cosmology; perhaps it will answer Fermi's question as well.

An End To Malaise

"Mass poverty, malnutrition and deterioration of the planet's water and atmosphere resources—that's the bleak government prediction that says civilization has perhaps 20 years to head off such a world-wide disaster."

Thus began a typical story reporting *Global 2000*, a study commissioned by President Jimmy Carter. More than one million copies of the *Global 2000 Report To The President* were distributed. Before the report was completed, President Carter used its conclusions as the basis for discussions with other world leaders. The disaster was rushing upon us; something had to be done.

There were even news stories with headlines like "We have to get poor quick."

We don't hear so much about *Global 2000* any more; but it's still out there, still used by government agencies as a basis for predictions. The AAAS meeting in 1984 featured a panel called "Knock down drag out on the global future." The idea was to have optimists face pessimists; the pessimists in general accept the conclusions of *Global 2000*.

The Resourceful Earth (Basil Blackwell, 1984) was edited by Julian Simon and Herman Kahn just before Kahn's untimely death. The book is a collection of essays whose central thesis is simple: *Global 2000* is dead wrong. Where *Global 2000* sees dead-end problems, *The Resourceful Earth* sees challenges and opportunities. Julian Simon is an economist; and though economics is known as "the dismal science," there is nothing gloomy about his views of our potential future.

As an example: when England was denuded of forests, many predicted doom and poverty. Instead, England turned to coal, and entered a period of prosperity unequalled in human history. We stand at such a crossroads again. We have the resources, we have the science, we have the technology; do we have the will to solve global problems? Or must we despair and die?

From population to pollution, crops, water, energy, and minerals, *The Resourceful Earth* presents an alternative to doomsday. The era of limits and the time of national malaise are over. The only limit to man's vast future is nerve.

EDITOR'S INTRODUCTION TO:

NUCLEAR AUTUMN

by
Ben Bova

On March 23, 1983 President Ronald Reagan proposed that the United States employ our technological resources to develop defenses against ICBM's. Let us, he said, use our technology to make these terrible weapons obsolete and irrelevant.

The press reaction was nearly unanimous. When a number of Democratic congresscreatures called the President "Darth Vader," and derided strategic defenses as "Star Wars," the newspapers and television networks hastened to trumpet those epithets to the world.

The public had different views. When pollsters asked about "Star Wars," nearly 80% of the American people said "Damn right, and about time, too."

Meanwhile, Carl Sagan and others brought forth something else to think about. If Lucifer's Hammer (well, it was probably an asteroid, but it might have been a large comet that hit the Earth a few million years ago) killed the dinosaurs by throwing up so much dust and dirt into the atmosphere that plants died and the big lizards starved, might not a large nuclear war bring about the same result? That is: set enough fires, and pulverize enough dust, to bring about atmospheric conditions that would bring about, not merely a new ice age, but something even worse? The possibility has become known as the Nuclear Winter.

These and many other issues of importance are discussed at length in Ben Bova's book, *Assured Survival* 1984, Houghton-Mifflin. In that book Ben gives me credit for inventing the phrase "assured survival." Alas, his publisher was already advertising that title when we announced my own book on the subject: Jerry Pournelle and Dean Ing, editors: *Mutual Assured Survival*, Baen Books, 1984.

Both books are worth reading. Although differing in detail, both reach much the same conclusion: It's better that nuclear weapons don't explode at all, but if they're going to, space is the best place for that to happen. If nukes are intercepted in space, they won't set fires or pulverize dirt, and thus won't bring about the nuclear winter.

One of the advocates of strategic defense is Lt. General Daniel O. Graham, U.S. Army (Ret.); because he is identified with defense against the ICBM most people assume he was in the Air Force. He wasn't. Dan Graham was, in his words, "a gravel agitator," which is to say an infantryman. He is, as I write this, neither grizzled, nor old, nor yet chief of staff; but all things change.

NUCLEAR AUTUMN

Ben Bova

"They're bluffing," said the President of the United States.

"Of course they're bluffing," agreed her science advisor. "They have to be."

The Chairman of the Joint Chiefs of Staff, a grizzled old infantry general, looked grimly skeptical.

For a long, silent moment they faced each other in the cool, quiet confines of the Oval Office. The science advisor looked young and handsome enough to be a television personality, and indeed had been one for a while before he allied himself with the politician who sat behind the desk. The President looked younger than she actually was, thanks to modern cosmetics and a ruthless self discipline. Only the general seemed to be old, a man of an earlier generation, gray-haired and wrinkled, with light brown eyes that seemed sad and weary.

"I don't believe they're bluffing," he said. "I think they mean exactly what they say—either we cave in to them or they launch their missiles."

The science advisor gave him his most patronizing smile. "General, they *have* to be bluffing. The numbers prove it."

"The only numbers that count," said the general, "are that we have cut our strategic ballistic missile force by half since this Administration came into office."

"And made the world that much safer," said the President. Her voice was firm, with a sharp edge to it.

The general shook his head. "Ma'am, the only reason I have not tendered my resignation is that I know full well the nincompoop you intend to appoint in my place."

The science advisor laughed. Even the President smiled at the old man.

"The soviets are not bluffing," the general repeated. "They mean exactly what they say."

With a patient sigh, the science advisor explained, "General, they cannot—repeat, can *not*—launch a nuclear strike at us or anyone else. They know the numbers as well as we do. A large nuclear strike, in the 3000 megaton range, will so damage the environment that the world will be plunged into a Nuclear Winter. Crops and animal life will be wiped out by months of subfreezing temperatures. The sky will be dark with soot and grains of pulverized soil. The sun will be blotted out. All life on Earth will die."

The general waved an impatient hand. "I know your story. I've seen your presentations."

"Then how can the Russians attack us, when they know they'll be killing themselves even if we don't retaliate?"

"Maybe they haven't seen your television specials. Maybe they don't believe in Nuclear Winter."

"But they have to!" said the science advisor. "The numbers are the same for them as they are for us."

"Numbers," grumbled the general.

"Those numbers describe reality," the science advisor insisted. "And the men in the Kremlin are realists. They understand what Nuclear Winter means. Their own scientists have told them exactly what I've told you."

"Then why did they insist on this Hot Line call?"

Spreading his hands in the gesture millions had come to know from his television series, the science advisor replied, "They're reasonable men. Now that they know nuclear weapons are unusable, they are undoubtedly trying to begin negotiations to resolve our differences without threatening nuclear war."

"You think so?" muttered the general.

The President leaned back in her swivel chair. "We'll find out what they want soon enough," she said. "Kolgoroff will be on the Hot Line in another minute or so."

The science advisor smiled at her. "I imagine he'll suggest a summit meeting to negotiate a new disarmament treaty."

The general said nothing.

The President touched a green square on the keypad built into the desk's surface. A door opened and three more people—a man and two women— entered the Oval Office: the Secretary of State, the Secretary of Defense, and the National Security Advisor.

Exactly when the digital clock on the President's desk read 12:00:00, the large display screen that took up much of the wall opposite her desk lit up to reveal the face of Yuri Kolgoroff, General Secretary of the Communist Party and President of the Soviet Union. He was much younger than his predecessors had been, barely in his mid-fifties, and rather handsome in a Slavic way. If his hair had been a few shades darker and his chin just a little rounder he would have looked strikingly like the President's science advisor.

"Madam President," said Kolgoroff, in flawless American-accented English, "it is good of you to accept my invitation to discuss the differences between our two nations."

"I am always eager to resolve differences," said the President.

"I believe we can accomplish much." Kolgoroff smiled, revealing large white teeth.

"I have before me," said the President, glancing at the computer screen on her desk, "the agenda that our ministers worked out. . . ."

"There is no need for that," said the Soviet leader. "Why encumber ourselves with such formalities?"

The President smiled. "Very well. What do you have in mind?"

"It is very simple. We want the United States to withdraw all its troops from Europe and to dismantle NATO. Also, your military and naval bases in Japan, Taiwan and the Philippines must be disbanded. Finally, your injunctions against the Soviet Union concerning trade in high-technology items must be ended."

The President's face went white. It took her a moment to gather the wits to say, "And what do you propose to offer in exchange for these ... concessions?"

"In exchange?" Kolgoroff laughed. "Why, we will allow you to live. We will refrain from bombing your cities."

"You're insane!" snapped the President.

Still grinning, Kolgoroff replied, "We will see who is sane and who is mad. One minute before this conversation began, I ordered a limited nuclear attack against every NATO base in Europe, and a counterforce attack against the ballistic missiles still remaining in your silos in the American midwest."

The red panic light on the President's communications console began flashing frantically.

"But that's impossible!" burst the science advisor. He leaped from his chair and pointed at Kolgoroff's image in the big display screen. "An attack of that size will bring on Nuclear Winter! You'll be killing yourselves as well as us!"

Kolgoroff smiled pityingly at the scientist. "We have computers also, professor. We know how to count. The attack we have launched is just below the threshold for Nuclear Winter. It will not blot out the sun everywhere on Earth. Believe me, we are not such fools as you think."

"But . . ."

"But," the Soviet leader went on, smile vanished and voice iron hard, "should you be foolish enough to launch a counterstrike with your remaining missiles or bombers, that *will* break the camel's back, so to speak. The additional explosions of your counterstrike will bring on Nuclear Winter."

"You can't be serious!"

"I am deadly serious," Kolgoroff replied. Then a faint hint of his smile returned. "But do not be afraid. We have not targeted Washington. Or any of your cities, for that matter. You will live—under Soviet governance."

The President turned to the science advisor. "What should I do?"

The science advisor shook his head.

"What should I do?" she asked the others seated around her.

They said nothing. Not a word.

She turned to the general. "What should I do?"

He got to his feet and headed for the door. Over his shoulder he answered, "Learn Russian."

EDITOR'S INTRODUCTION TO:

TALION

by
John Brunner

I first met John Brunner in 1964, at the World Science Fiction Convention held in the Leamington Hotel in Oakland. It was the largest Worldcon ever: over 400 people, as I recall. I was at the time a county chairman of the Republican Party, and my wife was chairman of the county Citizens for Goldwater campaign. Mr. Brunner was a dedicated adherent to the socialist wing of the British Labour Party. By September of '64 it was pretty obvious that Senator Goldwater wasn't going to win. I forget how the Labour Party was doing.

(They told me in 1964 that if I voted for Goldwater, my money wouldn't be worth anything, there would be riots in all the major cities, and we'd have half a million men overseas in a land war in Asia. Alas, I voted for him, and it all came true.)

Brunner and I met at a party held by the late Tony Boucher. It should be obvious that we didn't get on—except that we did. John Brunner has always been polite and willing to let his opponents have their say. We did argue a bit, with an odd result: one of Tony Boucher's (thoroughly inebriated) young guests, totally devoted to the cause of the pacifist left, decided that I might in fact have won some points in my arguments with Brunner (and Boucher, who sided with John). It was therefore clear that I was far too eloquent; and since I was clearly dedicated to a totally evil cause, it being common knowledge that Barry Goldwater was a fascist warmonger, it was the young man's civic duty to kill me. Mr. Brunner was one of those who helped restrain him.

I have met John Brunner many times since. We do not argue much any more; perhaps we each despair of persuading the other. Moreover, I do not live in Britain, and it is not my task to teach others how to run their countries.

However, Britain is a NATO ally, and Brunner doesn't much care for the implications of that. His position is simple. Britain should get rid of the nukes—and also adopt a Swiss defense system, in which every citizen of Britain has a rifle and is trained to use it.

"I would rather see Britain an indigestible lump in the communist empire than a cloud of nuclear vapour," John once told me. It's not an unreasonable position. I think of arguments against it, but I don't know what I'd think about that if I lived over there. It doesn't matter. I live here. I believe that a U.S. strategic defense program can give John Brunner—and all the Brits—more alternatives than guerilla war vs. nuclear doom.

John Brunner believes that governments not only can, but *must* do good things for their citizens.

John Brunner
TALION

It is a commonplace that our civil defense is, and must always be, hopelessly inadequate to cope with the slaughter and destruction which would be brought about by thermonuclear bombardment ... It seems a reasonable guess that for every "megacorpse" caused by blast, fire and radiation, there would in a few weeks be another megacorpse caused by the epidemics and starvation resulting from the breakdown of transport and industrial production. No drugs, no drains, no food. "Fortitude" or "the will to resist" under thermonuclear bombardment would be as much use as swordsmanship against a heat wave.

—Wayland Young (Lord Kennet):
Strategy for Survival, 1959

There was going to be another spring after all, and even summer might yet return to Britain's grey and ravaged land. Muffled in cumbrous synthetic furs, despite their thickness having to strive not to shiver as the Optica survey plane droned on its way, Reginald Curtis clung to that belief with might and main, and stared at the veiled disc of the pallid May sun as achingly as any pagan worshipper. Almost a year had passed since it had been visible at all.

Shifting in the left seat, nominally the co-pilot's— but pilots were too scarce for two to fly together, just as they had been in the days of Lancasters and Stirlings, a fact Curtis remembered vaguely from his childhood—Tanner muttered, "He must have been seeing things!"

"Who?" countered Smith from the middle of the cabin.

"Ellis! The man who made the report!"

"Oh, him!" Smith's tone reflected proper military contempt for Ellis, whose most demanding pre-war task had consisted in ferrying holiday-makers to and from Majorca. He himself was a career RAF officer, promoted Air Marshal for lack of anyone better, although he still wore his old flying-suit with the stripes of his substantive rank, wing commander. "Yes, either that or he was off course. My guess is, he was miles adrift from where he claimed. Everyone knows this area was contaminated past hope by the ground-burst at—at—" He tried to snap his fingers, but his heavy gloves permitted only a dull patting noise. "Oh, that nuclear plant with the impossible name!"

"Not *everyone*," Tanner said with snidely daring over-loudness, tilting his head ever so slightly rightward. The plane seated three abreast, and normally there was plenty of room for all, but his bulky garments and the need to avoid nudging against the pilot meant that the Minister felt as tightly packed as well-stowed cargo, a condition that would normally have made him temptingly irascible.

This time, though, he did not rise to the bait. He had given up listening with more than half an ear. He sat with maps on his knee and a stub of pencil poised above them, not because he imagined himself a better navigator than Smith, nor even because he expected to spot anything previously unrecorded, but simply to occupy his mind.

Only the stratagem had failed, and it was long since he had moved the hand whose limp fingers clutched the pencil, the arm which lay slack on the map-board to prevent it sliding when they turned at the prescribed corners of the aircraft's search-pattern. His heavy-jowled face, too, was as still, and blank, and desolate as the land beneath.

Whichever way he gazed through the plane's huge windows, what he saw blurred over in moments and forced him to blink away tears.

My country! Oh, my raped and ruined country!

He wished he did not have to look, because such a sight implied the ultimate indecency. He felt he was uncovering the nakedness of his mother, once beautiful, wasted into a parody of herself. And worse than nakedness—*oh, God!*—for the very flesh was failing now, to expose the lewd bones. Almost he would have preferred the snow to fall again, freezing mists to roll in from the ocean as they had throughout what by the calendar should have been last summer. In a way, what was happening now was like watching a corpse arise from its grave, its shroud foul with rot and spilling worms. The return of the sun was bringing on a thaw, because so much of the dirt hurled skyward by the ground-burst bombs, and of the smoke from all the cities, forests and oilwells set on fire, had been washed back out of the sky as the air chilled and countless drops of water were precipitated around myriads of ionizing particles. Until last year he had never seen black snow, nor dreamed it might be possible. Then it had drifted down during July, and August, and September . . .

The surviving scientists at Corsham looked on the bright side. They said that if so much detritus had not been trapped and carried down to earth, but gone on floating round and round the world, or if the snow-layer had been virgin white, another Ice Age might have ensued. As it was, just enough dust had fallen back to let the sun show through, and correspondingly the ground-cover had grown dark enough to absorb its feeble radiation: hence this thaw.

But what horrors the snow was melting to reveal!

Some people appeared immune to their impact: Smith, for example. He seemed to be concentrating exclusively on his controls and charts. Tanner was more affected; he was talking over-often, sometimes shrilly, and this was so different from his usual meek behavior Curtis suspected it must be a defense mechanism ... *Defense?* Ah, how useful jargon was—had been!

For himself, this was as bad an experience as emerging from shelter after the war, perhaps worse. Even the stinging air of that smoke-saturated spring had not called tears so readily to his eyes. Then, trees still stood and bore their leaves, and recovery could be envisioned. Of course, one knew that land which man had tended for centuries must sink back into the wild, but one spoke with confidence about the decay-rate of the fallout, and made plans.

And then the summer froze.

Abruptly the radiation-counter gave two measured clicks; it was set to its slowest rate, for obvious reasons. In Curtis's mind it was like the double slam of an auctioneer's hammer: *going, going—*

"Minister!"

The saw-edged voice of the pilot rasped Curtis's ears. He was obsessively studying the landscape in the dim gray light, seeing no sign of movement save what was brought about by the harsh wind, and the shift of great masses of discolored snow as the streams threading their way across this countryside of ridge and notch undercut them on their way to the poisoned sea. Because they were flying low, to conserve the fuel they would expend on attaining greater altitude, he had been able to note accidental dams of half-burned tree-trunks, hurled from higher on the hillsides, whose charred substance turned the water to the hue of ink. Around here, he remembered, there had been mines of some sort. Slurry from them must have done much the same to just these rivers . . .

He roused himself, painful with cramp, and uttered a gruff response.

"How much longer do we have to drag out this fool's errand?" Smith demanded. "We haven't seen a sign of what Ellis said he spotted, and we have barely an hour's juice left before we'll absolutely have to make for base!"

"What's more," Tanner chimed in with nervous defiance, "during the pass closest to the old nuclear plant, we picked up a lot of hot dust!"

The Minister too would rather have headed for home than gone on quartering the ruined countryside like a bird of prey—but so far this year no hawks had been recorded, and few of their cousins, save gulls driven inland by storms. The time for doing as one liked, though, was long past, and it was futile to hark back to it.

Hunching forward, but not turning his head, he said, "What are you after, Tanner—a transfer to manual reclamation duties?" And thought as he spoke of the harsh reality defined by those abstract polysyllables: slow-moving figures clad in rags amid the rubble and crusted ice of empty cities, condemned by military courts for looting and suchlike offences, but buying a few more months of life by doing the same with official approval, venturing into hot areas in search of reusable scrap . . . That was just one of the ways his government had had to copy the enemy; they had long had punishment battalions, and in wartime used them for clearing minefields. Sometimes, as in that former case, the guards who had to drive them on at gunpoint rebelled. There had been six executions so far this year—six more wasted, out of how few . . . ?

A haunted look came and went in Tanner's eyes, and he stared ahead again, trying perhaps to imitate Smith's customary dumb—and sometimes not so dumb—insolence. But trained pilots, being so rare, could get away with almost anything, while Tanner had only the outdated office skills of a civil servant.

Curtis did not need to feign the anger that colored his voice as he continued.

"Get this through your head, will you? Until Ellis's report is proved false beyond a doubt, we follow it up! He described a small town, an inhabited town, surrounded by newly-dug ground! He saw smoke rising not from wildfire but from chimneys! He saw people dodging for cover—that's what he said! And that was at the very beginning of the thaw, two weeks ago! We're looking for survivors who may need help! If that doesn't touch you, try thinking about it the other way around—we may need something they've got!" He made sarcasm crackle in his voice like an electrical discharge, as though he were addressing some bothersome heckler at a political meeting in the old days. "Now shut up and just keep flying!"

"As you say, *Minister*." This from Smith, whose tone had the mock formality of a warrant officer perfectly aware he was better informed than the junior lieutenant ordering him about. "Only trouble is, 'just flying' is going to take us over the ocean in ten or fifteen minutes. What heading do you wish us to try next?"

The bastard, the bastard! Jumped up ex-sergeant pilot, promoted because he survived when others didn't . . . All my life I've been plagued by snotty yobs like him, even when I was Head of School because by

*then they'd let the rabble in! You'd think they'd be
glad of someone trained to keep his head and take
them in charge!*

But at the same moment Curtis felt a cold iron
hand closing around his guts. He withstood the
pain long enough to formulate an adequately blis-
tering answer.

"If you're incapable of setting course to cover
the last part of the search area, I'll have to find out
what you're doing in charge of our best remaining
survey plane, let alone calling yourself an Air
Marshal! Is that clear?"

Then the iron hand clamped tight, and he had to
double up and grope for the supply of tablets bur-
ied deep inside his layer upon layer of clothing. He
crunched a foul-tasting pill and endured the three
or four minutes it took to master the agony trans-
fixing him. As usual, the pain was not only in his
belly but in the roots of his remaining teeth, in his
eyes and behind his forehead.

The ulcer would never heal, of course. He had
been told so. He was too old, and even though he
had spent the war in the deep shelter at Corsham
he had been exposed once too often.

When he came back from his blank abyss of
pain, there was a change in the atmosphere of the
cabin. Both Smith and Tanner were leaning forward, staring through the front window, and the
first thing he heard clearly when the rushing in
his ears faded was Tanner's voice shaping words
he hardly dared believe.

"That looks awfully like what Ellis said he saw!"

*God, Let it be, let it be! Let there be proof that
people can survive and have survived outside the
shelters!*

With vast effort Curtis craned forward to peer

past Smith, to the left and downward. Here the ground was rolling in character, rounded hills and shallow vales succeeding one another like petrified waves. Snow still lay on the uplands, but it was melting fast, and—and someone had set up a water-mill in one of the streams!

The sight of it made him so giddy he almost blacked out. The pills sometimes had that effect. He barely heard Smith say, "Well, something's going on here, at any rate. Look, that field's been ploughed this year, or I'm a Dutchman."

Forcing his eyes wide, Curtis stared desperately at the gray land—and discovered Smith was right. There was a level patch of soil, scratched into untidy furrows, with a sprinkling of bright green on it, random as pepper-grains.

"Thank God!" he whispered. "But who did it? Find them! We need to know who they are!"

"What do you think I'm doing?" was Smith's curt reply as he swung the plane over the next ridge at the lowest speed it could sustain without a stall.

Then they saw it clear: a little town, built of slate and drab gray stone, along the sides of a slanting valley. It was deep enough between the hills to have credibly survived any nearby blast, and some accident of weather might well have ensured that the heaviest fallout was carried over it to drop elsewhere. But what counted most was that the wan daylight glinted on a long shed roofed with glass.

"My God!" Tanner breathed. "I thought there wasn't a greenhouse left in Britain!"

He reached for binoculars, but Curtis for once was quicker, and almost before he had adjusted the focus he was able to say, "Nor did I! And I don't think that's pre-war. It looks as though it's been patched together from ordinary house-windows."

"But last summer there wasn't any sun!" objected Tanner.

"I know, I know!"—frantically scanning the area. "But look! There is smoke coming out of chimneys, just as Ellis said!"

"People?" Smith offered sourly, reaching for the radio to report their position—and was answered on the instant.

There was a noise like an angry bee and a clang from the starboard wing. The wings held their remaining supply of fuel; the long-range tanks slung underneath were long since empty, only retained, despite their extra drag, because they could not be replaced if they were jettisoned. Smith jerked his head around with a cry of alarm. A thin clear spray of petrol was spurting from a neat round hole, and it must be one of two, for the bullet would have gone right through.

"They're trying to shoot us down!" the pilot barked.

Tanner uttered a whimper of animal terror and bent to retrieve from the floor their only weapon, an army carbine. Curtis shouted at him.

"Idiot! How can they be sure who we are? RAF markings don't mean anything nowadays! We could be bandits who stole this plane, couldn't we? We don't shoot back—we land and talk to them!"

"We don't have much choice about landing," Smith said grimly. "With that much free juice blowing around, it's a marvel we're not on fire already. If we're going to make it back to base, we have to patch those leaks at once!"

"I think we're being invited," Curtis muttered. "Look, there's a level bit of road and someone's waving to us."

At the lower end of the town's single street, between abandoned houses whose roofs, unlike those higher up, still bore a layer of frost, the roadway was indeed relatively intact, and wide and long enough for the Optica to use as a runway. Luckily the wind gusting over most of this region today was diverted by the nearby hills.

Nonetheless Smith swore to himself as he made a wide turn and set the plane down with a screech of brakes. By the time it came to a halt, the briefly-glimpsed figure who had signalled an invitation to land had disappeared.

Since the shot rang out everything had happened so rapidly Curtis had scarcely had time to feel frightened. Smith at least retained his sense of priorities, and demonstrated the fact by seizing a pack of emergency repair patches. Climbing over the minister without ceremony, emerging with hands half-raised to show he bore no weapon, he strode to where he could seal the holes: *slap* below, so the dribble of fuel ceased; then, using the starboard tire for a step, *slap* above, at the maximum reach of his arm.

"They haven't shot me yet," he said gruffly. "But they could be covering us from any of those empty houses, and at least one of them is bloody good with a gun. You'd better get down too."

There was a rattling noise, so distinct that at first Curtis imagined it to come from the radiation-counter. But it was Tanner's teeth—or rather, his false ones. Like most of the survivors at Corsham he had lost his own, and dentistry was low on the urgent list.

The sound gave Curtis an excuse for spurious courage. His own, starboard, door being ajar, he snapped at the younger man to open the port one also, and added: "Pull yourself together! What do you think we've run into—a gang of psychotic killers? If they merely wanted to wipe us out they could have done it by now! It looks more as though they want us to advance and be recognized!"

He slid to the ground, afraid it might be icy, but it was only wet. He secured a good footing and looked around. The nearest houses were small and cramped into rows; their doors were gone, doubtless for firewood, and their windows presumably to build the greenhouse. On higher ground to the west there were other and larger buildings, a church, a school perhaps, a town hall, a probable nonconformist chapel sited arrogantly almost in the shade of its older-established rival. Up there, too, the slate roofs appeared to be in good repair, and he caught a whiff of sulphur-tainted smoke.

Then suddenly he recognized something on the flank of a lowering hill: under a half-melted mask of snow, the shape of that kind of oblong gallery which typically sheltered the entrance to a driftmine, where a seam could be worked on the level without hoisting gear.

For a moment he was proud of himself; had he not already remembered that there had been scores, maybe hundreds of villages like this one folded among the westerly hills, whose people had been glad to turn from the uncertainties of raising sheep when mineral wealth was discovered underground? Then he realized he didn't know for sure what had been dug in this area. Was it coal? Or was it lead or tin, or even silver? He reproached himself for being so ignorant of the country he claimed to love so much, yet had paid attention to only when it was past repair.

Stop: he must not think such thoughts! He cupped his hands to his mouth, wishing he could have brought a functioning loud-hailer—but there were no batteries left to power those—and shouted, "Hello! We're friends, we've come to help! We're from the Emergency Government! I'm the Minister of National Recovery!"

The words died away into faint echoes among the stark facades of the abandoned houses. Abandoned—but probably not empty. Noticing how many windows and doorways might offer vantage-points to hidden snipers, as Smith had hinted, he shivered, not from the chill.

"That worked a bloody treat, didn't it?" the pilot growled, rejoining him. A hot retort boiled up in Curtis's mouth: any approach to a survivors' group was always supposed to include references to a ministry or a government department, which would combine overtones of pre-war normality with the implication of authority to be defied at your peril. He himself had helped to draft the standard procedure.

Only here, now, on the first occasion he had had to put it personally to the test, it seemed to have been found wanting. Accordingly he held his tongue.

He gazed around, wondering whether to bring the binoculars, and suddenly a voice addressed them, seeming no louder than if the speaker were the other side of a room.

"Move away from the plane, please. You're covered by six first-rate markspeople."

Behind the words: the unmistakable snick of the bolt on an old-fashioned rifle.

"They can't order us about like that!" Smith exclaimed, tossing the repair patches back into the plane's cabin.

"It strikes me as proper defensive procedure," Curtis sighed. "I could have been lying, couldn't I? Come on."

Reluctantly, as though physical separation from the plane were a sort of amputation, they obeyed.

"Very sensible," approved the voice when they had covered a dozen paces. From shadow within a doorway the speaker appeared. One of his hands was empty; the other clasped a crutch improvised out of pieces of tubing such as in the old days might have been attachments to a vacuum-cleaner. On the same side his leg was shrivelled, pipestem-thin, the foot drawn up into a kind of claw which dangled pendulum-wise beneath his knee. Also that side of his face was scarred; the cheek was puckered and a keloid had formed along the angle of the jaw. That apart, he looked healthy, judging by what of his skin was not concealed by greasy tattered clothing. He was thin, but his eyes were bright, his face and hands were free of sores, and—an index of a functional community—someone had gone to the trouble of neatly sewing up his short trouser-leg, rather than just chopping it off and letting it fray.

How old was he? Curtis estimated he could not be much over twenty. However, his youth counted for less than the fact that he exuded confidence and self-possession.

A subaltern type! Wonderful!

"So you're not just sent by the government," the cripple said after looking the strangers over. "One of you is a minister, yet! Well, well!"

Sensing that Smith was about to snap back, Curtis caught at his arm. But suddenly there was a noise from behind and all three of them swung around. Smith uttered an oath and started back towards the Optica.

"Better not," warned the young man with the crutch.

"The hell you say!" the pilot roared. "Those bastards have no business monkeying with my plane!"

Curtis too felt a pang of alarm. From an alley between the low-built houses two people had materialized, probably young by the way they moved, but whether male or female it was impossible to judge because they were so disguised by their ill-fitting clothes. One had opened the engine compartment, while the other was peering this way and that inside the cabin. Smith made to rush at them.

"Wing commander!" the cripple said with force, and Curtis noted the fact that he had recognized the rank-stripes on the pilot's suit. "Stay where you are, please. They're entitled to do what they're doing. You might say they're agents of our Ministry of *Local* Recovery."

"Smith, don't be a fool!" Curtis forced out. "We haven't done much for these people lately, have we? And anybody who can bring land back under cultivation—Dammit, do you want to get us all shot?"

Tanner, looking sick, offered vigorous nods in support.

Dejectedly, Smith yielded. Closing the gap between him and them with three swift strides, the cripple said, "There's no need to worry about your aircraft, I assure you. By the way, I'm interested to see that you've kept at least one of the Opticas in serviceable condition. It must be much lighter on fuel than a helicopter. Anyhow, all my friends are doing is following—hmm! Let me see if I can get the jargon right . . . Ah, yes: they're following our SOP for this kind of case."

"You've been contacted before?" Curtis flashed.

"Oh, no"—with a lopsided shrug. "But we were resigned to it happening sooner or later."

"So what are they doing?" Smith demanded, clenching his fists.

"Immobilizing the machine, searching it for arms, and deactivating the radio so that it'll be we, not you, who determine what news about us reaches your headquarters. I suppose you'd call these precautionary measures, right?"

The cripple cocked his head, but remained otherwise expressionless. Curtis was still struggling to find an answer when the pair who had raided the plane reported with their booty.

"Took out the ignition leads," said the first, a man. "Not something you can replace with baling wire."

When the other spoke—a woman—it could be seen she had already lost most of her lower teeth, though she could scarcely be older than her twenties.

"The radio's demountable. Probably they're running short of parts, have to take out things like this and use them for other purposes when the plane isn't flying. But it's been well serviced. Oh, and there's a gun on the floor of the cabin. I removed the bullets." She patted her hip; if there was a pocket there, Curtis could not see its opening. With a meaning glance at him, she added, "We're not thieves. Just trying to protect ourselves."

"Well done, and thank you." The cripple shifted his attention to the newcomers again. "Now we can spare time for proper introductions. My name is Edwin Renshaw. I usually answer to Ed. And you are—"

Curtis cleared his throat.

"My name is Reginald Curtis. As I said before, I'm the Minister for National Recovery. This is my personal aide, Mr. Tanner. And this is—" He hesitated for a second, and Smith cut in.

"*Air Marshal* Smith!"

The cripple looked at his face, at his badges of rank, and at his face again. Just as Smith was reddening and about to erupt, Curtis broke in.

"I—uh—I must say I admire what little I've seen of your organization around here. Merely to have ploughed a field and sown it over is an achievement. As for your greenhouse, and your watermill—well! Am I right in assuming that—uh—you're more or less in charge?"

"Me? I'm not in charge of anything," Ed answered. "It's just that I'm better employed talking and thinking than doing anything more strenuous. For reasons which ought to be obvious."

He jerked his wasted thigh. The shin and foot beneath swung obscenely in mid-air.

"But how did you—?" Curtis began, meaning to ask how they had survived unaided. Ed was ahead of him.

"Cora, you said you found a gun in the plane?"

The woman nodded.

"Where there's one there may be more. Andy, they'll have to be searched before we take them up the hill."

Eagerly Curtis said, "That was our only weapon, I assure you!"

"So you managed to let them all off?" Ed countered. "Didn't even save a few for World War IV?" He waited for a second; then, as though not expecting an answer, went on: "And don't forget the crotch. According to pre-war thrillers that's a favorite hiding-place."

"I'm not going to have bastards like you groping me in public!" blurted Smith.

"Put up with it!" Curtis snapped. "Don't these people deserve our respect? It's a hell of a job retaining any sort of order in the middle of chaos, and they've done it without any help from us!" He could hear his voice shaking with the excitement he felt at having found an enclave of civilization in what he had imagined to be a barren waste.

"Oh, hell! I'll take my balls out and wave them around, how about that?" Smith muttered, but sulkily allowed the body-search along with his companons.

"Clean," Andy grunted at last.

"So far, so good, then," Ed approved. "It's an advantage not to be caught out in a silly lie. When it comes to overall credibility, I mean. Since your statement about being unarmed has been borne out, I'll accept that you are who you say you are: the Minister of National Recovery. Now the crucial question. What brings you here?"

Curtis drew a deep breath, fighting to control the tension in his gut that must eventually bring on another spasm from his chronic ulcer. He said, "As and when we can spare the fuel and a pilot fit enough to fly, we've been scouring the whole of Britain for survivors. A couple of weeks ago we had a report to the effect that part of this area had recently been put back under cultivation. The pilot took some pictures, but unfortunately the film was faulty—radiation-fogged—and his radio was on the blink, so we had only a vague idea of your location. Otherwise we'd have been here sooner."

"I see. Yes, we did notice an overflight a while ago, didn't we?" Ed glanced at Andy and Cora for confirmation, and they nodded. "Well, I suppose it was unavoidable. But tell me this: do you always send a cabinet minister to visit newly-found survivors?"

Was there mockery in that gentle, polite tone? To his dismay Curtis realized he could no longer judge; he had spent too long in the company of those who spoke only to issue orders or—more often—to convey despair.

How to explain, anyway, that he *had* to make this trip personally? Minister or not, regardless of what objections his despondent colleagues raised, he had come to prove what he had always believed: that people could still live and flourish in the midst of devastation!

Then, displaying his civil servant's taste for masking an awkward pause with empty phrases, Tanner spoke up with a little bob of his head and a nervous hand-washing movement.

"My Minister judged from the pilot's report that you were managing astonishingly well. Naturally he wanted to inspect your achievements for himself."

Tanner, you're a worse fool than I feared.

What he ought to have stated at once, Curtis thought, was that his own title and that of the person he served were both near as dammit meaningless. "Minister"—faugh! The truth was that the three of them, like everyone else who had survived at Corsham of whatever status, were each like one man trying with his bare hands to plug a breached dyke that needed a million tons of rock. The days would never come again when a cabinet minister sat in an air-conditioned office and deputed subordinates to carry out his wishes. There weren't enough subordinates to go around—though admittedly some of them had a sight more sense than this nitwitted Tanner . . .

But he still hadn't framed his thoughts in proper words when Ed gave a lopsided shrug and spoke again.

"It's much too early for us to quit work at this season when every daylight hour is precious, but some of us can spare a while to hear what you have to say. Come up the town."

As though that were a code-word, the nearby houses uttered people: four, five, six of them. Smith drew in his breath with a hissing sound, for although two of them looked like mere children each bore a gun—a couple of rifles, three twelve-bores and a .410.

And they had other things in common, too. They had the haggard cheeks of those who had gone long without decent food; their expressions were sullen and hostile; and their gaze was honed to sharpness with distrust.

Most stood apart, warily, but a man in his fifties who carried a rifle approached in response to a gesture from Ed. He was addressed as Mervyn; he wore a tweed suit, much torn and stained, but no overcoat, despite the cold. His hands shook constantly; his face was thin and nervous, and like Cora he had lost a lot of teeth.

With terrible difficulty he posed a question: "Y-y-you w-w-want m-m-me to c-c-come along?"

"At the ready," was Ed's dry answer. And, with a glance at the strangers, he added, "Don't be misled. Mervyn is an excellent shot, as the damage to your plane will testify. I believe the technical term is 'intention tremor.'"

Mervyn gave a vigorous nod and a gapped smile.

"I shot you d-down," he said, patting the stock of his gun. "The t-t-trouble g-goes away when something important has to be d-done. It's a kind of P-parkinson's D-d-d ..." He shut his eyes for a second, and concentrated. "Disease!" he achieved at last.

"Surgeons used to operate in spite of it," Ed commented with a sad chuckle. "So don't think of making a break, will you? Not that there's any place for you to go."

So they trudged up the single street, which shortly grew far narrower than the section where Smith had been able to set down the plane. As they climbed, they had a bitter view of the mouth of the gallery leading to the mine, and infuriating bells of memory started to ring faintly in Curtis's brain. Also, as they passed between houses in good repair, he had the unpleasant sensation of being constantly watched, even though those who had ambushed them had dispersed—back, he assumed, to their usual work.

He clung for reassurance to the fact that they did have organized work to do, and went about it, rather than declining into apathy. How in the world had they survived last winter? He must find out!

A dense bank of cloud masked the sun, restoring the world to the gloom he had become accustomed to over most of the past year. In the temporary twilight he heard familiar noises—or rather, noises that used to be familiar: the cluck of hens, the baa-ing of sheep, the squeals and grunts of pigs. Unable to contain himself any longer, he rounded on Ed, who was keeping pace with his fitter companions up the steeply slanting road.

"Do you still have breeding stock of all your animals?"

The cripple halted and stared at him levelly, until he had to drop his gaze.

"I take it," Ed said at last, "that you do not."

"Well, we do have—"

"Probably as little as we do. Even the hens' eggs are rarely fertile, though the pigeons seem to have done all right. As for the piglets—! But that's enough for the moment. You're fat, to my amazement, and this is a steep hill. Save your breath until we get to the school."

"You have a school?" Curtis exclaimed. "It's in use?" That above all was the index he had chosen to mark out a survivable community: educating the next generation was the touchstone of confidence in the future. Hope flared for a second in his mind.

Then Ed said bitterly, "You mean pupils memorizing the classics by rote? As they would have said in the old days, thou hastest to be jokingest. Why can't you hold your politician's tongue for just a minute?"

Bridling, Tanner started to say something about due respect, but Curtis scowled him down, aware of a curious sense of anticipation. Could it be that these isolated people had found a solution to what had baffled all the brilliant brains for whom places had been reserved in the deep bunkers, who had emerged on the surface and for the most part thrown their hands up in despair, not knowing where to start again to build a civilized society?

Behind him, Smith was muttering curses against those around him and their ancestors. Curtis bit his lip.

Civilized?

They reached the building which was quite obviously a school; at any rate, before it lay a wide asphalt playground, with a merry-go-round, a slide, and a tall iron frame from which still hung three swings made of plain wooden boards on thick ropes. Assuming this to be their destination, Curtis slowed. But Mervyn, following close behind, hastened him on towards the largest house of all, atop the rise adjacent to the church.

"Isn't that the school?" he demanded of Ed,

panting; the pace the cripple was setting on the slope was tiring him.

"That? No, we use it mainly to store turnips and potatoes—not that we have much stock of either left."

"But it was a school, surely!" Curtis cried.

"Was," Ed echoed, and reached out with his crutch to tap Curtis on the buttocks, as though goading a sluggish ox. "And that other building we just passed *was* a chapel, only now most of us live in it because it's easier to keep warm when you all huddle together."

Trying not to stumble, Curtis half-turned to glance back at the chapel. It was built of the same stone as most nearby houses—a variety of granite, was his guess—but it had a line of pointed windows either side and a pointed door. He said, imagining he had guessed the explanation for what Ed had just told him, "Ah! Under the stress of the war, everyone came back to the older church. Was that the way of it?"

"Church?" said a female voice at his side. It was Cora.

"Yes, church!"—feverishly. "That church!" He gestured ahead, indicating the steeple silhouetted on the darkling sky, the long shape of the nave. He even fancied he caught a polychrome gleam reflected from stained glass.

"Oh, you mean the big barn," said Andy, coming up behind him. "That's where we keep our cows and horses."

"Where you—? *What?*" And Curtis registered from the corner of his eye the horror that Tanner was displaying.

"If only we had donkeys too," Cora sighed. "I always hoped we might breed at least a few mules,

but we only had one jack, and he died." She
sounded genuinely sorrowful.

Ed rapped on the road with his crutch, as though
to signal a warning, and she fell silent.

Gulping, Curtis ventured, "It sounds as though
you've set out deliberately to change the old
usages." And added, when no reply was forthcoming: "What have you turned that into? It looks
like the town hall."

"You're halfway right," Ed conceded. "But we
didn't plan it that way. We just took—had to
take—a fresh look at what was left to us. We didn't
have a hospital, and that was what we needed
most, and the town hall was the best choice. And
the old rectory with its nineteen rooms became
the school."

"School?" Curtis echoed in bewilderment. "Nineteen rooms? My God, how many of you are there?"

"Just over two hundred. There may have been a
birth or two today; we're expecting four about this
time."

"And you need a school with nineteen rooms?"

"I told you: not the kind of school you're accustomed to! In this foul new world, doesn't everyone
have to learn how to stay alive, all over again? The
war made students of us all, Mr. Minister—all that
are left!"

Waiting long enough to be sure his point had
sunk home in Curtis's mind, he concluded, "But
my father is the one you need to talk to. By now
he'll be expecting us. Come in and meet him!"

He strode ahead along a frost-deformed path-
way of slate slabs, traversing what must once have
been a handsome garden but now was trenched in
hope of growing potatoes. The few haulms that
had sprouted were wan and yellow. At least, though,
Curtis told himself, an effort was being made.

"I don't like this," Smith muttered. "I think it's a trap!"

Tanner's teeth were chattering again, but he contrived to say, "He said his father's expecting us. How's that possible? I didn't notice any phone-lines, I didn't see anybody run ahead of us—"

"Shut up and don't be such a fool!" Curtis snapped. "From here you can overlook the whole damned town! Are you so used to living underground that you've forgotten about windows with a view?"

Conscious of a petty triumph, he marched ahead through the main door of the house, which Ed was politely holding.

"On the right," the cripple said, and at the full reach of his crutch thrust a front-room door ajar.

"Come in!" called a husky voice.

Tanner and Smith hung back. Determined to shame them, Curtis advanced as he was bidden.

The room stretched from front to rear of the house, with windows at either end. In spite of that it was dark, not—like so many he had seen in the past year—because its interior had been blackened by smoke, but because its walls were lined and crammed with books in discolored bindings, no doubt salvaged from every library within reach, whether public or private. Some were neatly arranged on shelves; far more lay in stacks on the floor. A pair of trestle tables, that narrowed the floor-space, groaned under yet more books. One which caught his eye was a volume of the *Britannica*, its front cover folded back to reveal that its blank flyleaf had been torn out. Covered with dense writing, a sheet of paper which might be that flyleaf poked out from between the pages.

There was also a desk. On it reposed a pile of

scrap paper weighted with a brass statuette, a jar
holding a few pencils and several sticks of charcoal,
a bedpan, and a medicine-glass with a teaspoon in
it.

On its other side sat a man in a wheelchair.

Curtis experienced a curious temptation not to
see him: thin, his skin almost yellow, very tightly
stretched on the bone beneath, wearing a blue
dressing-gown with astonishing red lapels over a
thick undervest buttoned to the neck. That neck
was bird-thin, corded, the Adam's apple prominent.
Hands whose backs were corded, too, with bluish
veins, sprang from cuffs of the same red as the
lapels. Eyes sharp, keen, dark preserving a fire
which perhaps had once burned in the whole of
the wasting body, looked out of the gaunt face as
though from another world. However—

Having glanced at him only once, the minister
stared past him towards the far window, not
through it at the snow-streaked hillside beyond,
but at something pinned to its frame: a tatter-
edged sheet of paper bearing a broken cross in-
verted within a circle, blue on white.

Entering on Curtis's heels, Tanner saw it at the
same time and gave a strangled moan of dismay.
Then followed Smith and Smith's anger.

"What the hell have we wound up in? A nest of
stinking traitors, by God!"

He strode forward, hands raised as though to
tear down the paper with the symbol and trample
the man in the wheelchair on his way.

"Smith!" Curtis found his voice just in time.
"Stop it, damn you!"

"Don't you know what that is?" Smith roared,
rounding on him. "Have you forgotten what it
means? Cowards! Traitors! I've put up with all I'm
going to take from bastards like that!"

"I said *stop it!*"

For a terrible instant Curtis thought Smith was going to defy him. Then the bluster faded. The pilot turned his back in a pose of idiotic theatricality and stared fixedly out of the opposite window—which did indeed offer an overview of the whole town, past the school playground and the chapel clear to where the Optica had landed, perhaps even beyond on a clearer day than this.

There was a faint chuckle, most likely from Ed. But the cripple had closed the door and left them alone with his father.

Curtis found he was shaking with relief. It had been a shock to him too to find that long-banned symbol in this place. The last time he'd seen it had been—when? Oh, yes: cut with a knife on the naked breast of that woman the mob had lynched at Castle Cary. A traitor's sign? After the war it had been made more of a traitor's brand . . .

Yet chancing on it here might not be so incongruous after all. It was an arguable claim that the people who adopted it had thought more about the outcome of another war than anybody else save those like himself whose business it had been to plan for the catastrophe. And given that some of them, at least, had been possessed of a healthy urge towards survival—

He dragged his eyes away from the symbol and looked at his unexpected host. The latter's only response to Smith's outburst had been to adopt a stiff, out-of-practice smile. All the teeth had gone from both his jaws except five on the left upper side.

"Mr. Curtis!" he said. "Why, you've changed less than I have. When Olwen ran up here with the news, I wondered whether I'd recognize you from your old pictures in the papers. But I see the likeness plainly. What are you doing now that your constituency is—how shall I put it? Ah! A rotten borough? You used to be my Member, you know. As Ed would put it, my 'erected member'!"

Curtis suppressed a start and peered more closely at the skull-like face. Doubtfully he said, "I don't recall . . ."

"You wouldn't, naturally." The man attempted a chuckle, but it turned to a hacking cough, and it was seconds before he managed to continue. "As a matter of fact, we never actually met. But you once had the pleasure—as it were—of putting me in jail. My name is Eric Renshaw."

Click.

A photograph enclosed in a confidential dossier, its cover stamped RETURN TO NEW SCOTLAND YARD, SPECIAL BRANCH. A voice heard on the tape of an intercepted phone-call. A secret memorandum to a judge, insisting that he pass a heavy sentence on this dangerous subversive. . . .

Curtis felt the iron hand clasp his guts again, and had to steady himself with a touch on Tanner's shoulder. The contact informed him that the younger man was shaking like an aspen-leaf.

Aspen? How many aspens are in leaf this year? How long before no one will know what aspens look like?

"I see you do remember," Renshaw said. "In case you need further prompting, I should say that my offense consisted in leading two thousand people into the area designated for a Civil Defense exercise and demanding that they receive treatment as though they were genuine casualties, in hope that the government would prove it could be done. They'd promised it would be possible for millions, and my offense, in the last analysis, was to doubt that promise. Most of the others were

fined twenty pounds. As a ringleader, I was sin-
gled out for preferential punishment."

Again that forced, unhabitual smile, seeming to
be dredged from far in the past.

"Well, Mister Reginald Curtis, Member of Parliament?" There was the same note of mockery in this
voice that there had been in his son's—(Son? Vague
memory of a boy sent down from university because he missed a term's study when he likewise
got sent to jail after a protest demonstration . . .
but no recollection of him being crippled. Maybe
more than one child, then. What happened to the
others?)—only now the mockery wasn't veiled, but
overt.

"Well?" Renshaw taunted. "Which of us was
right—*Minister?*"

Curtis's vision swam. He heard, and felt, a gasp
break from his body. It was as though he stood at
one remove from himself, detached in space and
time as well. He barely reacted when Tanner spoke
to him.

"Here, sir! Here's a chair!"

Feeling it thrust against the backs of his knees,
he folded compliantly, fumbling again for his box
of tablets. He was supposed to take not more than
one every four hours, but this was an emergency.

As from a vast distance Renshaw's thin voice
reached him. "How rude of me not to have invited
you to sit down before. Mr. Tanner, do be seated—
and you, Wing Commander!"

Smith, half-turning, spat in the direction of
the open volume of *Britannica*, but missed, and resumed his glaring out the window. Renshaw gave
an exaggerated sigh.

"Well, when you get tired of standing . . . Mr.
Curtis, are you feeling better? Good! Well, you've
seen a sample of what I've been up to since our

paths last crossed. So, as I was going to say: how about yourself? Your electors can't be demanding much of your time these days."

How does he pack so much ghoulish cheerfulness into his voice? As though he were meeting an old friend after a trip abroad!

He said with an effort, "I gather you find the fate of my constituency amusing. I don't. I haven't been able to joke for a long time."

"Granted," Renshaw said. "It wasn't very funny, was it?"

"No one expected it to be!" Curtis flared, feeling a resurgence of his spirits as the tablet took effect. "But as for who was right—wasn't that what you just asked me?—*We* were! There was bound to be a nuclear war, and no one could make it go away by wishing! Anyway, that doesn't matter any more. The only thing that counts now is to make the best of what's left to us!" He realized his voice was too shrill, and forcibly lowered it. "Which, as far as I can tell, is what you're trying to do here. That puts us on the same side, doesn't it?"

"I'm not sure I'd entirely agree with you." Renshaw's fire-bright eyes, live embers in his ashen face, flicked from Curtis to Tanner to Smith's obstinate back, and settled on Curtis again. By then all mockery had vanished and his voice grew level and dry, like the bed of a stream in time of drought.

"Are you really a full minister now? When I last heard of you, you were only the Home Secretary's PPS."

Curtis nodded. He said thickly, "I was—uh—as you know, I was chairman of the House of Commons Committee on Civil Defence. I was . . . well, best qualified, I suppose."

"Of the survivors?" Renshaw needled.

"Yes, damn it!"

"I see. And where are you operating from—Corsham?"

"So you do know about the Emergency Government!"

"Of course. We had a couple of old-fashioned valve radios capable of surviving an EMP, and we rigged up some pedal-powered generators. We've been listening to you ever since the war."

"Then I'd have thought"—Curtis picked his way with care among words that might be as treacherous as land-mines—"you could have set up a transmitter too."

"Would you?" countered Renshaw noncommittally. "Well, we didn't. But we've monitored your broadcasts regularly in the hope of finding out something which in fact never gets mentioned. Maybe you can tell us."

Curtis felt sweat gather on his forehead. He ran his finger around the collar of his coat, for it suddenly felt far too tight.

"What?" he achieved at last.

"The present population of the British Isles."

Tanner stifled—half-stifled—a groan. From the corner of his eye Curtis saw that he had put his hand over his mouth as though to prevent himself uttering a reply. But what purpose did deception serve? He delivered the truth in a defiant tone.

"As near as we can tell: two hundred and eighty-five thousand."

"What?"

It was a source of grim satisfaction to Curtis to find that he had shattered Renshaw's mask-like composure. *Let him ponder what it's been like to live with that knowledge!*

But the other recovered rapidly. He said after only a brief pause, "I see. Those who made it to deep shelters with plenty of provisions, is that the way of it? So what became of your 'millions of probable survivors'?"

I knew it when I crossed the threshold and saw that symbol. It felt like walking into the past . . .

But—worse than that—abruptly it was like having the past stand up and speak to him. The promise of "millions of survivors" was as ridiculous as the peace symbol pinned to the window-frame, in this harsh real world.

He countered in the steadiest voice he could muster, "Do you mean how were the casualties caused?"

"I mean: how did more than fifty million of us die, Mr. Curtis? Casualties? That's a word we don't use. Dead bodies is what we say. Corpses!" He leaned back in his wheelchair. "How many were killed by what? That's plain English. I want an answer in the same blunt terms."

Oh, hell. . . !

"Tanner," Curtis muttered, "quote our estimates."

The civil servant's teeth were chattering again. But he took hold of himself and began to recite in the impersonal tone he frequently adopted when he was worried or had been reprimanded.

"We assess that twenty-four million died in the initial attack, from direct blast-effects or the subsequent fires. The weapons used were mostly of one-half to three megatons' yield, air-burst in the first wave, ground-burst in the second. Approximately another fourteen million died from the immediate effects of fallout during the next few weeks. Some otherwise uncontaminated areas, particularly in Wales, Ulster, the West of England and the West of Scotland, were more severely affected by fallout arriving later from North America, and intensive fallout from the battlefields on the continent is known to have drifted over southern and eastern counties."

At some point during Tanner's recital Renshaw had raised his hands and folded them on the desk as though in a sketch for prayer. He had not otherwise reacted.

Like a record being played, unemotionally, Tanner went on. He said, "What we refer to as the third strike, consisting of a salvo of kilo-ton weapons submarine-launched from the North Sea, resulted in approximately one million further deaths in the evacuation zone between Leominister and Stourbridge. This was about a week after the effective cessation of other hostilities."

He stopped.

"Go on," Renshaw said in a grating tone. "We began with over fifty million, and you've left a good many of them unaccounted for."

"Oh, for God's sake!" Curtis exploded. "What do you think? Starvation and sickness killed the rest of them! Contaminated water, deficiency diseases— wild dogs, come to that! Even before the freeze, epidemics were going through the survivors like machine-gun bullets!"

"The freeze," Renshaw repeated thoughtfully. "Yes. We feared that most. That's why we took such precautions."

Sensing the chance to switch the discussion on to a more positive track, Curtis said, "How do you mean?"

"Short of emigrating to the southern hemisphere, there was only one sane choice. Ed and I studied all the maps we could find, especially official ones showing probable targets and fallout patterns, and then I realized every penny we had and some on top, and bought a coal-mine."

"What?"

"You heard me! A worked-out coal-mine, with too little left in it to be economic. Enough, though, to keep a handful of people warm during the nuclear winter, if they didn't squander it. You passed the entrance on your way up here."

"And you used it as a shelter?"

"That as well, for the first few weeks."

"My God!" Curtis flung both hands in the air. "I wish we'd had a million like you!"

Renshaw bared his remaining teeth again. "What a far cry from the days when you called me one of Moscow's dupes!"

"That's what you always were and always will be!" Smith shouted, swinging round.

"Smith, *hold your bloody tongue!*" Curtis roared. "Stop living in the past! We need to find out more about what was done here. It might lead us to other pockets of survivors, and heaven knows we need every able-bodied person!"

Tanner drew Smith aside to soothe him, and Curtis was able to continue.

"You stocked the mine with food and—and medicines, and so on?" Receiving a nod: "How did the local people feel about what you were doing?"

"Oh, some of them thought we were crazy—the ones who had swallowed your propaganda. But there was forty per cent unemployment, and a good few had stopped believing in goverment promises ... Towards the end, naturally, almost everyone pitched in. We've come to be quite accepted now."

"I should hope so! Mr. Renshaw, I truly am impressed! If there's anything we can provide to help—I don't want to make you imagine we plan to take you over, because frankly all of us have our hands full, and more—but if there's anything you need ... Well, we're running short of almost everything, but we have reclaimed a lot of useful scrap, for instance."

"Bees?"

"I beg your pardon?"

"I said bees! Butterflies would be useful too, but I imagine all the butterfly-farms were wiped out. We're going to have to do one hell of a lot of hand-pollination, because we only managed to save two of our hives, and both the swarms are pretty sickly after months on sugar-syrup."

"Well—ah—I must confess I'm not sure. Tanner?"

"I don't think so, Minister," Tanner admitted.

"Oh, hell. Oh, hell. Oh, hell." Renshaw put his hands to his temples and squeezed so hard it seemed he might crack his skull like a walnut. Alarmed, Curtis leaned forward.

"I'm sure you don't need to despair so. Like I said, you've done miracles already!"

"Miracles? Oh, yes—miracles! Like the freak of the wind which spared us the worst of the fallout, is that what you mean? And were you too under the special protection of Providence?"

"I wasn't under anything," Curtis sighed. "Except—ground."

"You said a moment ago you couldn't make jokes any more!"

"I thought I couldn't. And it wasn't very witty anyway, was it?"

"True."

There was a pause. During it, Curtis glanced towards Smith, who stood drumming his fingers on his biceps, and realized that vast clouds had turned the sky beyond the window almost black. Casting around for something else to say, he chanced on a spark of memory.

"I shouldn't be calling you 'Mr.' Renshaw, should I? Weren't you a doctor in general practice?"

"You've no idea how general it's become!" Renshaw gave a harsh laugh, which as before turned into a cough. "Now I'm a bo'sun tight and a midshipmite and everything by turns: teacher, ecologist, agronomist, town clerk . . ."

"In other words, you're the leader of this community."

"Leader? Heaven's name, man! The opposite!"

Curtis blinked incomprehension.

"Oh, I'm sure you'd love to pin that label on me, but I can't oblige. Why should the people here choose to take orders from a stranger who fled to them for refuge?"

"But you must have some sort of—of organization?"

"I suppose you could say we live under a system of primitive communism . . . Ah, Wing Commander Smith has turned around! Why don't you sit down now? It's getting too dark to see much out there."

"Did you just say you were a communist?" Smith flared, taking an angry pace forward.

"I did not. I never bothered much with party politics. Though I did once point out to an American that in order to recover from a nuclear war it would be necessary to adopt all the practices he regarded as unforgivably socialist: central control of all resources, for example, direction of labor, confiscation of private property for the general good, and so on. 'From each, to each, according—' I forget the precise wording. But I imagine it's much the same everywhere now."

For a second Curtis was afraid Smith might dispute Renshaw's statement, but it was incontrovertible even by him. With a shrug, he seized a chair laden with books, tilted it so they crashed to the floor, and sat down at last. There was no discernible reaction from Renshaw, who resumed where he had left off.

"And, speaking of America: are they sending any aid?"

Curtis felt himself flush, and was glad of the dimness.

"Not so far. The weather seems to have been even worse there than in Europe, but they say they have a lot of uncontaminated farmland, and with only about twenty million people left to feed—"

"Stop it!" Smith bellowed. "Stop playing up to this son of a bitch! Don't you see? That's what he wants to hear! He wants to be told how bad it was for us, and the Yanks, and everyone else in the free world, so he can sit there and gloat about it! Why in hell don't you tell him what we did to the buggers on the other side? That'll wipe the grin off his face!"

Rounding on Renshaw, he poured forth words like vomit.

"Why don't you ask what happened to the commies that you love so much? Well, I'll tell you! We burned them, by the bloody millions we burned them! Whatever they gave us we gave back double, only worse! They died like goddamned flies when we were through with them! Christ, I wish I could send you to join 'em! What the hell did you do to help out when the crunch came, tell me that? Oh, you ran for your cosy bolt-hole, didn't you? While *I* was out there finishing off a whole division and damned near getting killed in the process, *you* were sitting on your arse whining for your beloved Russkies to protect you from the wicked British government!"

"What was that about finishing off an entire division?" Renshaw said. Only his lips moved;

the rest of him was still as a statue carved in stone.

"Smith, be quiet!" Curtis shouted.

"I will not! He's a traitor—a traitor—a lousy stinking *traitor!*" Leaping up from his chair, he planted his fists on the desk and leaned so close that flecks of spittle from his lips landed on the older man's face.

"I'm proud of what I did, d'you hear me? I was a Jaguar pilot, and I bombed the bastards between Chemnitz and Plauen, and I hope I killed a hundred thousand of them, *and* I made it home to go on fighting! But you! *You. . . !*"

He locked his fingers together as though around a throat. His joints cracked like dry twigs breaking.

"I never before met a man who could drop a nuclear bomb," Renshaw said after a pause that was like the moment between the lightning and the thunder. "But I must say you're exactly the kind of person I always pictured."

"What the hell do you mean by that?" Smith screamed. Curtis, struggling to his feet, cast around for some way to stop him physically attacking Renshaw, but before he could shape words the doctor himself found a solution. His thin claw-hand dropped momentarily out of sight under the desk; when it reappeared, it was holding a revolver.

"Sit down," he said to Smith, a trace of perspiration on his parchment forehead catching the last glint of daylight.

The pilot stepped back. He said mockingly, "You'd never have the guts to use that thing."

"Oh, you mistake me. I've never been a pacifist by conviction, any more than I'm a traitor. There are situations where a threat of force will persuade rational men to adopt a wiser course of action. I'm sure you're a rational man—aren't you?

But just in case you're skeptical, I assure you this is a real gun, with real ammunition. And . . . Well, while I've killed fewer than you, I too have killed."

Smith, face suddenly paling, lowered himself back to his chair. His expression reflected total incredulity.

As though returning from an immense distance, Curtis felt himself slip back into a different mode of existence. Desperate to deflate the tension, he essayed jocularity.

"Well, well, Dr. Renshaw! How strange to find you a convert to the theory of deterrence!"

"Oh, deterrence can be made to work." Renshaw did not withdraw his dark gaze from Smith. "As between rational individuals, that is. But a government is not an individual and there are excellent grounds for claiming that it can't be rational, either. A thousand otherwise intelligent and sober people can become a mob with an IQ lower than an animal's. So can an army, which is another kind of mob. The whole can be made to act like less than the sum of its parts. The wing commander here has acted logically in face of what you're pleased to call my deterrent. He has removed the factor which would have led to his destruction by sitting down. The old governments, of one of which you once had the honor to be a minor representative, never behaved as sanely as that, did they? On the contrary! Mr. Smith would have acted like one of those governments if, for example, he had continued to approach with hands raised as though to strangle me, saying the while, 'You can't scare me!' And his death would inevitably have resulted, as have so many billions of others. I remember saying, Mr. Curtis—if not to you personally, at least to other members of your party—that the rational course for governments facing each other under the threat of annihilation was for them mutually to admit that they had made a mistake and set out in search of a better alternative. Since their collective intelligence, however, was by then at a somewhat lower level than that of the barbarians who followed Genghis Khan, they went right on doing what they were used to doing, much as an animal will batter a wall with its head till it's unconscious, instead of learning to lift the latch of a door."

"Don't rub it in," Curtis said wearily. "We miscalculated, that's undeniable. But we're doing our best to make amends."

"You remind me of a story they tell about Napoleon," Renshaw said. "I seem to recall that you admired Napoleon in the old days, so you probably know this anecdote. It seems he had dismissed one of his generals, and friends of the disgraced officer came to plead for him, saying, 'He did his best!' And Napoleon said—"

" 'Show me a man who has not yet done his best,' " Curtis supplied. " 'For him there is still hope.' "

"Yes."

There was a short silence, almost complete save that they heard trudging footsteps on the road. No doubt it had become so dark that people were having to return from outdoor work. Moreover it was growing cruelly cold.

When the pause became unendurable Curtis forced out, "You said you're not the local leader, because you came here as an outsider. Was there not a mayor, or somebody—uh—*before?*"

"Are you referring to the chairman of the council?"

"I suppose so."

"He was assigned a place in a deep bunker. He

took it, and left his family. Since then we've heard no more."

"Well, then!" Curtis racked his brains. "There must have been—ah—a vicar, or a parson!"

"Indeed. But they expelled him from the shelter."

Curtis jolted upright, unsure he could believe his ears, but Renshaw locked eyes with him.

"Yes, you heard right. He was an outsider, as I am, but he had done nothing to help—nothing but praise the Lord for granting to his faithful flock this triumph over the hordes of unbelievers. So they decided his was a mouth not worth feeding, and told him to cast himself on the mercy of God. . . . Of course, he was deranged by the war, but he was not alone in that. If we did win, as Mr. Smith would doubtless claim, the victory was Pyrrhic. The people here come of a very old stock, Mr. Curtis. For century upon century they have demanded that their priests and lords produce results. And when they don't . . ."

The thin hand that did not hold his gun folded in mid-air, as though closing the cover of a book.

"An equally sad fate overtook someone you'd doubtless want news of: the local Civil Defense organizer. We were told about him by refugees who'd been shot at when they sought admission to the county emergency headquarters. Not that any of them survived for long, poor devils.

"At any rate, they reported how, when he realized what sort of task he was facing now the bombs had actually fallen, he took poison. He was probably the first victim of the war in his home town. Not, naturally, the last."

Curtis felt another twinge from his ulcer. He said angrily, "Much more of this and I'll have to agree with Smith! You *are* gloating!"

"I'm trying to confront the facts, that's all. As I

told Mr. Smith: I too have killed. And I have—
mostly with a bubble of air injected into a vein,
because air costs nothing. I've had to give release to
the aged, and the incurably radiation-sick, and the
hopelessly burned, and now I'm having to dispose
of malformed babies: so far, nine. I've betrayed all
the ancient tenets of my calling, just about. But
we do have over two hundred people, and they're
mostly fit, and even cripples like my son have
been given the chance to contribute to the community—Yes, of course! The word I should have
used, to avoid offending Mr. Smith, was *commu-
nalism.* What we have left belongs by consent to
whoever makes best use of it. We've had to be so
careful about waste, you know . . ."

He shook his head repeatedly as the last word
died away.

"Mr.—ah—*Dr.* Renshaw," Tanner ventured, "may
we go back now? Mr. Curtis has told you we don't
plan to interfere, but really it's getting very dark,
and . . ." He swallowed noisily, more air than saliva.

"And I've had the ill manners to offer neither
food nor drink since your arrival," Renshaw said,
recovering his poise. "Well, I'm afraid it's not in
my power to grant you anything, you see. The
people must decide."

Before Curtis could ask what was meant by that
extraordinary remark, there came a knock and the
door swung open. Turning, he saw Ed.

"We're all ready, father. Shall I push you down?"

"Ready?" Tanner echoed in a querulous tone.
"For what?"

"You are to meet the people," Renshaw said,
returning his pistol to its drawer. "Since it's neither snowing nor raining, they have assembled in
the playground. There will be torches to see by. I
trust you have no objection."

"On the contrary!" Setting his shoulders back, Curtis climbed to his feet. "It's a chance I welcome!"

"I regret I don't feel up to the strain of accompanying you," Renshaw went on with a sidelong glance at Ed. "I was severely radiated while tending the refugees, you see. More and more my son has had to take over. I hope you won't feel slighted if I remain here."

"Don't trust him!" Smith barked. "This cowards' hideout reeks of trickery! It makes my skin crawl!"

Curtis ignored him. To Renshaw he said with awkward deference, "I really meant it—sir—when I said I admire your achievements. Particularly since . . ." He mistrusted the next words that sprang to his tongue, but Renshaw divined them.

"You were perhaps going to say: since it's been done by cooperation, not compulsion? I suspect you've based your work in recovery and reconstruction on the threat of force: am I right?"

"Well . . ." Curtis licked his lips, finding his mouth as dry as Tanner's sounded. "Well, a nucleus of disciplined organization—"

"I see. 'Do as you're told, or I'll kill you!' Well, that's never been my way. But one thing I beg you to remember, Mr. Curtis—beg you!" Abruptly his tone was fierce.

"I came here late, and what little I've been able to accomplish has been done in a short time and under terrible difficulties, whereas what you and your kind did has been going on for centuries. Don't blame me for other people's failings, though heaven knows I have plenty of my own!"

Elbows on the desk, he dropped his face in his hands and finished in a muffled tone, "I said I'm not the leader of these people, and that's true. No more is Ed. We had to put up with the only terms on which they'd let us settle here. Like I said, they come of very ancient stock, and they've seen too much deceit to put their trust in strangers readily . . .

"No! All I know how to be is their servant!"

Curtis remained staring at Renshaw for a long time before he was distracted by a glare of yellow light. Still carrying his rifle, Mervyn had come to join Ed, and behind him, each with a flaring torch, stood two more men, alike enough for brothers, with full black beards, red cheeks and heavy canvas aprons, looking like blacksmiths fresh from the forge.

It had been in Curtis's mind to ask about food, drink, and beds for the night, but something in the bearded men's faces made his heart quail. With what spirit he could muster he approached the door.

Smith caught his arm.

"For God's sake, are you out of your mind? You're a bloody minister, aren't you? Order 'em to fix the plane and let us go!" He swung to face Renshaw. "You! Tell 'em to put our radio back so we can contact our base! Or it'll be the worse for you!"

Renshaw did not react. After a moment Ed answered for him.

"Apparently you weren't listening. He doesn't tell any of us what to do. That's up to the individual to decide."

"Now see here, you snivelling pup!" Smith began, and clubbed a fist.

Balanced on his crutch, Ed looked down at the fist, then up at Smith's face.

He said evenly, "Okay, go ahead. I've always imagined that the sort of man who could drop a nuclear bomb could hit a cripple."

Smith hesitated. After a moment, seeming

ashamed, he drew back. He said, as though the point had just struck him, "How did you get like that, anyhow?"

Ed gave his one-sided shrug and turned to the door. Over his shoulder he said, "Ancient history. Come on."

"The way he got like that," said one of the black-bearded men harshly, "was dragging a kid out of a wrecked house. A burning beam fell on them. We lost the kid but we got him back—just. Satisfied?"

Smith shook his head, as though stunned by that same beam, and started off in Ed's wake. Tanner followed like a puppet on strings, and then, with a last puzzled look at Renshaw, so did Curtis.

More flaring torches on poles marked their destination in the old school playground. As before, Ed set a brisk pace despite his crutch. This time, though, to Curtis's astonishment, Smith kept level with the cripple and cast glance after sidelong glance at him, as though winding up to say something. He found the right words just before they drew abreast of the playground gate.

"Hey, whatever your name is—Ed! I keep thinking I've seen you before!"

Ed nodded. "Very likely. Weren't you based at RAF Paulton Vale, about twenty miles from Oxford?"

"Yes, I was!" Smith tensed.

"While I was up at the 'Varsity I went on an all-night disarmament vigil at the gates of your station. Coming back from the pub, you and a couple of your chums pelted us with beer-bottles, and scored a lot of hits. We tried catching some in the hope they might be full. No such luck, I'm afraid . . . Well, here we are."

He gestured with his crutch, and at the same

moment the torch-bearers hoisted their flares aloft, dispelling the unseasonable dark. Curtis caught his breath. It had been so long since he saw so many people gathered in the open air, other than casualties—

But here, he forced himself to remember, that word wasn't used.

Shapeless as fungi in what clothing they had salvaged, but with their faces visible in the flickering glow, the entire population of the town appeared to be present, down to babes in arms. Unsurprisingly, there were no very old folk, the likeliest victims of radiation-sickness (and Curtis re-heard in memory what Renshaw had said about killing . . .), though many were leaning on sticks and sucking bare gums. What struck him most about them, however, was their utter stillness. He did not even hear a foot shift on gravel, let alone a child's cry.

There was a medieval feeling about this assembly, he realized, what with blacksmiths—he glanced at their escorts—plough-hands, butchers, most likely shepherds and carpenters and masons, all in basic trades . . . Miners too? No doubt. But winning coal now only for the local folk, no longer wage-slaves to a distant and anonymous master, be that a land-owner or the State. A shiver stole down his spine, as though the thought portended something ominous. What Renshaw had said about the vicar haunted him: to have deliberately driven a man of the cloth out of their shared refuge, leaving him to heaven only knew what fate . . .

"Over here, please," Ed said urbanely.

The playground seesaw had been propped at either end to form a bench. Having seen them seated on it, the cripple hopped nimbly up on the nearby roundabout and called out.

"You all know what's happened, don't you? We have visitors from the Emergency Government! Here's Mr. Reginald Curtis, and he's the Minister of National Recovery!"

He glanced down. "Mr. Curtis, say something, please, so they can recognize your voice. There are several people here who can't see you because they were looking towards the Trawsfynydd bomb. Tests at Johnston Island in 1958 showed that burns could be sustained on the retina as far as 345 statute miles from the explosion. Sorry. I'm forever quoting my father's books." He gave his usual twisted smile.

Sick, but not daring to flare up despite such needling, Curtis rose. Here was something he had always hated ever since he entered politics, the chore of addressing a working-class crowd. His natural accent was easy to parody, as had been proved by countless radio comedians. His home constituency had been mainly residential and dominated by the upper middle class, so he was accepted there. However, when it came to speaking in support of a colleague in another area . . .

But this was now and that was then. Distinctions of the old kind must be got rid of. Did he dare say "we're all in the same boat"?

"My friends!" he began, and paused to let that greeting register. "I've been here only a few hours, and I'm more impressed than I can say with your success in getting back to normal life in face of appalling difficulties. I think it's bloody marvellous, I really do."

And sat down, sweating of a sudden despite the chill.

"Also we have Mr. Smith, a pilot," Ed announced, and added under his breath, "Excuse me for not mentioning your rank."

Smith glowered, folded his arms, stretched out his booted legs and faked a yawn.

"And Mr. Tanner, the minister's assistant," Ed concluded. "I won't call on them to speak because I'm sure most of your questions will be addressed to the minister, right?"

There was a grumbling sound in agreement, and abruptly, despite the muzziness that second pill had created in his brain, Curtis realized what was going on. This wasn't just a town meeting. This was to be an interrogation.

This was a trial . . .

Pain blazed up from his stomach, ran through his limbs, exploded dazzlingly behind his eyes so that for a second he could not see.

"Oh, my God!" he whispered. "Justice is blind!"

"What?" Smith, scowling, glanced at him. "Can't you hurry them up with this farce, sir?"

He said "Sir," and he never says that unless he's scared . . . Why here, why now? This is a stupid man! He could never have the insight I just had, which is truly fearful!

But Smith was going on, offering a very real reason to be afraid.

"If we don't signal base, they'll assume we've been captured by invading forces! They'll order a search-and-destroy mission, and I've seen what those can do!"

Oh. They very well might, being rendered paranoid by the universality of affliction. And one can't just mislay a cabinet minister, even now—

But in the front row of the small crowd a woman was standing forth, who looked elderly and might not be, who looked blind and definitely was. Querulous, her voice was nonetheless loud, and rasped at Curtis's nerves.

"I want the minister to tell me—" And a gasp for breath, racking in her throat. "I want him to tell me what became of my sister as lived over to Reading. That's all I want. Just let him tell me that."

Curtis struggled to think of a reply, against an intolerable burden of pain. He said at last, "Well, I'm afraid more than one bomb was dropped in that area, so I don't really know what happened to your sister."

"Yes, you do"—matter-of-factly.

"I don't quite follow ..." Forcing a smile that felt from inside as naked as the grin of a skull.

"Yes, you do!"—not from the might-be-old woman now, but shrilly from a teenage boy at her side: her son...? Yes! "You know damned well what happened to my auntie! If she was lucky her house fell down and killed her quick. If she wasn't, she was burned alive in it, or got radiation-sick so her hair and teeth fell out and her guts rotted and she died slow. Or she starved, or she caught a fever, or else she froze to death. Ah, you know that!"

A kind of sad triumph showed in the woman's face, and those around her uttered soft agreement.

"How much of this do we have to put up with before they offer us a meal and a bed?" whispered Tanner.

"A lot more, I'm afraid," Curtis said resignedly. "But I'll do my best to talk us through it ... Yes?"—to a stolid-looking man leaning with one arm against the children's slide and the other tentatively raised.

Invited to speak, he suddenly coughed, and made two false starts before he forced his question out.

"Cousins of ours emigrated to New Zealand. And there are others here with kinfolk in Australia."

Again a struggle for breath; then, valiantly:

"When can we look forward to help from Down
Under, including food?"

"Yes! Yes!"—from half a dozen throats, and someone else said clearly, "That's what I'd like to know,
too!"

"You'll have to answer, Mr. Curtis," Ed murmured, leaning close. "How about the rest of the
world? It's been some while since we saw the TV
news, you know."

Bastards, traitors, sons of bitches— Words such
as Smith might have uttered echoed in Curtis's
head. *Mocking me, hitting me when I'm down! And
all the time this blasted pain making me so giddy . . .
or the pills . . .*

His old reflexes, however, took command, and
he heard himself say with the properly regretful
inflection, "Well, we are hoping for aid from Australia and New Zealand, and naturally now we
know about your community we'll make sure to
divert part of what we get to you, though we can't
predict when it will arrive because of course they
have problems of their own thanks to the Chinese,
and—"

He broke off before he started to ramble. Why
burden people like this with so much of the bitter
truth about the ruins that the last bulwarks of the
Old Commonwealth had fallen into? He was here
to encourage, not depress them.

Were there any more questions? He peered about
him in the flickering torchlight, and abruptly noticed that the little crowd was parting down its
center, to let pass with deference a man he had not
seen before. Elderly, of middle height, as shabbily
clad as his companions, there was little remarkable about his appearance save that his beard was
very long and very white. He walked with a
stick—to lean on, Curtis assumed at first; then

realized abruptly: he, like so many of the rest, was blind.

"That's Dewi Price," Ed whispered. "His family has farmed hereabouts for more than four hundred years. Rumor has it that they came of bardic stock. At any rate he has the *hwyl*."

"What does that mean?" Curtis mumbled. He was beginning to feel that today's flight had borne him not just across a landscape once familiar, now grown alien, but to a different century as well. Now, to baffle him still further, the language too was becoming foreign.

"You'll find out," Ed promised, and withdrew.

Guided by one of the black-bearded brothers, while the other followed, Price took station directly confronting Curtis. Planting his stick before him, he leaned forward on it, hand above hand.

"Blind I may be," he said in a high, penetrating voice. "Deaf I am not, thank the Lord. I heard young Ed say we had been here four hundred years, but that's only as long as we've held written title to the land. Say a thousand and you still might miss the mark. More likely, we were driven hither by the Romans. And we lived. Through the age of hunting and the age of herding and the age of mining it has been our land. Through fat years and lean years, through rain and drought and health and plague, it has been our fathers' land, their fathers', and then ours. And now at last it has been raped and robbed from us, with subtle poisons that will not decay for years."

As he spoke, his sightless gaze bored into Curtis's face and his words took on the character of a lilting chant. The minister summoned his scattered wits at last.

Who's this—some fanatical lay preacher who's

*found a rôle as local spokesman? I've met that type
at election meetings. Why do they always spell trouble?*

While he was still struggling to decide whether
this was actually a question, Smith spoke up
unexpectedly.

"We gave as good as we got, you know—if not
more!"

Feeling as though stones were about to be hurled
at him, Curtis closed his eyes. When he dared to
reopen them, he was amazed to discover that no
one had moved.

Except Price. Now he stood upright, shoulders
back, his stick held in both gloved hands and canted
across his body like a rifle at the port.

"We do not *haff* to be told that!" And he tightened his grip on the stick as though to twist it
until it snapped.

"We do not *haff* to be told there was a war! We
do not *haff* to be told how millions died, and land
was spoiled and cattle sickened from the tainted
grass, along with sheep and pigs and birds and
bees! The sun itself was stolen from us! My blind
man's bones could measure your abominations by
the lack of summer!"

He raised his stick head-high in his right hand,
and there was a sort of settling among the on-
lookers, as though they were watching a fixed and
ancient ritual, and some key stage had just been
properly attained.

"What you must tell us, you who call yourself a
Minister, is this!"—and his voice dropped, from a
pitch that might carry for miles across a mountain
valley, to a deep and thrilling boom such as could
once have made the rafters of a Great Hall ring . . .
or the dank recesses of a cave.

"Who started it?"

*   *   *

Curtis felt as though he were running headlong through dense fog, fleeing nameless horrors, striving to recall the pattern of the one safe path. What answer could he offer? Was he to recount how wheat and rice harvests suddenly failed all over Russia and Asia, so the scythe of famine cut down victims by the million, and a wave of desperate survivors welled out in all directions, including across the East-West border? Scarcely, for at that stage there had still been normal news; this must be known to everybody. On the other hand, people like Renshaw, or Price, or others here, might have been convinced by all those propaganda claims to the effect that blights had been deliberately spread, to win a war without beginning one. Even among the loyal handful left at Corsham there remained suspicions, because the Western powers had refused to send relief although its stocks of food were such that governments were paying farmers not to plough their land . . .

In the wan torchlight the faces of the people showed like gravestones, each the memorial to an infinity of lost hopes.

Curtis heard himself starting to babble.

"You have to remember we were faced with overwhelming odds! It was more like a massacre than warfare, and the defenders were being rolled up like a carpet! Besides—"

It was useless. Price was moving his stick back and forth in the air, like a magician's wand wiping away the echo of futile words.

"We seek the truth," he said, his tone reverting to the conversational as though he were conscious of having performed the rite required of him and cast the proper, necessary spell. "You know it. You must, or else you're lying about who you are. *Tell us who was the first to use The Bomb!*"

The crowd edged, as one, ever so slightly nearer, and a score of hands caught the faint light as they were cupped to deafened ears.

But while Curtis was still floundering, Smith burst out again.

"Even a bunch of peasants like you ought to know the facts by now! Mr. Curtis is right—there was a bloody massacre going on! We *had* to use our tactical weapons! *Had* to! Or else the Fourteenth Soviet Armored Division would have bust clear through between Bremen and Wesermünde before our forces could fall back on the Ems!"

Oh, Smith. You fool. You fool. You goddamned fool . . .

For a moment Curtis was afraid the audience would become a mob and tear them limb from limb. Yet when he looked about him—at Ed, and particularly at the keloid that had formed along his jaw; at the blind woman who probably wasn't old; at her son; at Dewi Price who said his forebears had lived here since Roman times—he saw no faintest sign of a reaction.

He was about to heave a sigh of relief when Price spoke anew. Then he realized why.

"And you were a member of the government that authorized that. How did you earn your position?"

Oh, Christ. The reason they didn't respond to Smith's admission was because they didn't need to ask. They knew already . . . And Renshaw said they killed their vicar!

He swayed on the child-narrow board of the seesaw, only vaguely feeling Tanner's hand offered in support, only distantly hearing Tanner's voice—*another damned fool! I'm cursed and plagued with them!*—explain to the crowd the story of his career, his qualifications, his right to rule.

As though that had anything to do with it . . .

*   *   *

Silence returned when the recital ended. It was broken this time by one of the black-bearded smiths. Smith: smith. Funny! Curtis wanted to laugh, but there was too much pain at the pit of his stomach.

The man said stonily, "So you knew what it was going to be like, and you didn't warn us."

"Nobody could be sure what it was going to be like," Curtis wheezed. "I assure you there was no intention to mislead. If you look at the record—"

"The record's been burned up. And you didn't just mislead us. You cheated and you lied. We found that out in the end. Ed here now—I recollect him before the war, and his father, always talking about what would happen.

"Me, I used to laugh at him. I said along with the rest of us, 'Ah, if it were like you say the government would let us know. And have they? So it can't be as bad as you make out!' But it was! Rot your soul in hell, it was a thousand times worse!"

Once, a long time ago, at a public meeting, someone like enough to Price to have been Price had risen with a similar charge, and Curtis had offered a facile answer about being accused of warmongering if they prepared the population with an intensive publicity campaign. He thought of quoting himself, and decided it wasn't worth the effort.

Something had happened by the time he reached that conclusion, though. A murmur of agreement seemed to have passed among the crowd. There was a shifting. Mothers with small children were heading for the gate. Mervyn had been standing apart with his gun at his side, butt on the ground; now he caught it up and held it alertly across his body, exactly as Price had held his stick.

Not noticing, Smith gave a snort and rose, wiping his face with the back of his glove. "What a bloody performance!" he muttered. "I expected some sensible questions, like about what we can do for them. I bet we'd have got there if you hadn't said it was us that lit the fuse!"

Did I? I thought it was you who put the fact into so many words . . . But why argue when it's too late?

"Well, we did," Curtis grunted. "And you can't say we weren't expecting what followed. Maybe you didn't get to read the umpires' reports from our joint maneuvers with the NATO forces, but I did." He felt very tired, and the griping from his ulcer was coming in rapid waves. "Besides—What is it, Tanner?"

His aide had uttered a wordless cry and pointed across the playground, towards the high iron frame from which the swings depended. The smiths were reaching up to unhook the ropes one by one. Another man stood by with ropes of a different kind.

"So it was a trial," Curtis whispered. "And they found us guilty."

"What?" Smith burst out, clenching his fists. A second later the truth dawned, and he rounded wildly on Curtis.

"You're crazy! I said you were leading us into a trap, and you were! Now you can damned well talk us out of it! Come on, tell 'em what'll happen if they do this to a cabinet minister! D'you hear me?"

Their brief task complete, the black-bearded brothers returned towards the seesaw: large men, with muscles accustomed to heavy weights.

"Curtis!" Smith raged. "This is what that smooth-tongued treacherous devil Renshaw really stands for! Here's the truth behind his prating about peace! Aren't I right?"

When Curtis failed to reply, he spun on his heel.

"All right, you bastards!" he shouted. "Come and get me! I'm not one of your milk-and-water pacifists! If you want to string me up you'll have to catch me first, and I swear I'll see one of you in hell when I arrive—and maybe more!"

"What does he mean?" whimpered Tanner. "What does he think they're going to do?"

Curtis guessed that he knew very well; that bar which had held the swings echoed lynching scenes aplenty from films and television. But he preferred to disbelieve.

As for himself . . .

Suddenly there was noise. Fighting. Smith had tried to run for the gate. It was futile, of course. Curtis closed his eyes again. He could barely think now, the pain plus the pills were so paralyzing, but words did bubble to the surface of his mind: words he wanted to speak aloud, only somehow they wouldn't cross his tongue and reach his lips.

He wanted to say: *Smith, you're wrong. All the Smiths have always been wrong, and the Curtises too. What you said just now, about what lies behind Renshaw's words—it isn't true. Oh, I'm sure he knew what was likely to happen and that's why he preferred to stay at home. But think of what he said as we left him: "All I've accomplished was done in a short time under terrible difficulties, whereas what you and your kind did has gone on for centuries."*

That's true, Smith-so-proud-of-giving-as-good-as-he-got, Smith-pot-calling-kettle-black, Smith-see-you-in-hell-first. It was done at leisure over generations, and in the end we made them proud that they too could slaughter people by the millions. Look at me, everybody! I can make babies come deformed, same as you can!

And now they've realized the consequences, and

since they're ordinary decent people they're ashamed. Worse, they're angry. And they only know one way to set things right: the way we've taught them all their lives.

When they came for him, Curtis kept his eyes closed. He kept them shut even when the rough noose coiled around his neck and he heard the order given to jerk him off his feet and let him hang.

EDITOR'S INTRODUCTION TO:

PETROGYPSIES

by
Rory Harper

Several years ago I was invited to a conference with the NASA Administrator. Marvin Minsky, one of the founders of MIT's Artificial Intelligence Laboratory, was visiting at the time, and was to be part of the conference—indeed, he'd arranged my own invitation. The conference was to be held near Monterey, California, which is a six-hour drive from here; and since the conference site wasn't near an airport, and we'd have to rent a car once in Monterey, it seemed reasonable to drive.

In recent years they've completed Highway 101 which runs down the western part of California; but for many years there was a long stretch of 101 only one lane wide. The alternative in those days was Highway 99, a long boring route through Bakersfield and up the San Joaquin Valley. Neither route was very appealing, so I found another which led along the base of the Temblor Range. More to the point, my route went through the oilfields around Taft, California, and one of the sights along the route was an ancient wooden oil derrick: the first well drilled in that field. Wonder of wonders, it was still pumping a tiny trickle of thick sludge.

Minsky and I stopped to look at it. Marvin had recently been given a contract to develop computerized robotic aids for oil drilling, but he had never seen an oil well. Just north of Taft we came to another operating oil rig; this one was one of the portable steel towers that have taken the place of the picturesque wooden derricks. The drilling crew were pulling the drill string out preparatory to changing the drilling head. Marvin and I watched for nearly an hour; it's a fascinating process, with each man in the crew doing a precise job at precisely the right time. If one of them misses a cue, the others could get hurt—but the job isn't regular, because sometimes it takes a little longer to unscrew one of the pipes, or to stand the removed pipe in its stack. It wouldn't be easy to computerize.

I've since studied a little about oil drilling. It turns out you can get an undergraduate degree in drilling mud mixing, and the selection and use of oil tools is a complex subject requiring a lot of expertise and experience.

Rory Harper lives in Houston, Texas, home of many oil millionaires; and it's obvious that he's done some study of oil drilling. It's a little hard to pin down just when and where this story takes place; my guess is that it happens after a not very devastating nuclear war, or perhaps a plague. Whenever it is, it's obvious there have been some amazing advances in molecular genetic biology. . . .

Rory Harper

PETROGYPSIES

J K POTTER

I glanced up from a shovel full of pig slop just as the Driller made the corner down by the dried-up bed of Hanson's Creek.

The sun was about half set, so at first all I could make out was a long dark *something* churning up a cloud of red-dirt dust. It was wide as the road and then some. And long—the front of the Driller must have been more than a hundred feet past the curve before the cloud at the end trailed off and blew away. I never saw nothing like it in my life before.

I yelled out. By the time it drew up down at the cattleguard, all eight of us, Papa and Grampaw and us four kids, plus two dogs, were clustered in front of the porch steps with three squirrel guns, a deer rifle, a hayfork, and a slop shovel pointed in its general direction. It stopped at the cattleguard and the dust started to settle. The lower flanks were streaked red and gray from travel, but the rest of it was black as a moonless night, only all slick and shiny like the intestines of a fresh-slaughtered bull. Hundreds of stumpy feet marched in place all the way down its length. I had a thought that shooting it probably wouldn't do much more than tee it off if it decided to come through the gate and eat us and the farmhouse.

It stood quietly about forty feet away, with the people getting more quiet and the dogs getting more noisy every second, and then a head popped out of a hole that opened in its top near the front. The rest of a human body followed until a bearded man was free from its innards. He slid down the slope of its foot high flank and walked towards us. He was wearing a gray jumpsuit with colored patches sewed all over it. On his head perched a battered silver-metal hat with a wide brim all the way around.

"Howdy, folks," he called out as he walked toward us. "I'm Doc Miller. This'd be the MacFarland place, I take it." He tugged leather gloves off and offered his hand for a shake as he drew near. He was a big, strong-looking man. He came nearly up to my chin height, and I suspected if we arm-rassled, it'd be chore to put him down.

Papa nodded cautiously, handed me his gun, and stuck out his own calloused hand.

"Didn't mean to startle you folks. Pleasure to meet y'all." The man twitched his head back in the direction of the road. Holes had opened up in half a dozen places along the Driller's body and more men were climbing out of them. "We heard in Hemphill that y'all had been a little water-poor of late and came by to see if you'd be interested in a business proposition."

We hadn't seen rain for most of a month. We'd been managing to haul in barely enough water for man and beast, but the corn visible in the field behind the house had already started to turn from green and gold to brown and dead. Papa couldn't have said he wasn't interested even if he'd wanted to. Without water, and soon, this year's harvest would be ten acres of dry stalks. Last year hadn't been much to speak of, and this one just might be bad enough to run us off the land.

In the morning, Papa and the two youngest, Danny and Greg, took the buckboard to town after breakfast to see about getting a loan from the Grange Bank to pay the gypsies and buy lumber for the irrigation troughs. After I did my chores I wandered over with Towser at my heels to where the Driller squatted and watched while the gypsies got ready. They'd made camp at the far end of the pasture because the slope of the land was such

that it was the best place to start running an
irrigation system from.

Doc Miller stood on top of the head of the Driller
directing things. The pasture looked like the carnival had arrived. They'd pitched half a dozen tents
of various bright colors, and they fussed with piles
of strange equipment and odd-shaped boxes which
littered its shady side. Towser stayed close beside
me, every now and then growling half-heartedly. I
squatted off to the side for about five minutes
before I caught Doc's eye.

"Hey, boy. We been running a little short-handed.
You want to help out a bit? Drillin' is an exciting,
romantic business, and you might learn something."

"My name's Henry Lee, sir, and I'd be pleased to
help out."

"Hey, Razer!" he called out to one of the scurry-
ing men. "You take over while I give Mr. Henry
Lee MacFarland a tour of Sprocket." He slid down
the Driller's side and led me along its length, slap-
ping it affectionately on the flanks as he went.

"This here is Sprocket. There ain't too many like
him." He stopped where a bunch of large and
small folds in its dark hide stretched for a dozen
feet or so. "Oh, there's lots of them half-assed
water-well rigs wandering the countryside. They'll
go down a piddling five hundred or a thousand
feet. I'd be ashamed to be associated with one."

He rubbed an area about a foot above one of the
creases. The crease unfolded lazily and an eyeball
twice the size of my head poked out. It stared at us
for a long second, then slipped back under its
cover. Doc stooped and pulled at the blubbery
edge of a crease that ran knee high for eight or
nine feet. "Ol' Sprocket here ain't even in the same
goddam species. He'll go down twenty thousand
feet—that's four *miles*, Henry Lee. There ain't a

drilling rig in the world better than Sprocket at finding oil and making hole down to it." The crease split open and I took a step back. Towser had stayed back a couple of dozen steps, watching tensely. He's a good squirrel dog, but this monster had him spooked. Had me a mite edgy, too.

As the crease widened into a huge black and red pit and I took another quick step backwards, Towser broke into barking and making stiff-legged hops back and forth. A slick, sticky-looking white tube shot out of the pit and wrapped him up. It was so quick, all I really saw was a glimpse of a struggling, yelping blob half visible inside the tip before it sucked back inside.

Doc immediately commenced to beating on the creature with both fists. "Dammit, Sprocket! Spit that goddam dog out! You know better'n to act like this!"

After a second, the eyeball reappeared and blinked at us twice. Doc picked up a crowbar laying in the grass and started whupping on Sprocket with *that*. He jumped aside when a hole appeared in the crease right in front of him and Towser jetted out, still yelping. He hit the grass running and kept going.

Doc beat on Sprocket a couple more times before he threw the crowbar aside. Then he turned to me, grinning. "Hell of a drilling rig, Henry Lee, but I can't say his humor is always in the best of taste. So to speak."

Sprocket's enormous mouth gaped open again and he stepped up on its lip. "C'mon. Let me show you his guts." He saw me hesitate and grinned again. "Hell, don't worry. This ain't his eating mouth. It's his drilling mouth." He pointed down at his feet. "See? No teeth." He stepped off the lip and marched inside the monster. If he could do it, so could I. The mouth closed behind us.

It wasn't dark for more'n a second, because Doc pulled open a curtain of flesh a couple of yards further on. We stepped into a hallway almost twice my height that must of stretched just about the entire length of Sprocket. It was lit by lamps bolted into living flesh at regular distances apart. The walls were pink shot through with darker red veins and they moved in and out slowly. A musky smelling breeze shifted direction every few seconds.

As Doc led me down the hallway, he pointed out holes and creases along the way. "Now this here, Henry Lee, is my bunk room." He pulled it open and I looked over his shoulder. Inside was a small round room holding a couple of chairs and a bed with a lamp over it. Colorful tapestries covered the walls and floor. A bulky wooden desk stood next to a set of rungs leading to a hole in the ceiling which let early morning sunlight in. "Since I'm the tool pusher on this rig, I get the room that's most forward." He closed it and walked on.

"Most of the rooms front of the tongue base are living areas. You know, bunkrooms, mess hall, head, that sort of thing. Now here—" We'd reached the tongue, a long white snaky tube that lay in a groove in the center of the hall and gradually thickened as it led back to a hump about thirty feet further on. "Here is Sprocket's drilling tongue."

He peeled back white blubber from its tip and exposed a gleaming black bone, with three ratchet-edged pyramids angled off from its sharp point. "This is the drill-head and these here are Sprocket's drilling cones," he said, tapping one of the pyramids. "He twists 'em back and forth when he's making hole. They bite into earth and rock and chew it up." He let the blubber flop back over the cones. I'd gotten over worrying about being eaten alive and was starting to get interested in what he was saying.

We walked further down the hallway. The tongue got thicker, until it was higher than my head. At its very rear, it disappeared into the floor. Beyond it men hustled about, carrying things and calling to each other. "The tongue actually goes back almost all of the rest of Sprocket's length under the floor. It compresses when it's not drilling, then stretches out as far as it's needed the deeper we go. We're only going down to the aquifer on this one. Won't give it any kind of workout at all."

"Uh—no offense, sir, but how come you're finding water for us instead of being elsewhere drilling for oil?"

He leaned against the base of the tongue and pulled makings out of a pocket on his shoulder. "Well, Henry Lee, we just finished doing a couple of wildcat wells up north." He grinned humorlessly as he shook tobacco out and rolled. "They all come up dry and the operator went broke before he paid us. It damn near busted us. We're heading down to a field opening up near Odessa. Looks like it's gonna be pretty rich. But a man's gotta eat along the way." He licked the endpapers and struck a phosphorus match off his hat. "Probably drill a dozen fast holes around here on farmsteads and then move on."

A man at the far end of the hall yelled at us. "Hey, Doc! We're ready to spud whenever you are."

"Be right there, Razer." We walked down the hallway and out Sprocket's rear end. Doc made a final check of everything. A hose led from one crease to another and he yanked on it to make sure it wouldn't come loose. "Leads from his water bladder to his mud bladder," he explained. "Since we're going so shallow we'll just use fresh water for drilling fluid." Various machines and hoses were hooked into other creases and he checked all those.

Finally, we stood at Sprocket's head. A dozen men sat in folding chairs fiddling with various instruments in their hands. Doc stuck his arm in to the shoulder through a crease next to the mouth and felt around for a few seconds. "Pressure's good, Razer," he said to the man who'd called us and now stood next to him. "Let's get this show on the road."

Four men pried open Sprocket's mouth and walked inside. A minute later, they emerged carrying the tongue between them. Doc pried back the tip's cover for one last inspection of the cones, then laid it on the ground.

I'd been so interested watching him that I'd barely noticed the movements and sounds of the men in the chairs.

Doc walked over to a crate in front of them and handed me two carved sticks that were on it. "Here you go, Henry Lee. Time to work." They didn't weigh much, and when I tapped them together made a pleasant hollow sound. I felt like an idiot standing there with them. What kind of work could I do with a couple of sticks?

Doc picked up the crowbar that he'd used earlier to get Sprocket to spit out Towser, and commenced to beating on him again, this time in a more rhythmical pattern. "Time to get to work, you lazy bastard!" he yelled. "We're ready and you're ready and it ain't no use pretending you're asleep." This time I was far enough back that I could see it when both huge eyes opened and tried to stare cross-eyed at Doc. Satisfied, he backed off, reaching down to give the drilling tongue one last caress.

"Stokers ready?" he called out to a couple of men that stood next to a high pile of wood next to another opening in Sprocket's side.

"Bet your ass," was the reply.

He pulled a foot and a half long wand from a narrow pocket I hadn't noticed before that ran down his right leg. "Now, Henry Lee, I'm depending on you to help us out with this. You just watch my baton and hit those sticks together in time."

He raised the wand and took a deep breath. "Ah one and ah two and ah. . . ."

The men in the chairs started blowing and rubbing and pumping their instruments all together, as his wand moved in graceful curves through the air. I missed the first few beats, but after that I did fine, the sticks' mellow clear sound following perfectly.

Oh, it was wild, blood-stirring music. That tongue jerked erect for a minute and then plunged into the earth, twisting and squirming. Sprocket's eyes squeezed shut, then popped open again. His sides heaved gently and his hundreds of feet tramped in rhythm with the gypsy music. The stokers off to the side began to chant in a language I didn't understand as they chunked logs into Sprocket's eating mouth.

We played for what seemed to be hours. I was in another world.

We didn't make music all the while he was drilling, of course, and I had work to do anyways. Papa got back from Hemphill after lunch. The Grange Bank had give us the loan, so we spent the rest of the day sawing and hammering, making irrigation troughs. Sprocket drilled close to five hundred feet, going below the aquifer to leave a reservoir of water in the bottom of the well. They finished late that evening. I did get to watch after supper when they snapped twenty-inch surface casing onto his tongue and set it in the hole, then mixed and poured a dozen sacks of cement around the wellhead to make sure it stayed in place. I talked with Razer and Doc some while I helped mix the concrete in a trough. They planned to move on down the road to drill another water-well the next day at the Brewster place. Back to slopping pigs for me. I fell asleep listening to them partying in the pasture.

The next morning I'd already finished the morning chores before any of them stirred. The tents were still pitched where they'd been, but Sprocket had wandered over toward the back of the pasture. The dozen scraggly cows we owned gave him a wide berth. Doc was slouched over a campfire sipping from a battered tin cup when I walked up. "Hey there, Henry Lee," he called out. "You old enough to drink coffee?"

"I'm nineteen last month, Doc. I can do whatever I damn well please."

He squinted up at me. "Feeling kind of salty this morning, ain't you?"

I crouched and poured coffee into another tin cup. "Aw, I didn't mean nothing. I guess I'm sorry to see you going. Yesterday was fun."

"Like I said, it's a romantic, exciting way to live."

"Yeah. Looks like it beats dirt farming, anyway."

About that time the ground started to shake. A thunderous pounding came from Sprocket's direction. His hundreds of feet were stomping the back of the pasture into mud.

Doc jumped to his feet, looking disgusted. "Damned fool!"

"What's he doing?"

He threw the last third of his coffee into the fire. "Seismic testing." He shook his head. "Yesterday when we were drilling and he was marching in place he got one baseline. Now he's going for the other one."

"I don't understand." Sprocket's thumping speeded up.

"When he pounds the ground like that, it sends sound waves through the earth. Sprocket hears 'em when they slow down or speed up or reflect off different geological formations. Two baselines gives him a three-dimensional map of what's down there. The damned idiot's looking for hydrocarbons. Ain't no oil for two hundred miles in any direction."

Sprocket abruptly stopped and ambled back in our direction. The men had all woken and stuck their heads out of their tents cursing and groaning sleepily.

"Well, at least that foolishness is over," Doc grunted as he picked up the pot to pour himself another cup. Sprocket reached us in a minute and towered over us silently. Doc stared at his protruding, rapidly rotating eyeballs.

Sprocket's tongue shot out of his mouth and began to drill furiously not three feet from me.

Doc threw his coffee into the fire again.

Papa didn't approve of the whole thing, but his eyes bugged out nearly as far as Sprocket's when the company man for Exoco came around and showed him the numbers wrote down on the royalty contracts he offered. If the gypsies hit a good pocket of oil or natural gas, the first in an entirely undeveloped field, Papa and Exoco would get rich beyond any human cravings. Exoco would finance the drilling costs and get the biggest share. The drilling gypsies would make out, too, but not nearly as much.

Doc just shrugged when we talked about the deal. "Exoco's putting up some serious exploration money on this, Henry Lee. And we're drilling on property that your Daddy owns the mineral rights of."

"Yeah, but none of this wouldn't be happening without you and Sprocket! It isn't fair!"

He shrugged again. "You been around the oil-patch a little longer, you'd understand the economics of the situation. It don't matter a hell of a lot; anyway. We ain't in this for the money, much as I hate to admit it. It's the excitement and romance, son."

I thought the carnival had come to town when Sprocket first arrived. I was wrong. Within a week, the whole pasture was covered with strange beasts and strange equipment and even stranger people. The mud gypsies, the casing gypsies, the tool gypsies, the cement gypsies, and more—all converged on the MacFarland farmstead out of nowhere, all accompanied by one or more beasties that did something vital to the drilling of an exploratory well. In between chores and building and placing the irrigation troughs that led from the water-well to the cornfields, I usually only got loose after supper. I wandered among the tents and lean-tos they erected, breathing in the amazing sounds and smells and sights the gypsies brought with them.

The Exoco company man shouted and strutted about the camp like a little dictator. I started to understand why nobody knocked him upside the head for acting as obnoxious as he did when I realized that his company was footing the bill for everything and everybody in the pasture. Doc told him to go suck on sour gas, though, when he once made a suggestion about how to handle Sprocket.

Sprocket drilled twenty-four hours a day, his sides heaving with the effort. Illuminated at night by the light-poles set up all along his length, the stokers fed him continuously the first week. Then the first of a series of bloated brown tankers showed up on the scene and hooked up to him. I was there when Doc himself stuck the hose firmly into Sprocket's eating mouth and we stood back as he began to suck on it like a calf at the teat.

"Ol' Sprocket'll eat just about anything, Henry Lee," he said with pride, "But what he loves second best is that refined, high-octane, lead-free, pure sweet gasoline."

"What's he like best?"

He grinned evil-like. "Fresh dogmeat." I hadn't seen Towser since the day Sprocket almost ate him.

"Just funnin'," Doc said before I could ask the awful question. "What he likes best of all, of course, is heavy crude. Oughta see the way he gets to shaking and shimmying and moaning when he hits a producible formation. You don't think he's workin' himself into a lather just because we play pretty music for him, do you? That's just how we sweet-talk him into doing favors for us, like drilling your little water-well or trying out a wildcat some damn fool has a religious faith in, but he's in the business strictly to fill his belly with petroleum.

"And," he added, "For the romance and excitement of it all."

Eight nights after Sprocket started drilling, I snuck away from the house after bedtime. Papa

hadn't come right out and told us younguns to
stay away from them, but his mind was easy enough
to see. I guess the rest of them was born to farm,
but I'd lay in bed after breaking my back in the
damned, boring-to-death fields, and hear pagan
music, and the hum of many voices, and the
whining, trembling noise Sprocket made in his
search for the thing he loved best and I'd want to
cry for some reason.

Doc was talking to a couple of casing gypsies
when he spotted me coming. They stood in a half
circle in front of Sprocket, who was surrounded by
half a dozen other oversized beasts. Doc didn't
seem too surprised to see me. "Howdy, Henry Lee.
Just couldn't stand it any longer, could you?"

"Sir?"

"I recognized the symptoms the first day, son.
Not too hard to do. I got 'em myself about your
age. Still got 'em."

There wasn't nothing I could say to him.

He turned to the casing gypsies. The reason I
knew they were casing gypsies is they were all
women. Casing gypsies always were. They wore
dark green jumpsuits, but theirs fit a whole lot
better than the men's. Over the next few weeks
Doc told me stories about the wild ways of casing
gypsies that I not only didn't believe, but, due to
my lack of experience, couldn't even understand
half the time.

He spoke to the dark-haired woman that must
have been their crew chief. "Ramonita, we're gonna
be ready to start snapping on that twenty-six hundred feet of twenty inch surface pipe in less than
an hour. Big Red's hooked up and ready to cement.
How come I don't see your pipe here?"

She swayed a few steps forward and tapped his
chest with a black-tipped finger. "Because," she

purred, "your half-smart *segundo*, Razer, moved Big Red's pumper and his bulk cement holder onto location ahead of time. They're blocking us out, as usual. They're asleep, as usual."

Her purr deepened into a snarl. "And it's your goddam job to straighten it out, not mine. We've been ready since this afternoon."

About that time, I wandered off, too embarrassed to listen to the rest of the conversation.

Ramonita was actually pretty nice once you got to know her. That night I helped her and her casing crew to snap on the surface casing. Sprocket pulled his tongue out of the hole for it. Each joint of casing was a twenty foot tube of dark ceramic that their beast excreted and they baked until it hardened properly. It unfolded in half lengthwise. They placed the first joint right behind his drillhead, so that his tongue rested on a double trough, then snapped it closed around the tongue and sealed the seams with a special glue. Then they hoisted the rear end of the casing vertical into the air with a sling hung from a tripod scaffolding they'd erected, and fed the first joint most of the way into the hole. The end of the length of pipe tapered in, then flared out again. The next joint's front end snapped right over that nipple, and so on.

After a few hours of lifting and snapping casing, I guess I should have been tired, but I wasn't. We worked to the rhythm of the music made by gypsies from half a dozen specialties, and it made that casing feel light as goose feathers.

When we were done I collapsed into a chair and watched Ramonita and her girls dance to the music while Big Red pumped cement down the inside of the casing and out the bottom and back up the outside into the annulus between the casing and the hole, bonding it in place. Doc strolled over with a cup and a plate heaped with sausage and thick pieces of bread.

"Here you go, Henry Lee. Oilpatch work may feed the soul, but every now and then you gotta feed the body, too."

I took a big bite of the sausage and it felt like my mouth had caught on fire, so I took a deep swig from the cup and the flames leaped higher.

"You've killed me," I finally managed to choke out. "What *is* this stuff?"

"Just boudain and a little heart-starter, Henry Lee. Good stuff."

I took small bites of everything that was offered to me afterwards. That heart-starter kinda growed on you after a while, though.

I didn't get much sleep the next three weeks, what with working all day in the fields and being with the gypsies every night. I helped out on most all of the beasties at one time or another, learning how drilling mud was mixed and why, or helping the tool gypsies dress and move their tools when they were getting ready to run in the hole for a squeeze job, or unpacking float shoes and collars to attach to the bottoms of a string when they got ready to run it in. All of them was real friendly, answering all my dumb questions, and telling me stories about the far places they'd been and the wild things they'd seen and done.

But I kept coming back to Sprocket. The deeper he got, the more he had to exert himself twisting that long, talented tongue deep into the bowels of the earth, clamping his mouth over the well-head to fight downhole hydrostatic until they could weight up the mud, whenever he hit a high-pressure zone. I got to know him inside and out, literally.

Doc taught me how to care for him and keep him clean and feel inside his guts to monitor his vital signs so the stoking could speed up or slow down, or they could play music to calm him or spur him on.

They didn't need to spur him on much. He was drilling like his life depended on it.

The proudest moment for me came one night when we were down about ten thousand feet. We'd just started in the hole to hang some eight and five-eighths inch liner pipe off the bottom of a ten and three-quarter inch long string. I was standing at the well-head when it slipped a little. Displaced mud gushed out of the hole, drenching me from head to foot. The second pair of coveralls I'd ruined. I only had one pair left.

When we finished up and I was kicked back sipping on some heart-starter, Doc strolled up with a cloth-wrapped package under one arm and a silver-metal hardhat under the other and dumped them at my feet.

"I don't mind you getting underfoot ever now and then, Henry Lee," he said. "But I do mind you doing it in them damned old messy coveralls."

I set down the cup with unsteady hands and untied the string and shook open the package. Inside were two gray patched jumpsuits and a pair of steel-toed workboots.

"If they don't fit, you're out of luck," he said. "They're the biggest sizes we got."

"Thanks, Doc."

"Ain't a present," he said gruffly. "You earned 'em."

Then he strode off shouting curses at Big Red for not getting their cement down-hole fast enough. I hid the clothes under my bed during the daytime and wore them at night when I went to the gypsies.

                      *   *   *

Sixteen thousand feet, seventeen thousand feet,
eighteen thousand feet, and still no strike. Sprocket's
hide began to lose its sheen and get wrinkled and
rough looking, but he drilled on, heaving and
panting. He sucked gasoline in vast quantities, forcing his tongue through rock that grew harder and
hotter. The mud circulated up practically boiling
and we began to coat his tongue with special un-
guents when it came out of the hole, looking burned
and chafed.

The camp grew quieter when he passed twenty
thousand feet, his maximum rated depth. More
pressure, more heat, but no hydrocarbons.

I missed six nights while we got in the corn. The
weeks of no sleep finally caught up with me. I
simply couldn't anymore handle harvesting and
working all night, too. I worked like a zombie in
the fields all day, and couldn't bring myself to
visit the camp under Papa's watchful eyes when
sunset neared. I collapsed into bed right after supper each evening, sick as a dog, and slept without
dreams until Papa shook me awake at dawn. Being
sick don't matter when the crop's got to come in.
When I saw Doc or one of the other gypsies I
waved at a distance, but they only waved back
and hurried about their business.

I came back the seventh night. They stood around
Sprocket in silent little groups, no music, no laughing and joking.

Sprocket had somehow shrivelled. His hide hung
in loose rolls along his length and every few minutes a painful wheeze streamed from around the
edges of his drilling mouth where he'd mashed it
into the ground around his tongue. His head

twitched spastically and his eyes were squeezed shut in agony.

Doc turned a dead face to me when I touched him on the shoulder. "Oh. Hello, Henry Lee."

He fumbled at his shoulder pocket and came out with a tobacco bag. When he saw it was empty, he let it drop. "Sprocket's down somewhere around twenty-three thousand feet," he finally said. "We can't measure for sure, because he's refused to stop drilling for three days. We've got twenty pound mud in the hole and he's still having to fight the bottom-hole hydrostatic. He's had his mouth dug in for a blowout preventer since noon."

I was frightened as much by the slurred, toneless way he spoke as by the meaning of his words. "Make him stop, Doc. The oil ain't worth it."

"He won't stop, Henry Lee. We've played to him, and talked to him, and shut off his gasoline, and he just won't stop."

He reached out and rubbed Sprocket's mottled skin. "Sometimes it happens this way. They just go crazy and won't stop drilling." His hand dropped to his side. "Until they die."

We stood together not saying anything for a long time. Finally I knew what I had to say, even if it wasn't true.

"You're wrong, Doc."

"What?"

"I don't believe Sprocket's gone crazy. You told me he's the best Driller in the world for finding and getting down to oil. Either you were wrong then or you're wrong now. Sprocket's going for the deepest, biggest reservoir that's ever been found."

His big hands clenched, but I guessed angry was better than the way he'd been before. "You don't know what you're saying, boy. You're just a typi-

cal worm. You run around here a couple of weeks
and you think you know it all. You—"

"I know one thing, Doc. Sprocket ain't in this
business to kill himself. Like you said, he's in it for
the petroleum!" I was shouting now, leaning right
into his face, mad as hell for no reason I could say.
"And for the romance and excitement, too, you son
of a bitch!"

I turned around and started yelling at the other
gypsies. "What's the matter with you people? Did
you come here to find oil or not? How come you're
standing around like a bunch of—" I tried to think
of the worst thing I could call them and found it.
"Like a bunch of dirt-farmers!"

I rushed over to where the instruments lay in a
pile and started throwing them at dumbfounded
people. "Play, goddam you! Sprocket's doing his
part of the deal. Least you can do is give him some
music to work by if you're not gonna work yourselves."

I ran out of words and stood glaring at them.
Nobody moved. There was silence except for
Sprocket's harsh panting and mine. I whirled, with
a fist cocked to fly, at a scuffling noise behind me.
Doc had his wand in one hand and the rhythm
sticks in the other.

"I do believe you may be right, Henry Lee." His
voice rose. "Come on, people. It ain't over till it's
over!" In a lower voice, "I'm damned if I'll hold
Sprocket's funeral while he's still alive."

I helped them hook him back into the gasoline
tanker, and took turns massaging his heart muscle.
We played and danced all night. I don't know if
any of it did Sprocket any good. Along about day-
break I was sprawled against his side, right underneath an eye, beating my rhythm sticks together

drunkenly in time with his weakening gasps while half a dozen gypsies kept up on their instruments. The rest had fallen asleep where they stood or sat. A long shadow fell across me and I looked up to see Papa's grim face above me.

"He's dying, Papa," I said. "He wants it so bad nothing or nobody can stop him."

"The family's in the fields finishing with the harvest, son."

"Not today, Papa. I'll be a farmer tomorrow, but please not today."

Sprocket's breathing stopped.

For a frozen second I sat there. Then I lurched up, almost knocking Papa aside. "Doc! Doc! He's not breathing."

Doc had fallen asleep in a chair, his baton slipping from his fingers to lie in the dirt. I frantically yanked him erect and dragged him to Sprocket. Shaking his head to clear it, he inserted his arm into a crease and felt around. "Pressure down to nothing," he muttered.

Finally, blessedly, I felt the tears streaming down my face. "It's over."

Then Sprocket's body started to shimmy, quick little waves travelling along his body. Doc jerked his arm out as the first real convulsion hit. Sprocket's eyes popped open, nothing but the whites showing. His body began to jerk and twist and hunch, carrying dozens of his feet off the ground at once.

Then a deep growling sound like a hurricane grew in the air and Sprocket's body began to tie itself in knots as we all backed away.

"Jesus, Son of God!" Doc yelled. "The well's coming in on us!"

I looked down at Sprocket's mouth and saw it grinding in the dirt, squeezed tightly around his tongue, and knew Doc was right. In addition to the normal bottom-hole pressure, Sprocket had drilled into a *real* high-pressure formation and the upward force was trying to blast everything out of the hole. Sprocket was fighting it with his last remaining strength.

The wrinkles in his hide disappeared as he swelled up. Doc began to backpedal. "He ain't handling the kick! His bladders are filling with mud coming up. Head for the tall grass! Blowout! Blowout!"

We all turned and ran like the devil was after us. The gasoline tanker, which was the only beast next to Sprocket, ripped loose, crashed through the fence into the woods bordering the pasture, and left a wake of shattered pine trees behind him. The rest of the beasts took off in whatever directions they were already pointed in. In the midst of the turmoil, I caught a glimpse of Papa high-stepping his best. He was fresh from a night's sleep, so he was just about leading the pack. He didn't know what the hell was going on, but he was willing to find out from a safe distance.

I glanced back over my shoulder and saw Sprocket bloated like an enormous black balloon. Then he blew out. It looked and sounded like a tornado erupted full-grown from the top of his head. A stormy dark gusher fountained a hundred feet in the air. I kept running. If it caught fire, I'd be fried to the bone in a second.

Finally, I fell face down between two furrows, exhausted. It started to rain on my back and I turned over. The rain was black. It was oil.

Fifteen minutes later, the gusher gradually grew smaller, and finally sank back into the ground. Cautiously, we slipped and scrambled among drenched wreckage until we came to Sprocket.

Somehow, he'd held on and finally shut it in. He squirmed and wiggled happily in the middle of the mess, a deep dynamo hum vibrating his entire length.

Three mornings later the gypsies had washed off and repaired their belongings as best they could. The pasture and cornfields were covered with petroleum, black, clumpy globs of it drying in the summer sun. A welter of intersecting pipes and valves called a Christmas Tree guarded the hole that Sprocket had drilled. I stood on Sprocket's head and turned all the way around slowly. Papa and Grampaw and my brothers clustered in front of the farmhouse.

A trail of dust led down the road back to Hemphill and places beyond, marking the departure of all of the gypsies except Doc's crew. Doc's head popped out of the hole beside me.

"About time for us to go, Henry Lee," he said.

I slid down Sprocket's side and walked slowly toward my family. Behind me Sprocket's legs started to churn in place, limbering up for the march ahead of him.

When I hugged him, Papa tried his best to smile, because he loved me.

Sprocket's drilling mouth opened instantly when I tugged on it. We were halfway to the cattleguard before I made it through Doc's room and up his ladder.

As we looked back and waved good-bye, Doc said, "Damned if I understand you, Henry Lee. That well's gonna produce a whole lot of oil, and it's gonna be the only one around here, 'cause I don't think anyone else is crazy enough to try to get into a reservoir that deep. You could stay and be one of the richest men in this state."

I dropped my hand and turned to face the road. "Money's fine for them that value it, Doc, but I'll take the romance and excitement any day."

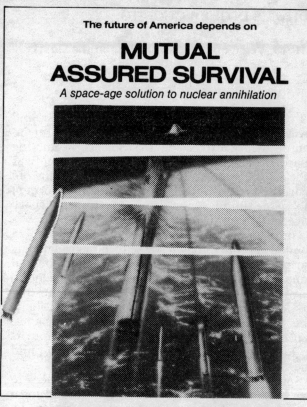

IRAS, Vega, and Intelligent Life in the Galaxy

by
Robert W. Bussard

I've long been known as a space enthusiast, and several years ago I was invited to become a member of the Board of the L-5 Society Promoting Space Development. In those days the name was shorter; it was just "The L-5 Society," and the old guard still refer to it that way. As the long form of the name implies, the L-5 Society is a "space advocacy" organization.

The short form is even more telling: the L-5 point, sometimes known as the fifth Lagrangian, is the point in the Moon's orbit 60 degrees behind Luna. Objects placed in orbit at that point tend to stay there. It was for some years thought that would be a good place to put the first space colony. The L-5 Society is definitely for space colonies, hence the name—although, alas, the L-5 point is no longer considered the optimum place to build one.

Space colonies are just that: artificial places to live in space. The concept has been around for a long time; the first mention I am aware of was by the Russian astrodreamer Tsiolkovsky, who also said "Earth is the cradle of mankind, but we cannot stay in the cradle forever." One of the first detailed views of life in a space colony was Robert A. Heinlein's "Universe." An early nonfiction examination of the concept was written by Dandridge Cole. The first engineering analysis of space colony requirements was published by Princeton physics professor Gerard O'Neill, which is why space colonies are sometimes known as "O'Neill Colonies," although it would be as appropriate to call them "Cole Colonies" or even "Tsiolkovsky Colonies."

Heinlein's space colony was special: it wasn't just a colony. If you have a self-sufficient space colony and a means of propulsion, you have a star ship. It will take many generations to cross the vast distances between the stars, but given sufficient sources of energy it ought to get there. Heinlein's "Universe" was such a ship, which travelled for so long that its inhabitants lost all record of a time when they had lived on planets.

I have written elsewhere of mankind's hundred-billion-year future; a future that is possible, but only if we are able to survive the death of our Sun. Space colonies are one key to that future; which is why I have worked hard for the L-5 Society, and once called L-5 "the advance planning department of the human race."

Alas, the politics of space advocacy are tricky and varied, and can be vicious.

In late 1983 IRAS (Infra-Red Astronomical Satellite) observed cold matter surrounding the star Vega. As it happened, I was at that time preparing the report of the fourth meeting of the Citizens Advisory Council on National Space Policy. Dr. Robert Bussard, "inventor" (possibly "describer" would be a better term) of the Bussard interstellar ramjet and former Director of Fusion Energy Research at Los Alamos National Laboratory, is a member of the Council; and we were in telephone contact about his contribution when I read about the IRAS discovery.

I asked Bob if he would do an article about IRAS and cold matter for the L-5 News.

"Sure. Technical on IRAS, or general and philosophical about implications?" he asked.

"General. Connect the discovery to the rest of the universe."

"Right. Next week be okay?"

I assured him he could take his time. In due course the paper arrived and I sent it off to the L-5 *News* editor. I thought no more about it until months later when I recalled I hadn't seen it. By that time the L-5 Society was racked with an internal power struggle that seemed to involve me; I solved my part of that by withdrawing from any management of Society affairs. Alas, that didn't really end the matter, and the article was rejected by L-5, which is their loss.

In this article Dr. Bussard presents a theory of the relationship of CroMagnon to Neanderthal man that is not highly regarded by most paleobiologists, and which I cannot myself accept. However, I find that some experts with better credentials than mine find his view possible if not convincing; and in any case that particular sentence is not necessary to the balance of Bussard's argument. Bob offered to excise it for the L-5 *News*; I thought it best to leave the article intact.

Herewith Robert Bussard on the significance of the IRAS discovery.

IRAS, VEGA, AND INTELLIGENT LIFE IN THE GALAXY

Dr. Robert W. Bussard

President, Energy Resources Group, Inc.

The most generally accepted theory of planetary formation is based on the idea, first put forward by Kant and LaPlace, that cold gas, collected by gravitational forces in star formation, led to a rotating ellipsoidal-shaped gaseous nebula around the proto star. This nebular "pancake" heated as it contracted under gravity, speeded up as it contracted, and formed planets by accretion around mass/density concentrations found within the nebular matter. The planets so formed would, of course, be in Keplerian orbits around the star.

The planetary accretions nearest the star occur in a nebular region of small volume and mass, and at high temperatures relative to the volume and mass available for "sweeping out" the colder, denser matter at great distances. Because of this, the innermost planets would be expected to be formed from the condensation of materials with high vaporization temperatures, such as rock and iron; thus the "terrestrial" planets. Conversely, the outermost planets would be formed by condensation and collection of low boiling point materials, such as methane, ammonia, hydrogen; thus the "Jovian" planets. The whole process of planetary accretion—given the initial nebular conditions—is thought to require only a few tens of thousands to a few million years, once started.

Detailed analyses of this process have been carried out on large computers (on models of star formation) over a wide range of conditions believed plausible for starting the process. These studies all showed the formation of multiple terrestrial planets near their stellar source, and multiple Jovian planets further out, sometimes with one or two Pluto-like planets still further, beyond the cold giants. Thus it has been shown that planetary formation is an almost automatic adjunct of stellar formation on the neo-LaPlacian model. If so, the key question as to the likelihood of other planets (we know there are other stars!) would be, "Is the neo-LaPlacian model correct; does stellar-formation really appear in this mode?"

At last we have the beginnings of an answer, from data obtained by the IRAS satellite. This space observatory is built to detect infrared radiation from radiating sources other than stars. It has recently reported the observation of an extended infrared-radiating mass of considerable extent surrounding the star Vega. By all analysis this seems to be a gaseous nebula ready for or in process of planetary formation around Vega. Other such bodies now seem probable. Of course, if the star is too hot its nebular envelope will be too tenuous and extended for planetary formation on the model of our solar system, while if too cold its planets will be formed small and close in. No matter; space is filled with F, G, and K type stars (we are G-type) of the general temperature range which allow formation of Earth-type planets somewhere in the nebular contraction/condensation process.

What all this means is that we now have evidence of the existence of conditions elsewhere for the formation of planets around (nearly all) stars, and thus reason to support speculation that the galaxy is filled with planet-bearing stellar systems. Taking 10^{11} stars as a reasonable estimate for the stellar population of our galaxy, and $1/10$ as the fraction in the "right" spectral/temperature class for life-of-our-type (LOOT), we estimate 10^{10} planetary systems as possible. Suppose only $1/10$ of these contain planets capable of supporting Earth-type life; then there will be only(!) 10^9 planets capable of supporting creatures like ourselves, or LOOT.[1]

The consequences of this now-nearly-validated estimate are truly staggering. If, as generally agreed, life evolved on Earth in ca. 10^9 years, Earth is ca. 4.6×10^9 years old, and our galaxy is $10\text{-}15 \times 10^9$ years old, then we Earthlings are very latecomers in galactic history and are quite likely *not* alone. In fact, a simple estimate suggests that *at least* 10^8 planets should be out there with our type of life abounding; and most of these should contain intelligent life far, far older than our own. For the size of our galaxy this gives an average distance between intelligent species of our type of about 100 light years. Of course, the stellar/planetary density is *not* uniform. It is concentrated towards the galactic center and lesser in the outer regions (where we live, far out in the Ophiucius arm), so mean inter-LOOT distances should vary accordingly.

---

[1] This apparent preoccupation with "life-of-our-type" or "-as-we-know-it" is *not* an example of anthropocentricity. It is simply that it seems fruitless to speculate on the imagined infinite array of life-form possibilities which we do *not* know and therefore can *not* assess.

If all this is so—as the new IRAS evidence gives us new reason to believe—then where are "they" and who are we? If they exist so thickly why do we not see them? This famous question, first posed by Enrico Fermi[2] can be answered only by several possibilities: (1) The detailed genetic evolution of LOOT is so improbable, even with Earth-like conditions, that we are nearly the first in all the galaxy, or; (2) Nearly all LOOT committed suicide upon reaching a state of control of sufficient planetary energy resources, so the LOOT lifetime is too short to allow galactic exploration or; (3) Densely populous LOOT exists, but chooses to conceal itself from us, or; (4) We are so far out in the galactic countryside that no one has bothered to look our way yet, or; (5) Interstellar transport is forever impossible. Let us examine each possibility, in inverse turn.

(5) Interstellar transport cannot be forever impossible simply because even *we* (new-born and illiterate on the galactic scale) already know how to go about it. Whether by interstellar ramjets, laser-driven sails, or anti-matter rockets (or their ducted ramjet versions) we already have enough physics and—soon[3]—enough technology to make starflight work; and we *will* go out as soon as we can build the requisite machinery.

(4) It is not hard to find us, nor would it take long—if they are there we should have been found long ago. Given star-flight by any of the above means it is easy to show that the rate of expansion into the galaxy from a LOOT source outbound for exploration and colonization will be at a rate of

---

[2] In 1955, after a dinner party at then-Livermore Labs Director Herb York's house in Livermore.

[3] Within 100 years or so.

about (c/1000). That is, the sphere of LOOT-occupied planets will expand at about one-thousandth the speed of light, once started. Thus reaching us, even from the galactic center, would take only 10^8 years at most; a time quite small compared to the galactic age. We should have been found long, long ago.

(3) Many reasons have been proposed for the unwillingness of an exploratory galactic colonization to show itself to us. Would *we* attempt to communicate with an island colony of destructive, semideranged, and apparently suicidal baboons carrying laser guns and using nuclear weapons? Better to let them find their own destiny. *If* they settle down, stabilize, and find their way off their island in peace, then we talk; otherwise, we watch—and guard. Or perhaps there has not been any concealment at all. Perhaps quite the opposite; perhaps *we* are *they*. They landed here long ago by accident or design, descended into savagery in the corrosive atmosphere of Earth, which destroyed all ships, equipment, and non-sustainable technology, and became Cro-Magnon man, doing away with Earth's natural creature, Neanderthal. If so, our efforts at spaceflight are only the long echo of a lost dream of home.

(2) Will *we* succeed in going out into the galactic darkness rich in new worlds suitable for us, or will we die before we go? Perhaps the nature of aggressive species which reach planetary dominance is such that the energy sources they control—which can make starflight possible—are used first among themselves in a pattern of destruction so complete that the race can never break out of its confining solar system shell. The bomb over Hiroshima gave us both the power to kill (nearly) all of ourselves or to escape to the stars. Which will we do? This is the preeminent issue of this most exciting of times.

Which did *they* do? Simple calculation shows that the probability of surviving this condition *must be less than* one part in a million, else the galaxy must be densely populated, and we may well be they. If so densely populated we should see them again, with a high frequency of contact. But do we (the UFO's?), or are they hiding (?), or did they all self-destruct?

(1) Or, finally, are we truly alone; the first intelligent species in the galaxy, the product of an immensely improbable chain of hundreds of thousands of sequentially coupled geological, chemical, biochemical, biological, and parallel astronomical events? Very simplistically, if 100 events of each type each had 10 possible outcomes only one of which was on the chain of success to life, the probability of success through the end of the event chain, over all the stars and the life of the galaxy would be only 10^2 (1%). Ergo, we are the only intelligent planetary-energy-dominating handiwork of God in all the galaxy. But this is just a numbers game, and we all know what those are! Much more compelling is the data from our Mars and Venus probes. Both planets seem *nearly* (but not quite) able to support LOOT. They are each just a bit beyond the one-sigma point for people like ourselves. Thus we see within our own solar system a probability far higher than any version of the "numbers game" would give.

On balance it seems probable that life exists, that LOOT *is* out there, and that we will find it (if it does not signal us first) when we go out within 100 years or so. All we have to do is live without global nuclear war for this time, ours and our grandchildren's, and we will be saved—from ourselves—and will find again our fellows and our new/old galactic homes.

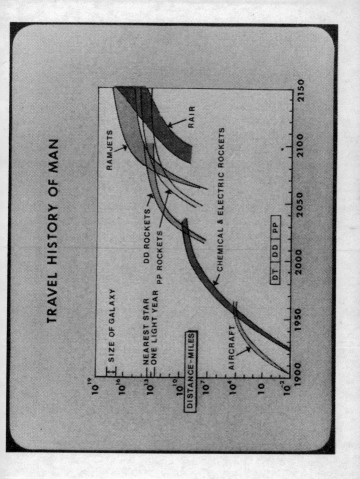

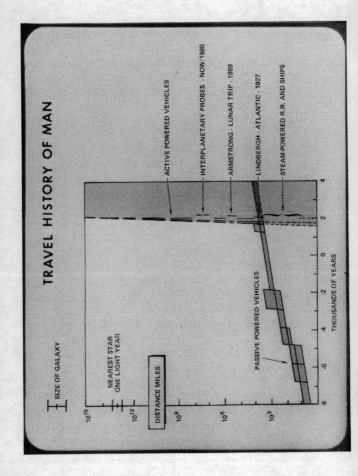

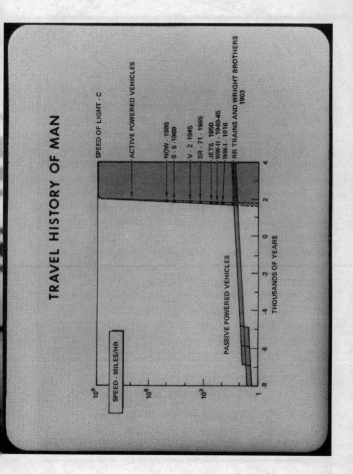

TRAVEL HISTORY OF MAN

EDITOR'S INTRODUCTION TO:

A CURE FOR CROUP

by
Edward P. Hughes

Edward Hughes, communications engineer, lives in Manchester, England. He has created a new twist to the post-disaster story.

The disaster isn't completely spelled out. Certainly there has been a war; there appear to have been environmental disasters as well. If so, they must have been enormous, and acted in a synergy of destruction with effects of the war. The Earth is, after all, pretty big, and it's not all that easy to affect it permanently and globally. Any given hurricane expends megatons of energy, while a large volcanic explosion, such as Krakatoa, releases more energy than all of mankind has been able to expend in war or peace.

This is not to say that we cannot, with ingenuity, muck things up. Harrison Brown long ago showed that if our civilization falls far enough, it will be exceedingly difficult to rebuild. Social structures are delicate. The late H. Beam Piper postulated two different ways for planets to "decivilize." If we work at it, we can make the Earth hard to live on. Hughes postulates that we did, and now must live with the results.

In Hughes' world everyone knows the magnitude of the disaster: but the inhabitants of Barley Cross are determined that life shall be normal for all that, no matter the cost. That cost has been high. For as long as most remember, the town has been dominated by the fortress known as The Fist, outside which stands the tank brought in by Patrick O'Meara, onetime Sergeant of Her Majesty's forces, now Lord of Barley Cross and Master of the Fist. O'Meara was the founder and savior of the town: and as such, exercised the rights of lordship, including *droits du seigneur*—the rights of the elder. He slept with every newlywed bride of the village.

Except for that peculiar arrangement, Barley Cross was as nearly normal as a village in a world of universal disaster could be; and all the men of the village were pleased to have it so, now and forever.

But nothing lasts forever.

Edward P. Hughes

A CURE FOR CROUP

The sound of a tolling bell woke Liam McGrath. He nudged his sleeping wife.

"Hear that racket, Eileen!"

Eileen McGrath stirred in her sleep. She had been up half the night nursing their one year old son through an attack of croup, and she was in no mood for conversation.

Liam frowned at the bell's clamour. *That* could only be the village church bell—and Father Con never allowed it to be sounded as a warning.

Eileen opened her eyes. "What time is it?"

Liam reached across her to consult the ancient wind-up alarm his mother had given them as a wedding present.

"Only half five, by God! D'you think there's something wrong?"

She said drowsily, "Sounds like a death knell to me."

He swung his legs out of bed. The Curry cottage clung close to the root of Kirkogue mountain, a cockstride out of the village of Barley Cross. From his bedroom window Liam could see along the village's one and only main street. He peered through the curtains. Figures moved on the distant roadway.

And the bell tolled.

He grabbed his trousers from the chair back, and put a leg into them.

Eileen raised herself on one elbow. "Where are you going?"

He buckled his belt. "I'm off to see what's happened. It may be an emergency."

She sighed. "Don't wake Tommy. I've only just got him off."

Liam nodded. Their son's harsh breathing and racking cough had demanded the village doctor's attention the previous night. Liam could hear stertorous respiration from the next room. He tiptoed downstairs, lifted his jacket from the newel post, and slipped out into the morning light.

Seamus Murray stood at the door of his forge. The smith's face was unduly solemn. He seemed not to notice Liam's presence.

Liam shook his arm. "What's happened, man? What's the bell for?"

Seamus' mouth opened and closed, like a fish in a jar. Then the words gushed out. "The O'Meara's dead! They found him at the foot of the stairs when the guard went in to report the 'all clear' this morning. He'd had a heart attack."

Liam stared, his brain refusing to accept the smith's news. Patrick O'Meara, Lord of Barley Cross, Master of the Fist, and focus of village life for as long as Liam could remember, dead? It was like hearing the village clock had vanished.

He said stupidly, "How come they found him so early?"

Seamus Murray shot him a pitying look. "The Master always wanted a report as soon as it grew light enough to see the O'Toole cottage. We've done it for years—though I doubt a lad of your age would appreciate why."

Liam knew why. He had suffered the saga of Barley Cross versus the Rest of Ireland from his elders ever since he had been old enough to pay attention.

He ignored Murray's dig. "So who found him?"

The smith scanned the road. Liam's face appeared to be the last thing he wanted to look at. "Christ, man—how should I know? I don't stand guard at the Fist any more. Does it matter? We've lost our protector—the man who kept us from death and destruction in the years gone by—and all *you* want to know is who found him!"

All Barley Cross went to the funeral, that being the villagers' normal procedure. But many a wife shed more than customary tears for the deceased. Patrick O'Meara, the ram of Barra Hill, had left no widow to mourn his passing, but in a very real way he had been a father to the community, and many of the women had peculiarly fond memories of him.

The O'Meara's henchmen met in the dining hall of the Fist as soon as the obsequies were done.

General Larry Desmond drained a tumbler of *poteen* with scant regard for its potency. He wiped the back of his hand across his mouth, then set the empty glass on the carpet between his feet. "Well," he said. "We're in a pickle now."

At the other end of the broken backed settee, Kevin Murphy the vet stared gloomily into his own glass. "God dammit!" he muttered. "I loved that bloody man. Why could it not have happened to one of us instead?"

Celia Larkin, MA, schoolmistress and spinster, sipped a cup of herb tea brewed specially for her by Michael, the O'Meara's servant. Neglected runnels in her face powder showed where the tears had flowed. She sniffed. "Maybe it's the Lord's judgment on our presumption. Father Con ranted about it often enough."

Denny Mallon, MD, dwarfed in the great, shiny armchair, sucked at an empty pipe. "Father Con's views on delegated procreation don't necessarily reflect those of our Maker. Think about Judah's advice to Onan in Genesis. And, anyway, this is no time to be questioning tenets. But for Patrick O'Meara, Barley Cross would be a futureless dormitory by now. I can't imagine even Father Con would want that."

General Desmond refilled his glass from the bottle on the floor. "Denny, you are overly pessimistic as usual. A few of us here still have a kick or two left in us. Point is—where are we going to find a man to father the next generation of kids in Barley Cross?"

"That child of the Kellys—" began Celia Larkin.

Kevin Murphy grunted. "Christ. Celia, he's only ten or eleven years old. We're surely not counting on adolescent precocity to—"

General Desmond choked over his drink. "God love us! Let the little fellow grow up first! We're not even sure he's fertile. The Kellys' never had any more kids."

Celia Larkin compressed prim lips. "You misunderstand me, gentlemen. It was the father I had in mind. And my idea was for it to be done surgically. Presumably the way Kevin achieves it with his beasts."

Kevin Murphy jerked upright. "Hold on, now! I'm no gynecologist. Better ask Denny about that kind of maneuver."

Doctor Denny Mallon lowered his pipe. "The Kelly boy might be a possibility in a year or two—if he *is* his father's son. But Con Kelly never managed another child. As for artificial insemination, I have no equipment and no skill—nor the wish to employ either. We have discussed this idea before, and rejected it. We agreed, if I rightly recall, that women are not cattle. And, anyway, to go in now for clinical insemination would explode our carefully nurtured fiction that the husbands of Barley Cross are the fathers of their children. No, my friends, what we need is a new *seigneur* to exercise his *droits*."

General Desmond's eyes narrowed in sudden suspicion. He glowered at the doctor. "Just *what* have you hidden up your sleeve, Denny lad?"

Denny Mallon picked at the charcoaled bowl of his pipe with a black thumbnail. He closed his eyes, as though weighing a doubtful course. Then he shook his head.

"It's not professional ethics to betray a patient's confidence."

"Denny!" squealed Celia Larkin.

"But if you'll each give me your word to preserve—"

"Christ, man! Yes, yes!" interrupted Kevin Murphy.

Denny Mallon swivelled arched eyebrows at the general and the schoolmistress. "You, too—both of you?"

"God, man! Give up! Yes!"

"Anything, Denny. Just tell us!"

The doctor tapped his pipe on the heel of his hand. His listeners strained forward to catch his soft-spoken words.

"Eileen McGrath tells me she's missed her menses for the second month in succession. I think she's pregnant of her *second* child!"

Larry Desmond's breath came out in a low whistle. "Young Liam McGrath?"

Denny Mallon nodded. "Who else?"

Celia Larkin's eyes flashed behind her rimless spectacles. "What exactly does that mean, Denny—you're the expert."

Denny Mallon grimaced. "It could mean that our dear Patrick passed on his fertility to Liam McGrath—for which mercy I would be grateful. Or it could be that our ozone layer is repairing itself since we stopped assaulting it with fluorocarbons. Which is unlikely. Alternatively, it could be that some of our children have developed an immunity to heavy ultraviolet doses. And that would be the best answer of all."

"But you don't know which?"

Denny Mallon shrugged. "Only time will tell. Meantime, I think we should make full use of young McGrath."

Kevin Murphy said, "Will he oblige?"

"Give me a chance to ask him!"

Celia Larkin pounced. "You'll do it, then?"

Denny Mallon grimaced. "Seems like I've got the job."

The general snorted. "Seems like we'll have to get ourselves an interim government."

Kevin Murphy looked doubtful. "D'you think they'll take orders from us?"

"They'll take them from Larry," Celia Larkin pointed out. "He still runs the army. And he can delegate duties to us. It will work 'til we get a new Master."

Denny Mallon got out his pouch, and poked his pipe bowl into it. He said casually, "I have to visit the Curry cottage tomorrow. The McGrath infant is not well, and I have a theory to check. I'll find an opportunity to talk to Liam." He rolled up the pouch and slipped it back into his pocket. "But we've got to offer him everything—Lord of Barley Cross, Master of the Fist, the lot—or it won't work. He must replace Patrick in every way. Anything less would confuse the village."

Kevin Murphy grunted doubtfully. "I'm not sure the village will accept him."

Larry Desmond drained his glass. "I'll guarantee the army's acceptance."

Celia Larkin smiled acidly. "And *I* the school children."

The vet said, "But how can we justify his taking the O'Meara's place? He's no more than a boy. They're used to an adult tyrant like we built Pat into."

The general chuckled. "Those in the know won't need any justification other than his fertility."

"But the others? The O'Connors, the Toomeys, the Flanagans—?"

"If Pat had only left a will nominating young McGrath . . ." Denny Mallon began pensively.

Celia Larkin sniffed disparagingly. "That would be too good to be true."

The doctor fumbled inside his jacket for one of the last ball points in Barley Cross. "Get us a bit of paper, Celia. I'll write one out straight away that meets the bill."

The following afternoon, Doctor Denny Mallon found Liam McGrath's donkey standing by a peat stack on the main road out of the village. The doctor rested an arm on the animal's rump and waited. Liam appeared from behind the stack, arms piled with turves.

Denny Mallon waved a salute. "God bless the work, Liam. 'Tis a soft day we're having." He shielded his pipe bowl from the drizzle, and struck a home made match.

Liam pitched his turves into the panniers borne by the donkey. "Are you looking for me, doctor?" His voice was sharp with anxiety. "You're not worried about our Tommy?"

Denny Mallon puffed smoke into the moist air. "I want another look at him, Liam. And maybe take a sputum sample. But nothing to worry about. I want a quiet word with you first."

Liam's face set hard. "About what, doctor? Is there something wrong with my son? If there is, there's nothing you can't say in front of my wife."

Denny Mallon cocked an eye at the white cottage perched on the toe of the mountain. Up here, presumably, Eileen McGrath went about her wifely duties. The top of Kirkogue was lost in mist. The nearest house in Barley Cross was a drizzle masked shape. Doctor and youth might have been the only inhabitants of a nebulous, rain-soaked, peaty landscape. Which was the way Denny Mallon had planned it.

He said, "Well now, Liam—I wouldn't be in such a hurry to make such pronouncements meself. What if I was to say I'm here on an errand for General Desmond?"

"Like what?" Liam demanded guardedly. "I'm not old enough to serve as Fist, yet. And if someone wants help with a job, he don't have to get the general to order me to—"

"Now . . . now," soothed Denny Mallon. "No one is complaining about you, son. And the only person seeking your help is the general himself."

Liam frowned. "What can I do for him?"

Denny Mallon put away his pipe. Home grown herbs didn't burn well in damp weather. He said, "I believe you had an interview with the O'Meara when you got married?"

Liam McGrath grinned at the memory. That particular day, he reckoned, he grew up. "The Master told you about it, did he?"

Denny Mallon turned up his jacket collar, and dug his hands into his pockets. "Let's say I had his confidence. Did he happen to let you in on a certain secret, about which I would be reluctant to expand any further?"

Liam's grin disappeared. "If you mean, do I know who fathered our Tommy—yes."

"Ah!" Denny Mallon's hobgoblin face creased in what Liam identified as a grin of satisfaction. "But *who* fathered your *second* child?"

Liam goggled at him. "Eileen is really going to have another?"

"I'm her doctor, aren't I?"

Liam was abruptly babbling nonsense. He rolled down his shirtsleeves, and pulled a scrap of tarpaulin from the top of the peat stack. "Come on, doctor— let's go! Thanks for the news. Eileen suspected she might . . ."

Denny Mallon raised a damp hand. "Hold on now, Liam. You've not heard the general's message yet."

Liam pulled the tarpaulin round his shoulders, gripping the donkey's rope. "Make it quick, doctor. Can't we talk on the way?"

Denny Mallon shrugged. "I'll put it bluntly, son. You're aware precisely what our recent Master's most important service to the village was. And I've just told you that you've fathered your second child. Well, since your little Tommy will be the only child in Barley Cross with a sibling—"

Liam frowned. "A *sibling*?"

"A brother or sister."

"Oh!" Liam's mouth made a circle. He said guardedly, "And so?"

"So you are the only male in Barley Cross capable of taking over from the O'Meara. Because you are the only one who has inherited his peculiar talent."

Liam glanced nervously towards the cottage on Kirkogue. "What are you trying to tell me, doctor?"

Denny Mallon inhaled, like a man preparing to plunge into icy water. Inwardly he berated Celia Larkin for lumbering him with this pest of a job. He said, "Our recent Master has nominated you in his will to be his successor. And since all the kids in Barley Cross are his children, you have as good a claim as any to his title. The general has charged me to invite you to take up your new role immediately."

After what seemed to be several hours' thought, Liam said, "He can't ask me to do that, doctor!"

Denny Mallon shrugged. "He can, Liam. Haven't I just done it for him?"

"But what would folk in the village say?"

The doctor shrugged again. "You might have to put up with some comment. Even the O'Meara was criticized. You can't expect to please everybody. But you'd have General Desmond and his men behind you."

Liam flicked another glance at the cottage on Kirkogue. "What if I have to—you know . . . ?"

"That would be your own problem, son."

Liam squared his shoulders. "And if I say 'no'?"

Denny Mallon stared impassively from beneath drizzle bedewed eyebrows. "Then Barley Cross goes down the drain."

Liam grumbled. "It's not fair to expect me to—"

The doctor's face was sphinx-like. "Who told you life is supposed to be fair? Do you imagine Pat O'Meara enjoyed playing a libidinous tyrant? Sometimes there's a need to subordinate personal inclinations to the wishes of the community."

"I'm not sure the community wants me to—"

The wizened, bent figure straightened up. "I'm not just talking about our village. There are bigger communities."

Liam said weakly, "Can I talk to Eileen first?"

"That might be the best idea," agreed the doctor.

Eileen McGrath said, "If you think I'll agree to your taking over from the ram of Barley Cross, you've another thing coming, my lad."

"But Eileen! Didn't you tell me that O'Meara was a civil man, and that it was an honor to be chosen for his *droit du seigneur*?"

"*You* and the O'Meara are two different people,"

his wife pointed out. "The O'Meara had no wife to object to his shenanigans. And you do!"

"But wouldn't you like to be the First Lady of Barley Cross, and live up at the Fist?"

Eileen McGrath's honest face grew sober. "I suppose any girl would say yes to that—although there's a great deal needs doing to that barn of a place before *I'd* hang my hat in the hall."

"Well then—"

"There is no well then," she affirmed decisively. "One wife is enough for any man, and one wife is all you're going to have."

Liam found Father Con shining brasses in the village church. The priest had aged in the short time since Liam's wedding. He now walked with a stoop, frequently clutching his side.

"Well, Liam," he greeted. "You've come to help me with these dratted brasses, no doubt?"

Liam grinned. He was fond of the old priest. He picked up a rag and a candlestick. "If you like, father. Actually I called for a bit of advice." He told the priest of the general's proposal.

" 'Twould be a fine promotion for you."

"It would be. . . ." Liam hesitated. How aware was Father Con of the reasons for the O'Meara's promiscuity? One had to be discreet.

"But you're bothered about certain aspects of the job?" added the priest.

Liam let out a sigh. "That's about it, father."

"Hmm." The priest put down the vase he had been polishing, and squatted in a pew. "I think we discussed this matter before? And I refused to condemn our recent Master's conduct—much to your dismay?"

Liam nodded. "That's true."

The priest sighed. "Well Liam, if you decide to take on the O'Meara's job, I might also refuse to condemn *your* conduct. One day you may learn there are higher loyalties than those between husband and wife." The priest examined the candlestick thoughtfully. "Jack Ketch is not necessarily guilty of murder when he carries out the state's commands. Nor the starving woman of theft when she steals to feed her hungry children. So maybe our recent Master was innocent of adultery when he exercised his seigneurial rights—for surely our fine school would be empty of scholars, and our church short of sinners, had he not done so." The old man rested his head on the wood of the pew.

" 'Tis a problem that's given me little peace these last few years. And I'm no nearer the solution now than I was at the start."

"Perhaps if you appealed to someone higher?" Liam suggested diplomatically.

The priest snorted in derision. "'Twould be a marvellous day that I hear from a superior, Liam—supposing there are any left. And remember, they too would be only men, with men's limping insight into ethical matters. Sometimes 'tis better to pray, and take your answer on trust. Desperate situations demand desperate remedies, lad. And Barley Cross is surely in a desperate situation."

Liam put down the polishing rag. "Are you saying it is okay for me to take the O'Meara's job, Father Con?"

The priest grimaced. "If you didn't want it, and I said 'yes,' would you take any more notice than if you did want it, and I said 'no'?"

Liam shrugged. Father Con could be pretty vague when he didn't want to come right out with things. He said, "I suppose you are right, Father Con."

"Suppose?" The old man raised his head angrily. "Is that the best you can say? Consider, Liam, who gives *me* comfort and advice? Do you think you are the only soul in Barley Cross with a problem? On this matter you will have to be guided by your conscience, and make your own decision. The days of dogmatic religion are gone. Soon you won't even have this remnant of Mother Church to steer your footsteps."

Liam sidled toward the church door. Father Con with the miseries was a person to avoid. He needed someone more cheerful to talk to. Someone like— Liam clapped his hands. Of course! Eileen's mother. He muttered, "I'll think about it, Father," slipped out of the porch into the sunshine, and was off, running.

Brigit O'Connor was in her kitchen, floury to the elbows over a batch of soda bread. She said, "Mister O'Connor is down at the mill. He'll be making a new blade for Mick McGuire's water wheel. Did you want him badly?"

Tom O'Connor being a joiner by trade was often called upon to fix bits of Barley Cross' machinery. Liam got on well enough with him, but he would not deny that he had half-hoped to find his mother-in-law alone. He said. "No sweat, mam-in-law—I'd just as soon bring my trouble to you."

Dumpy Brigit O'Connor beamed fondly at him. She had always fostered a soft spot for Maureen McGrath's lad. "Will I be making you a cup of tea?" she asked. "While you tell me what's bugging you."

Liam hoisted himself onto a corner of the table. He swung his legs for a moment, in thought. His mother-in-law might not be as well informed as Father Con. He said, "Doctor Denny says the O'Meara has left a will naming me as the next Master, and General Desmond has asked me to take over."

"Well now . . ." Brigit O'Connor hefted, one

handed, a steaming, black, iron kettle from the stove top. She poured boiling water into a dented aluminum teapot. "That would be a great step up for you, Liam."

His legs stopped swinging. "You wouldn't mind, mam-in-law?"

She stirred the pot vigorously. "Indeed no! Wouldn't you make as good a Master as the O'Meara, after you've had a bit of practice?"

Liam sneaked off the corner from a loaf cooling under a towel. He popped the bread into his mouth. "I wish Eileen felt like that."

His mother-in-law studied him with bright button eyes. "Does she not fancy living up at the Fist?"

"It's not that." Liam hesitated. The Master's actions were not supposed to be discussed, although the deeds were public knowledge. "There's an aspect of the job she's not keen on."

Brigit O'Connor's eyes gleamed—possibly with the memory of a night at the Fist a bride was supposed to endure with fortitude. "You mean the O'Meara's bedroom antics?"

Liam nodded. Somehow his mother-in-law always understood. "I don't think Eileen is too happy about me doing that sort of thing."

Brigit O'Connor poured out two mugs of herb brew. She pushed one towards Liam. "Well, surely the sexy bits are optional? You don't have to do it, do you?"

He grimaced. "I'm not so sure. Doctor Denny says the village brides will expect it, because it's an honor. And Brege O'Malley gets married in a fortnight, so the question would crop up straight away."

His mother-in-law lodged her elbows on the table to study him. Liam McGrath was a good lad:

nothing prurient about him. But if being Lord of Barley Cross meant he had to take each village bride to bed on her wedding night, then Liam would do it, conscientiously. "I wonder why the Master picked on you," she murmured.

He grinned with embarrassment. "I dunno." He glanced slyly at her. "Eileen is pregnant again."

Brigit O'Connor's eyes opened wide. "Liam! You clever boy!" She darted round the table, and hugged him. "I'll have a word with our Eileen for you. Meantime . . ." She stood back to smile at her reflection in the glass on the sideboard. Mother of the First Lady of Barley Cross! That would shake them. And no harm if some of the dignity rubbed off onto Biddy O'Connor. She said, "Is there any way I can get a glimpse inside the Fist? So I can tell Eileen what it will be like."

Liam said, "I'll have a word with Doctor Denny."

General Desmond ushered Brigit O'Connor through the door at the end of the landing. "It'll be twenty years or so since you saw the inside of this room, won't it, Biddy?" he asked, smiling.

Brigit O'Connor gave the general the gimlet eye. Twenty years ago she had been bright eyed Brigit Callaghan on the eve of her wedding night. She remembered the bedroom well enough, and the man who had awaited her there. She said, "That's quite enough from you, General Desmond. What passed between me and the O'Meara that night is no business of yours, or anyone else's."

General Desmond feigned alarm, and backed off.

Brigit O'Connor stared about the room with a grim nostalgia. Same old wooden bed. Same old yellow roses on the wallpaper. Same view of tree-tops from the window overhung with ivy to render easy clandestine entry and exit. Same worn carpet edged by bare boards. She sighed. For all his

tyrant's power, Patrick O'Meara had never looked
after himself properly. She gave the general a quick
belligerent glance. "If you want my opinion, Larry
Desmond, the place is a pigsty. Typical bachelor's
pad. Sure, you wouldn't get me living up here for
all the tea in Chiny. And you'll not get our Eileen
so easy."

The general's smile faded. "What's to do, then,
Biddy? Between you and me, it's essential we get
young Liam installed up here as Master. And the
sooner the better."

Brigit O'Connor planted knuckles on her hips.
"Then you'd better throw out every last stick of
furniture and scrap of carpet in the house. Get
some women up to scrub the place from top to
bottom. Repaint every bit of woodwork. Hang new
curtains at every window. Then fill the house with
furniture a woman could be proud of."

Larry Desmond rubbed his jaw thoughtfully.
"Denny said you'd give me some advice."

She laughed harshly. "It don't take a clarryvoyant
to spot a dirty dump. I'm ashamed to think you let
the poor devil live and die in this midden."

Larry Desmond studied the carpet. For once his
assurance seemed to have deserted him. At length
he muttered. "You loved him too, Biddy?"

She sniffed. "Didn't we all? D'you think we'd
have put up with his antics for a minute if we
hadn't?"

Larry Desmond sighed. "That maybe explains a
thing or two. I'll let Denny Mallon know what you
recommend. It'll mean mounting a raid for the
first time in years, but we'll have to get furniture
from somewhere."

The expedition had the village lads hopping with
excitement. Reared on stories of the glorious days,
they saw the opportunity for an adventure. They

pleaded with the general to be let come. Straws drawn from a cap decided who got the hard greased rifles resurrected for the occasion. And the general insisted on personally leading the raid.

Liam watched them march away, slit eyed with envy. Thirty men, all armed, and three horse drawn carts for the loot.

Eileen came to stand beside him. "And why isn't my bold bucko going with them?"

He grunted bitterly. "General Desmond says he daren't risk me getting killed."

Eileen McGrath pursed her lips. Liam guessed she was perversely pleased with his answer. She said, "But you haven't told him you'll be the next Lord of Barley Cross?"

Liam shrugged. "I don't have to, love. The O'Meara left a will naming me. The general posted it outside the church this morning. As far as he's concerned, I *am* the next Master."

She said quickly, "Where are they off to?"

He slumped against the door jamb. "There are some fine houses outside Oughterard. They are seeking some furniture for the Fist."

"And who's going to live there when it's all dolled up?"

He studied the boggy landscape mutinously. "No one—unless you agree to me being the Master."

Her voice rose. "Liam McGrath—"

He turned his face away. "Forget it, Eileen. If you don't want it, neither do I!"

Their son had another attack the following day. Liam went down to the doctor for a bottle. He seized the opportunity for a quiet chat.

"How long d'you think the raid will take?"

Denny Mallon corked a small sample of his croup mixture, and stuck one of his precious labels on the bottle. He handed it to Liam. "Depends on how fast they are at furniture removing. Remember now, tell your Eileen: a teaspoonful only, when the little fellow starts to breathe hard."

Liam took the bottle. He said, "I'm afraid they are wasting their time. Eileen won't hear of me being Master."

Denny Mallon got out his pipe, and polished the bowl on his sleeve. "Does she know why the general wants you?"

Liam shrugged. "If she knows, she doesn't care. No way do I get to have seigneurial rights with the future brides of Barley Cross."

The doctor grinned. "I'm not sure that I'd agree to it, either, in her place. D'you think the Fist might tempt her, when we've got it done up?"

Liam rolled his eyes. "She'll be tempted, all right. But no way will she put up with me doing what the Master is supposed to do."

Denny Mallon stared at his pipe. "Maybe she'll have to be let into the secret. I'll be wanting a chat with her soon about the baby. I think we have an allergy on our hands. But I need to make a few more tests before I'm sure."

Liam looked startled. "Can an allergy cause croup?"

The doctor lodged the cold pipe in the corner of his mouth. "Indeed it can, son. But so many things can set them off. I'm trying to pin down the hapten or allergen responsible."

"And if you find out, we could do something about it?"

Denny Mallon nodded. "That's the general idea, son."

The raiding party came home the following day. The village turned out *en masse* to welcome its warriors. General Desmond led the column, feet first, on a cart piled high with loot, one leg wrapped in bandages.

Celia Larkin stood beside Denny Mallon. "What's the old fool done now?"

"Got himself shot in the leg, I should imagine." The doctor waved a greeting as the cart bearing Larry Desmond went past. "I hope he doesn't want the damn thing chopped off."

"They must have been more lively in Oughterard than he expected."

"Maybe those old ones with a kick left are not confined to Barley Cross."

"Don't be snide, doctor," chided the school-teacher.

It took the rest of the week to clear out, clean up, and refurnish the Fist. The village's unofficial ruling caucus met at the weekend in a splendidly furbished dining hall. General Larry Desmond, crutch on the new carpet at his feet, said, "I've posted a notice in the village proclaiming young McGrath as Master. Everybody is asking when will he take over. She can't ignore that."

Celia Larkin perched primly on a bright, bro-cade tuffet. "That's your trouble, Larry. You never married. You don't understand how a woman feels about a husband's fidelity."

"She can't put young McGrath's fidelity before the future of Barley Cross!"

Kevin Murphy ran a palm caressingly over the pile on the arm of the settee. "I have known ani-mals refuse to breed."

The general's eyebrows went up. "Are you tell-ing me we've wasted our time? And me with half a dozen slugs in me leg!"

Denny Mallon waved his pipe. "You've done your part well enough, Larry. I think it's now time for diplomacy. Let me have a chat with Eileen Mc-

Grath. Maybe I can talk her round to our way of thinking."

The same day, Eileen McGrath got a note from the doctor, asking her to bring the child in for an inoculation. The doctor also made other preparations.

As they walked down to the village, Eileen said, "I hope you are not expecting to go out all the way out to Killoo farm to visit your parents as well? It's bad enough having to bring him out to the doctor."

Liam said, "We can go straight back home if you want. I was hoping we might leave Tommy with your ma while we take a squint at the Fist. I hear they've done marvels with it."

She lifted a corner of the shawl covering her son's face. The infant snored peacefully. She said, "I'd like to see it. My ma thinks I ought to let you accept the Master's job, so we can move up there. She says they've made it into a real palace."

He said, "Let's do that, then. We can call at the doctor's afterwards."

Brigit O'Connor got to her feet as they entered her living room. She curtsied to Liam. "Come in, me lord. I'll take the little fellow."

Eileen stared, dumbfounded. "Ma—you *bowed* to Liam!"

Her mother puffed out a pouter pigeon bosom. "And isn't he our new Lord? I always bowed to the O'Meara."

"But—" Eileen stared from her husband to her mother. "I haven't agreed—"

Her mother laughed shortly. "My girl, 'tisn't you that appoints our lord and master. We have the O'Meara's word as to who's to follow him."

Tom O'Connor entered from the kitchen, a saw in his hands. He halted, removed his cap, and said, "Good day to ye, sir. Hullo Eileen, me lady."

His daughter was wide eyed, "But, da—!"

Her father said hurriedly, "I'll fill the kettle for a brew." He vanished back into the kitchen.

Eileen stamped her foot. "I don't want to be First Lady of Barley Cross!"

Her mother shrugged. "You'll be the only person in the village who feels that way."

Later they walked up to the Fist. Villagers stepped out of their path. Men doffed caps, or saluted. Women bowed or curtsied. Eileen grew redder and redder. She murmured, "I can't stand much more of this."

Liam gripped her hand. "It isn't far now."

Just past the O'Meara's old tank, now blooming with bindweed and woodbine, a voice called, " 'Tenshun!"

A small Fist Guard stiffened.

Sergeant Andy McGrath bellowed, "Present arms!"

Rifles came smartly to the fore. Liam's stepfather came to the salute.

Liam muttered embarrassedly, "Thank you, sergeant." All those other salutes and curtsies might have been part of an elaborate legpull, but no one made Andy McGrath act the fool. Especially on duty.

General Desmond, limping with a crutch, met them at the drive entrance. He sketched a left handed salute for Liam, and addressed Eileen. "Excuse me not bowing, me lady. I'm still in a bit of a state. May I conduct you round your new home."

"But it's not—" Eileen began. "I haven't . . ." She let the words trail off. General Desmond was limping ahead of them, running on about the recent raid and how a spry Oughterarder had got him in a shotgun's sights before he could take cover.

They passed through the newly oiled and polished doorway into the great hall. Candles flickered in a shimmering chandelier overhead. Glass gleamed from a glistening oak sideboard. Underfoot the carpet was softer than a field of spring grass.

Michael, the O'Meara's man, appeared. He still wore his grubby flyaway collar and stained green waistcoat, but his hands were spotless. He said, "Can I get you some refreshment, sir? Madame?"

Eileen eyed him, wordless. "Some tea?" Liam suggested. A good stiff jolt from the *poteen* bottle would have been more to his taste, but Eileen held firm views on alcohol.

"Very good, me lord." Michael turned on his heel.

"Perhaps we could take it in the library?" suggested the general. "This way, me lady."

He opened a door on the left. Liam saw a room lined with more books than he had ever envisaged. Denny Mallon got hurriedly to his feet. "Good day, me lord, me lady." He pulled out chairs for them.

"I'll leave ye a moment," said the general. "While I make sure Michael knows where to bring the tay."

They sat down with the doctor. He placed both hands on the baize covered table. "Well, sir, madame—how d'you like your new home?"

"But Doctor Denny!" Eileen's face was scarlet. "I haven't agreed to move up here. We only came for a look."

"But sure, it's all been done specially for you and our new Master." Denny Mallon's voice was gentle, persuasive. "And doesn't the whole village want you living up here? It hasn't been the same without a Lord of Barley Cross domiciled at the Fist. So the sooner you move in the happier we'll all be."

Eileen's expression grew stubborn. "If we move in, you mustn't expect Liam to exercise his *droit* or whatever when that O'Malley girl gets married next week."

"But, my lady—he may be expected to do just that."

"Expected or no, I'm not having adultery in my house."

Denny Mallon seemed to shrivel even smaller. Perhaps he saw a carefully constructed edifice crumbling despite his bravest efforts. "My lady—could you tolerate it elsewhere? Out of sight?"

Eileen McGrath's mouth set firm. "Indeed I could not, doctor. And you've no cause to be tempting me so. What's important about these rights of the Master? They're just a tradition we could very well do without."

"But we really can't, my dear." Doctor Denny Mallon was suddenly down on his knees before Eileen McGrath. "I beg of you, my lady. Let your husband inherit his title and duties. For without him we are doomed. While the O'Meara lived we could hope. But now he is gone we have only Liam."

Eileen McGrath whimpered. The sight of Doctor Denny Mallon, a pillar of the community, on his knees before her, pleading, seemed to unnerve her. She grasped his hands and tugged. "Doctor Denny, stop! You mustn't kneel to me. It isn't dignified. Please get up!"

Denny Mallon resisted, head bowed. "My lady Eileen—if I get up without securing your consent to our wishes, all the work of the last twenty-odd years will have been wasted. Will it help persuade you if I get the general, the vet and the schoolmistress to kneel here beside me?"

Eileen McGrath's voice broke in a sob. "Doctor Denny, please get up. It is not fit that you should act like this. The O'Meara wasn't worth it. Everyone knows he was an old lecher with an appetite for virgins—"

"Eileen!" Liam was shouting. "You are talking about your real father!"

She paused. Her hand flew to her mouth, her eyes suddenly frightened.

Liam lowered his voice. "Listen to Doctor Denny, love. He's trying to tell you something dreadfully important. Patrick O'Meara was Master here only because he could father children. No one else in Barley Cross—or the whole world so far as we know—was able to do that. And now the doctor thinks I've inherited the man's fertility. So General Desmond has asked me to take over as Master."

Eileen's eyes grew big. "You mean the O'Meara did it out of *duty*?"

"My lady—" Denny Mallon interrupted urgently, "—let me tell you about two villages. One is a backward place dominated by a medieval type tyrant and his clique of sycophants. This tyrant's father debauched every bride in the village on her wedding night on the pretext of exercising his *droit du seigneur*. And the tyrant himself hopes to pursue the same lustful course despite the protests of good folk like yourself.

"The other village is the only place I know of where babies are suckled, infants play in the street, and children go to school as they used to do the world over. Moreover, it's a place where married couples can hope to have a child of their own to love and cherish. In fact, it's a village with a future to look forward to.

"Both these communities exist because of a fortuitous arrangement of one man's genes, and the determination of people to practice self deception on a heroic scale—because they are aspects of the same place. And it depends on your prejudices which one you choose to inhabit. Because, my dear, you can live in either, depending on what you believe. I, silly old fool that I am, just happen to believe we live in the one with a future."

"Doctor Denny!" Eileen tugged at his wrists, her lips trembling. "Please get up, and say no more. Liam will do it, and I'll try to see things your way."

One hand on the table, Denny Mallon got awkwardly to his feet. There was no triumph in his face. His eyes were solemn. He said, "Thank you, Eileen McGrath, for finding the courage to make the right decision."

She was dabbing her eyes. "Hadn't we better be getting down to your house to see about inoculating our Tommy?"

A ghost of a smile flickered at the corners of the doctor's mouth. "Sure that won't be necessary now, my lady. I've ascertained that the little fellow's croup is an allergic reaction to fossil pollen grains blowing off the peat stacks near your cottage. I was going to suggest you move away from there to give him a chance. But now it won't be necessary. Up here at the Fist, away from those stacks, you should be all right."

Eileen McGrath smiled, her eyes inscrutable. "What a wise suggestion, doctor. It will certainly do for a reason to explain why I changed my mind, if anyone should ask."

Denny Mallon nodded wisely. "It might at that, my lady."

Liam McGrath, Lord of Barley Cross, attended

his first meeting with the caucus the following Saturday morning. Neat in his best clothes, he entered the dining hall through his private door.

General Desmond and the vet, Kevin Murphy, sat at each end of the plush new settee, a bottle of *poteen* and the general's crutch on the floor between them. Celia Larkin, the school mistress, perched on a dainty tuffet, sipping tea in silence. An armchair which matched the settee for luxury almost swallowed the shrivelled form of Doctor Denny Mallon. And, on the other side of the fireplace, an old sagging armchair, arms and back shiny with use, stood empty.

General Desmond cocked a casual thumb in the empty chair's direction. "That used to be the O'Meara's seat. We've kept it specially for you, son, so you'll know your place. Now, about the O'Malley girl's wedding. We've decided you'd better get down there early and show 'em your face—"

Liam slipped obediently into the Master's seat. He nodded, listening carefully to his instructions from the real Masters of Barley Cross. He knew his place.

EDITOR'S INTRODUCTION TO:

EVILEYE

by
Dean Ing

It's remarkable how little Dr. Dean Ing and I find to agree on. Dean lives in a small town in Oregon. The kindest thing I have ever heard him say about my home (Hollywood) is that I live in an anthill. We don't agree politically (except when it comes to major issues like defense), or on our picture of the future. We were able to work together on *Mutual Assured Survival* (Baen Books, 1984).

The world would probably be a better place if everyone thought as I do, but it would also be rather dull; besides, as John Stuart Mill said, you cannot understand your position until you have argued it with someone who does not agree.

Dean first introduced Dr. Victoire Lorenz, marine biologist, in a story called "Liquid Assets" in the pages of the much lamented *Destinies*. It's fitting that she returns in *Far Frontiers*, successor to *Destinies*. Since we last saw her, Vicki Lorenz has learned much, and is changing more.

Dr. Victoire Lorenz stood in the shadowed twilight silence of the visitor display room, cradling her kitten, and studied her enemy in the big floor tank. The light from high windows above the aquarium displays was scarcely enough illumination for human eyes. It was more than enough for the nocturnal vision of Evileye. Prowling rocky sea-bottom haunts, his kind had fed in darkness for ten times a million years. Crowded up against the heavy clear plastic of his circular tank, clearly aware of her scrutiny, her enemy stared back. Though the tank was over twenty feet across, its acrylic wall waist-high to a woman of Vicki's small size, it was barely enough for Evileye to move about freely.

It had been Gary Matthews, mate of the *Yaquina*, who'd suggested adding the inward-curving tank lip with sharp edges. The angular, rawboned Matthews had shown interest in Vicki from the first, despite the fact that her responses were barely civil. Gary had taken her turndowns with an easy grace that irritated her, yet he could still take an interest in her work. That acrylic lip idea had, at least, stopped Evileye from prowling.

Now and then, when some idiot visitor tossed popcorn or a candy wrapper into his open pool of sea water, Evileye might move off in a sidelong crawl, sand and tons of water roiling in his wake. At such times he used a lidlike structure to squint. But at other times he could open his eyes round as a barracuda's. When at rest, for example; or occasionally when studying prey.

He was doing that now. *Think I don't know what goes on behind that pitiless gaze?* she thought. *But this concrete floor is my turf. And I know you, mister . . .*

In fact, most marine biologists knew him—or his kind. Proper name: *O. dofleini*. At her last research station across the Pacific in Queensland, they'd pronounced it "doe-flain-eye." Here in Newport at the Oregon State marine science center they said "doe-fleen-eye." But he'd earned his private nickname from Vicki by destroying a month's painstaking work with his insatiable lust for crab flesh.

A lab assistant had walked in one morning, horrified to find Vicki Lorenz's experimental tanks overturned, one smashed, with bits of *Cancer magister*, Dungeness crab, strewn on the concrete and too many carapace fragments in the octopus tank. Though the *dofleini* was again in his tank, the seawater trail was plain and the vast brute sported a cut on his mantle. Much of Vicki's salary came from a sea grant to study the diminished commercial crab catch. The ravenous *dofleini*, in one midnight foray, had wasted a third of her grant money and forced her to start anew. It *would* be a male! And afterward, to Vicki, he was Evileye.

His common name: Pacific Giant, the colossus of octopi. Larger specimens existed, but his body was the size of a medicine ball and at full span, those leathery tentacles could reach nine feet in any direction for the food, bits of crab or squid, introduced into the big display tank. Depending on his mood, Evileye might adopt a rusty hue or a grayish brown to match the sand. Few visitors appreciated his most subtle camouflage trick, the change of his surface texture from smooth to rough or even to nodular, as it suited this subtle hunter of the deep. He was a great favorite of the visitors.

"Oh yes," Vicki murmured, "they love a good safe scare. But what if they were your size, Scrapper?" At the sound of her name, the dozing tiger-stripe kitten waked for a languid glance at her mistress and, lying on her back in the crook of Vicki's arm, flexed tiny orange-furred paws.

"Think you're a predator, huh?" Vicki freed her left hand; moved it above Scrapper's face to tempt playful claws. "Well, that smart sonofabitch in the tank has two hundred pounds, and a lot of brain-power, and a few million years of evolution on you. You'd last about as long as a hermit crab." Her mind flashed in an unwelcome hallucination of the great beast plucking little Scrapper from her arms, encircling the tiny spitting ball of fur with a sucker-lined tentacle, plunging the kitten below to his own watery turf, pulling the pathetic sodden prey toward the beaklike jaws, lethal toxin from his salivary glands flooding the small body— She felt an unprofessional shudder; turned away toward her office and the experimental equipment it held. Acrylic lip or no, she would never again leave her tanks of gravid female *C. magister* specimens in the display room with Evileye.

Scrapper yawned and closed her eyes. "Yeah, me too," Vicki said. "And if I don't get those egg counts done tonight I'll be in a cock-up." While setting her desk in order she smiled to herself at the Aussie slang, an old habit of hers that grad students sometimes gently mocked.

Though Vicki was American, she'd found the peak of her life during her thirties after she and Korff landed jobs in Australia. Birding on unspoiled Heron Island near the small exclusive marine labs there, listening as Korff recited his latest poem— his "most recent literary offense," as he put it—and making love on the Tropic of Capricorn. When his tiny knockabout day-sailer was found capsized on the barrier reef, she could not believe at first that her best years were over.

The memory brought a familiar grief and, with it, a reaction that experience had caught her unaware. Anger, at least, she could handle. "Goddammit, get away from that," she muttered as Scrapper showed interest in the multicolored bottles of recording pen ink. The bottles were secure and the kitten had committed no offense but: "Make my desk a sack of arseholes, would you," Vicki said, lifting Scrapper by her scruff. She dropped the kitten a few inches to the waterproof carpet and resumed setting her notes in order for the morrow.

She knew that her anger was really at Korff, who'd betrayed her by dying. She'd learned from her mother that males weren't to be trusted, but she'd made herself deeply vulnerable to one, bedazzled by his mind, enraptured with his body. *He should've been more careful for my sake!* But he wasn't. Korff had been a gambler. And when he'd lost, *she* had lost. She sent the savage thought back across the years and the pelagic deeps to her long-dead lover: *Thanks for a valuable lesson, mate.*

Vicki slammed the upper left desk drawer too hard; heard a hard thump, probably the little nickel-plated Smith & Wesson she used to dispatch a thrashing shark when working at sea from one of the research vessels. An empty Nansen bottle, its heavy brass hidden with white epoxy paint, nearly toppled to the floor but Vicki caught it just above Scrapper's head. The massive specimen collection bottle would have obliterated her only friend. Certainly the only one she slept with. "Eight lives to go," she said with a shaky laugh, and swept the kitten up again.

A quick look at her wrist: past seven PM. She hurried to lock up, thrust Scrapper beneath her frayed pea-jacket, and headed for her rusted-out Datsun. The rules against dogs or cats at the marine center were supposedly strict. But because they had a problem with ants, the joke went, aardvarks were okay. One of these days an undergrad would show up with a real anteater, and then the joke would be ruined.

She took Bay Boulevard, ignoring the lingering Pacific glow that outlined Yaquina Bay Bridge, now a series of sinister spans arching against the bloody palette of the evening sky. Vicki hadn't time to drive to her cottage halfway to Waldport. But neither could she afford dinner at the nearby seaside places, so she turned toward The Anchor in Newport's heart. The food was good and, because they knew her, they'd ignore Scrapper so long as she stayed inside that pea-jacket. They offered other advantages too; when times were as hard as these, pride was your enemy.

She took a rear corner booth; made an effort to produce a smile because she knew the waitress slightly. "No menu, Fran; we're not all that hungry so, uh, a hamburger steak and iced tea. Make it a child's portion," she added, more defiant than pleading.

"You could eat a horse and chase the driver, honey," Fran accused, adding, "and child's portion it is."

Vicki nodded her thanks, knowing the finely drawn lines in her own face were more from overwork than from undereating. Besides, Fran obviously took pride in curves as exaggerated as an overstuffed sofa. Fran made no secret of her view: if you weren't blowsy, you were sickly. For a moment, Vicki's smile became genuine as she watched Fran's ample behind. By most standards, Fran was twenty pounds too healthy.

Then Vicki leaned back and closed her eyes, her hand stroking the fidgety kitten inside the jacket. She couldn't blame Scrapper; the restaurant smells had her juices flowing, too. It was probably the

shadow across her eyelids that made her jerk them
open.

"I bet you eat in bed, too." Gary Matthews's
voice was husky but light for a man of his size. He
saw the spark kindle in her face and raised his
hands, drawing back. "Cancel that. I mean, if you
sleep in restaurants, why then, ah—"

"Ho," she said gravely, "ho. And I wasn't sleeping."

"Minor surgery on your navel, then?"

She realized she was still stroking Scrapper and
jerked her hand from the jacket. One tiny paw
shot out, answering the challenge of quick movement, and by mischance caught Vicki's forefinger.
"Damn," said Vicki, and put the finger in her
mouth.

Matthews had seen the kitten. Still, "Ah; minor
surgery *from* your navel. It's little differences like
this that make you so intriguing, Lorenz."

He was still standing, because she was gauche,
because she needed to think about her grant work,
because it was all she had, because—"You're in
Fran's way," she said, "Sit." He did.

After an interminable pause of perhaps two minutes he leaned his chin on his knuckles. "You don't
talk me to death either. That's good."

"Maybe I just don't have much to say to you."

"Sure you do. How's the larvae count coming?"

The man had an unerring knack for divining
what was uppermost in her mind. Like Korff.
One strike against him. "Beg pardon?"

"Those Nansen bottles we brought you from the
escarpment. You know, planktonic larvae? From
Cancer magister? Basis of the local econ—"

"So I've heard," she replied drily. "It's too early
to tell, and thanks for doing your job, Matthews.

There's lots more lab work to do, mostly at night. I wish I knew why you cared."

"I've got friends in Newport, Lorenz. If the crabbing doesn't improve, a lot of furniture gets repossessed." His own job, of course, would be secure in any event; yet he spoke as if he really cared about people. Again, like Korff; strike two.

"Not about the crabbing. About me. I don't want to be bitchy, but why me?"

Fran was beside them, sliding a small plate with a suspiciously large aromatic meat pattie onto the table. She cast an appreciative eye toward the newcomer with his wide-set gray eyes and sun-bleached hair. "Something for you?"

"Doesn't look like it," he grinned up at her. He waited, watching Fran move off, amused at the cats-in-a-sack movement of her rump, and caught Vicki's glance before answering. "Why you? Well, you're dedicated; students claim you're tough, but fair. And you're a loner like me. You stay in shape. You don't party a lot." He paused to watch her separate a bite-sized piece of meat, saw Scrapper devour it from her hand. "And you read damned fine poetry, and you take in strays." He spread his hands again for her.

"Scrapper happens to be a female. No, I'm not lezzo," she added quickly.

"I never dreamed you were. I know about Korff," he said softly.

Now he was riding sidelong on a dangerous Pacific swell. "Then leave me alone with him!" She hadn't intended to say it that way, nor that sharply. More subdued: "I really just need to be left alone, Matthews. I really, really—" Momentarily, without knowing why, she was near tears with frustration.

"Forgive me," he said, rising. "You don't need

this. I just thought you might enjoy hunting agates on the beach sometime, or a steak at The Moorage now and then."

"I can't afford it."

"I can."

"I can't afford you, either."

"Ah." His answering smile was bleak now. "I suppose there's something to be said for traveling light. We *could* keep it light, you know." He got up slowly, favoring his back like an older man.

"Looks like you've put in a long day, too," she said to change the subject.

"They seem to get longer as we get older," he said.

" 'We are all her children, and age too soon; Yet our witch-mother sea is still bride of the moon.' "

A fragment of Korff; strike three. "Mister Matthews, you are now invading my privacy," she said, staring at her plate.

"I suppose it never occurs to you that others might miss him," Matthews said. "Or that his work belongs to us all—even if he did dedicate it to you."

He had already turned away when she spoke. "He gave himself too easily to the sea."

Pause. Then, over his shoulder: "Maybe you'll explain that sometime."

"Maybe I will. But I'm rotten company tonight, Matthews. I'm sorry."

He nodded and left her. Presently she withdrew a square of filmy plastic from her jacket; folded the remainder of the meat inside. "You'll want a midnight snack before I'm done," she muttered to the kitten, and counted out the coins for Fran's tip.

It was almost ten PM before Vicki had enough data on the *magister* egg counts. It was messy work with its own special odors. She washed up, setting out a few fragments of crab for Scrapper, and carried a tray of remains into the display room.

"Never say I'm not fair," she muttered as she emptied the tray into Evileye's tank. He reached one tentacle out, suckers flattening against the clear acrylic to anchor him, and sent two more of his powerful limbs after large morsels. He was in no hurry, but watched her warily as he began to feed.

Why had she told Gary Matthews she might explain her bitter memories of Korff? It would only make a bad situation worse. It was her firm conclusion that, among the more intelligent species, the female became the giver; a genetic bias, perhaps, in caring for the young. The male, biased toward the hunt, became a selfish taker.

She watched Evileye reach far across his tank for a remnant of *C. magister* with the tentacle that proved his maleness. Its underside had a faint groove from which, at mating time, a special appendage grew. This detachable pseudopod was his gift to the female. "And you wouldn't do it unless it felt damned good," she said, wondering for the first time about that particular tentacle.

Big specimens of Evileye's kind were in special demand for dissection, precisely because everything was so large. Fine structures, the optic nerve, even the circulatory and neural systems. Perhaps someone had already made a study of the nerve pathways of *O. dofleini* with respect to that special tentacle. If not, perhaps she would sacrifice Evileye to that end. It would be a great pleasure.

She noted the series of faint lines, perhaps abrasions from the stones in his tank, that marked the tips of three tentacles that were most directly in line with those evil eyes. "One day soon, you may

give your all for science," she warned, and took
the tray back to her office.

The far end of her narrow office held lab hardware and the sink. Presently she began to chuckle
as she completed her cleanup. It might be possible
for a man as honest as Gary Matthews to admit
that he had a selfish purpose in paying court to a
woman—herself, for example. But even under tor-
ture he wouldn't allow the comparison of his own
flesh, his sex tentacle as it were, to that of Evileye.
Still, that was clearly how it was. Basically, all he
wanted was his own selfish pleasure, regardless
who got destroyed in the process. Take a step or
two across the evolutionary ladder and you had a
cunning, highly intelligent male predator who made
not the slightest effort to please anyone in his
lust-driven pursuit.

You had Evileye.

Her wry amusement lasted until she had fed
new figures into her desk computer, saved the up-
dated data on a spare disk, and filed the disk
away. Then she remembered Scrapper's late snack
and, still sitting, reached for her pea-jacket. She'd
forgotten to shut the door to the display room, a
common occurrence. But then her gaze followed a
long trapezoid of light into the big room. In the
edge of the blade of light, a saffron bundle of fur
gamboled, fell over its feet, reared, pounced.

A runnel of water, a very small thing really,
edged into the light. Vicki wondered if the big
tank had sprung a leak, and then something else
flicked into the light for a bare, ghastly, enervat-
ing instant, and in that tick of time her heart went
as cold as primeval ooze.

She knew how suddenly, and with what lethal
precision, Evileye could lash out with that tentacle which now lay stretched over the lips of his

tank, its tip flicking in the edge of the light, tantalizing the innocent Scrapper into mock attacks. If she screamed or bolted into the big room, she would be too late. Evileye might have been luring the kitten forward for long minutes. Noiselessly, not daring to look away, Vicki pulled open the top left drawer of her desk and groped for the revolver.

But the cold metal object she grasped was not the revolver; it was merely a paperweight, long forgotten until this moment of mortal need. Now, straining to see into the gloom, she could see Evileye, crowded hard against the near wall of his tank, one huge eye wide, staring down at the kitten which was busily stalking the lure and did not see the second hawser-thick rope of muscle sliding along the floor behind it.

Biting her lip, mewling with desperation, Vicki wrenched open a second drawer, then a third, and then remembered with thunderclap clarity that she'd left the goddamn revolver in her apartment a month before. In her middle drawer was a dissection knife that she used as a letter-opener. If that was all she had for an attack on a monster twice her size, then that, by God, would have to do. She leaped to her feet, grasped the heavy Nansen bottle with her free hand and prepared to toss it against the tank in the wild hope that it might prove an instant's diversion. She took two steps, raised the metal canister, and paused.

Scrapper had already found her goal. The kitten had wrapped both forepaws around one leathery tip, and kicked with both hind feet against the tentacle in pretend ferocity. The second flanking tentacle had reached the kitten. Slowly, repeatedly, the tip of the second tentacle rubbed the back of Scrapper's neck, moving up between her ears and back again.

Vicki Lorenz, her knees failing, slid against the near wall of her office, so near collapse that she dropped the Nansen bottle. At the muffled clang, Scrapper came to her feet in a liquid gymnastic, then turned again to resume her little game. Evileye, staring expressionlessly from his world, seemed equally willing. Moments later he had the kitten on its back as he tickled its almost hairless belly.

As Vicki walked on unsteady legs into the room, slipping the dissection knife into a back pocket, Evileye moved one eye to keep her in view. Simultaneously, he slid his tentacles back with such guilty speed that one of them actually made an audible "plop" into the water. The kitten sat up and began to lick its breast.

"You didn't know I was watching, Evileye. So I believe you." Her voice shook so much, Vicki scarcely recognized it as her own. "Now I see how you got all those scratches. How many nights, I wonder."

Now he wrapped three of his rearmost tentacles around heavy stones in the tank; solid purchase for a quick retreat. Yet he stayed near the wall of the tank, watching as Vicki stooped to pull Scrapper into the crook of one arm.

"Scrapper doesn't know how sharp her little claws are; why do you let her scratch you up like that? Hell, why do *I*? Maybe friends all have claws, now that you mention it. You just have to be willing to bleed a little." Her voice, echoing in the big room, sounded doubly foolish. She didn't give a damn; at least it wasn't so shaky anymore.

Then she laughed aloud. "Let me tell you something, Evileye: I've pigged out on crab, too. Maybe we should pick friends for what they're selfish *about*, hm?" She didn't really expect the big brute to take her hand when she placed it in the water; and he didn't.

But when she squatted and eased Scrapper up against the clear plastic of the tank—the kitten did not care for its chill surface—one careful tentacle snaked out along the acrylic inside the tank, its tip moving as if in symbolic caress. Vicki placed her hand flat, fingers apart tentacle-like, opposite the appendage.

Later she would wonder if she had imagined it; but as the tentacle became still, Evileye did two things: he opened both eyes wide, and he changed from gray to a hue that was ruddy as her own sunburnt skin.

"That does it, buster; but it'll have to look like an accident."

Among the list of emergency numbers she found Matthews, Gary. He answered at the fifth ring. "If you're only watching Johnny Carson," she said, "how would you like to help me out here at the lab? Yes, tonight. The sooner the better."

During his reply she rubbed Scrapper's neck. Then: "It's not illegal, but you'll think it's crazy as hell. . . . Okay, twenty minutes, but one more thing: you must never, ever, tell anyone."

She listened a moment more. Then, with a sigh: "All right then: we're going to fishnap a two-hundred-pound octopus. Still with me? Right; fifteen minutes," she said, laughing.

She put down the receiver and strolled back into the display room with its horrific central exhibit. She leaned forward on the tank lip, certain that no member of *O. dofleini* could understand her words, saying them anyway. "I could set up subtle lighting and get videotapes; I know, don't tempt me. Maybe I will, with one of your brothers. But not with you, Evileye. It'll be a bitch to fake your trail, but we've got all night."

And maybe, she thought, one day she would tell the details to Gary Matthews, While sharing a London broil, or combing Agate Beach some summer evening. She nuzzled her kitten and winked at Evileye, her buoyancy an almost physical sensation. After long years of self-imposed exile in green twilight depths, she was rising now, soaring upward to the light and to her own element; to life. The least she could do was return Evileye to his.

EDITOR'S INTRODUCTION TO:

THE SOFTWARE PLAGUE

by
John Park

The computer revolution has only just begun.

Classical science fiction had few accurate predictions about computers. Most of the "golden age" stories pictured computers as enormous, and not very smart. Even Robert Heinlein, master though he was, continued to think of computers as expanded fire control systems until well into the '60s. The notion that computers would be small, and *cheap*, was a long time sinking into the collective SF consciousness.

In fact, science fiction was more willing to believe in robots than computers. Asimov wrote stories of robots almost indistinguishable from humans at a time when computers were still thought to be large and partly mechanical—although it requires little reflection to see that a robot is much harder to build than a computer, and any robot capable of acting like a human must have an excellent computer for a brain.

Even after home computers became more common, and some of us were using them, really imaginative stories of future civilizations built around computers were—and are—rare. Most tend to be about the giant computer that takes over the world; few tell much of everyday life in the computer age. I do recall at a meeting of the American Institute of Aeronautics and Astronautics in Baltimore several years ago that Dr. Charles Sheffield wondered whether, in future, TV announcers doing commercials might hold up, instead of a laxative to promote "regularity," a computer chip that you could plug into your nervous system to reprogram certain bodily functions; but I don't believe Charles ever wrote a story about it.

John Park is a Canadian writer who *does* have a feel for that future.

THE SOFTWARE PLAGUE

John Park

The clang of drowned bells and the prickle of cinnamon gravel: I was hooked into the ship's sensors, listening to magnetic fields and tasting cosmic rays, when Sheena's call came on line. The implant in my cortex sounded a faint chime and switched me to the navigation sensors. Over there, once more, was the glittering tangle of the starship complex, there the pale fat pillow of Jupiter; there lay Europa like a great fractured crystal ball, and somewhere over my imaginary shoulder was the cruel stabbing point of the sun. The implant hung a red circle around Dawson Base on Europa to show me where the call was coming from, and then Sheena appeared.

Just head and shoulders, her hair tied back, so that the streak of grey above her left temple was hidden among the black. The LED interface socket at her right temple was empty; for a moment I wished she'd used wide-band transmission. With the implants knitting into the synapses, wide-banding can be almost as good as real sex—some people claim it's better. In any case, it's the best you can do across twenty kiloklicks. But this wasn't the time.

She said, "You nearly through out there, Martin?"

"Just finishing Harley's data; it peaked four hours ago. Practically down to background again now. What's up?"

"I just got in from orbit. The backup for the communications net is down—software problems. Dave called to tell you: he thinks it's sabotage."

"Dave thinks metal fatigue and sunset and toothaches are sabotage. Why does he have to call me every time?"

"Be nice," she said. "And—we've got visitors."

"Oh yes? Who?"

"Surprise. And besides . . ."

"Yeah?"

"Miss you." She grinned. "Been dreaming of vampires again."

So I cut short the rest of Harley's data, and went into my nightflier mode. I spread my wings and planed through the eternal dark, watching the worlds turn about me and the stars hanging poised, and feeling just a little eternal myself.

With the ship parked at the orbital relay, I had to disconnect myself for the shuttle down to Europa. It's always disorienting, being penned in your own body again after your senses have been opened to the whole electromagnetic spectrum and more. The drop in free fall gave me time to adjust; and anyway, I didn't want to find myself addicted to using the implants.

The carways were less bright than usual when I made my way from the terminal; it took me a moment to realize that all the advertising holos were dark. Evidently the communications breakdown was more serious than I'd expected. And when I got into Number 2782 the IndiVid, which should have been ready to feed holos into our implants, was dead. Instead, the holo-vid was on, with a newscast from Earth showing riots and anti-tech demonstrations under smog-yellow skies. Sheena was curled up on the air-mat in front of it, but the wall screen was lit beside her. It was ablaze with enhanced stars and the immense glittering latticework of the starship construction bay, and I could tell from her posture and the look on her face that she wouldn't be awake to anything else. I watched her, then went over and took her hands. I whispered, "No, Sheena. It's not for us." We've got too many recessive genes; Sol is the only star we get to visit.

I studied her face as she turned to me. A broken

dream transforming to quiet joy in the curve of a cheek, the smoothing of a brow. Her face was thin, with a straight nose and high cheekbones. That evening she was wearing the brown jump suit that matched her eyes, and some of our magic jewelry: antique carbon resistors and metal oxide capacitors strung together as bracelet and necklace. Her hair was loose and it billowed behind her in the flow from the air mat, silvered by the unreachable stars. I wasn't using the RAM option on the implant, but some things stay in the memory. Whenever I think of Sheena now, that's how I see her.

We had an hour to ourselves, to play; we used our new invention which produced modulated radio-frequency radiation to stimulate certain neuron-implant interfaces. The generators were hidden in the antique jewelry; feedback and modulation were provided through our implants. The effect was like a direct line to the pleasure center. Away from the two foci, though, the interference patterns played absolute hell with any unshielded electronics—including other implants—which is one reason why emitters at those frequencies are illegal on Europa. But we'd shielded our bedroom meticulously, and no one ever found out.

Afterwards I left to see Dave and his theories about the communications breakdown and to deliver Harley's data, while Sheena went to meet our still-secret guests.

I found Dave Stromberg hooked up to an interface bank in the back of the auxiliary communications room. While I waited for him to disconnect, I stood by the window and watched a group of steelworkers from the starship marching under the fluorescents on their way to the red light district. I decided I could cope with Dave's paranoia today, as long as he didn't start whining or insisting on calling me Mr. Juarez.

He unhooked and came over, smoothing his white smock, his red hair flopping over his eyes. "God, it's a mess in there. Bastards are starting to play rough. I couldn't even get in far enough to do a proper diagnosis. I'm glad you came, Mr. Juarez; you don't know—"

"Call me Martin, Dave. Now, just who d'you think is starting to play rough?"

"I don't know, do I? You're in the reserve Militia, not me. I can't do it all, Mr. Juarez. But if we don't stop them soon, the whole city's going to be one big software crash."

I sighed. It seemed everyone in Dawson was in the reserve Militia, with nothing to do because it all came to me. "What makes you so sure this isn't just another power bump or something?"

"Look at this." He showed me a holo of the circuit bank, filled with a tracery of red lines. "Look, the thing's tied itself in knot. That doesn't just happen; someone fed a virus program into it. Only thing it could have been."

"You sure about that?"

"Of course," he said, tugging his sleeves straight, and I knew the whine was coming. "If only someone would listen to me, and tighten the defenses on the software. I've worked up codes that'll keep out anything on the market. Guaranteed. But they won't listen. They keep piling the whole system onto the same software base. They think I'm crazy. Just you, Mr. Juarez, you listen to me."

I swallowed a couple of things and said, "Dave, if this is sabotage, do you have anything that could give us a lead, any evidence at all?"

He frowned, gnawing his forefinger. "But it's so *obvious* someone's doing it.... Yeah, I've got it:

the way those latchings are used—it's like Amato-Singh's work."

"You mean the Mars traffic control program?" I said, managing to keep a straight face.

"They're like that, but the sequencing's different; someone who knows how to modify—"

The whine had gone again; he was starting to invoke the arcana of his art. I cut him off. "Okay, Dave, thanks. I'll see if I can get this checked out."

"Talk to them about my defenses, too, Mr. Juarez."

"Right, Dave."

I was sorry my patience with Dave had worn thin, but he had been finding sabotage and designing software defenses against it for so long that keeping him at arm's length was a reflex now. His holo of the circuit bank did not look peculiar, though.

After that I decided I didn't want to experience Harley as well just then, so I left a message with his cyber and went to find Sheena and our visitors.

The Arcade is the high-gravity quarter of Dawson; it's brought up to Earth normal by two old Blinc-Rigamonti generators, prototypes that hadn't tested out well enough in vacuum to meet the starship specs. The management charges three times a reasonable price for anything you do there, plus seventy-five a minute for using their gravity; but it's worth the cost just to keep in shape, for those of us who still think of going back.

Though Sheena had abandoned that dream for a less realizable one, she still wouldn't admit it to herself, and it was her idea to meet in Plato's Cave on the far side of the Arcade.

The cyber at the lock took my identifiche in its claw and passed it under its scanner. Its metal arm was still bright, and something in the way it moved suggested the whole cyber was new. I wondered briefly who it had been, and what he or she had been convicted of, or had died of. The cyber checked my prints, skin and breath analyses, and my implant code, then handed my fiche back. The lock rotated half a revolution and swung open.

I moved carefully through the gravity gradient at the entrance until my body had adjusted to full weight. Past the memorial fir trees in their hydroponics I came to the Square, where half a dozen steelyarders on two-year hitches at the starship were clustered around a news holo. They were identifiable by the lack of LED couplers in their temples, and by the way they watched the holo. It was showing the last stages in the trial of a hydroponics technician for embezzling air rations. Third offense. If—when—the cybers computed him guilty, he would be carted off to the meat shop, and the salvageable part of his brain turned into a useful cyber. The steelyarders obviously knew about our justice, and didn't like it; I could feel their eyes on my own LED coupler as I walked past.

A grizzled man in plumber's green in need of a wash stumbled across my path, his hands groping in front of him. He stopped with a sudden grin, and his head swung from side to side as though he were listening for something, while his eyes snapped back and forth in some kind of scanning raster. Then he went on again. I knew the symptoms. Going silicon, they called it, though the implants were all bio-organic semiconductors and had been for twenty years—which was why they could infiltrate the neural circuitry and start to take over.

Past the Square was an old-fashioned Earth-type dark alley, complete with garbage in the gutter and—this time—two fuel-tug jockeys, both male, linked temple to temple by an optic cable, and squirming together in electro-neuronic ecstacy.

One thing about the Arcade: you can be sure it's not going to change much from month to month.

I reached the Cave, and found Sheena as I'd expected, sitting by the starwindow, watching a fuel-scoop labor up from Jupiter, loaded with light isotopes for the starship. Two people were sitting opposite her: a blond young woman in a green jump suit—and Victor Sixl. I had known him for seven years, but I hardly recognized him. He was thinner than I remembered, his hair was tawny rather than red, and streaked with grey, and there were more lines on his face than I had ever expected to see. His eyes were sunken, and they held an expression I could not fathom. Wanting to ask, "My God, what's been happening to you?" I said, "Well, hi, Victor; it's been a hell of a long time."

He smiled broadly, transforming his face; then he jumped up and shook hands with a sudden nervous intensity. Under his heavy brows his eyes seemed to glitter.

"Three years, Martin," he said with a grin. "It's aged you. Made you look mature."

"Thanks."

We sat down; he introduced Greensleeves as Frederika, and explained that they had arrived on Europa three weeks earlier from the Ultra Longwave Telescope complex on Ceres, and had just found out that we were here. "Thought you two were still ice-fishing on Ganymede. Come on, the first bottle's on us. None of that wine you kept trying to poison me with; this is a celebration." So we punched for hard liquor at high-g prices. As we drank, I noticed his eyes again: intense and constantly searching, while Frederika's seemed to watch everything with ironic patience. He turned to Sheena. "You still piloting that overgrown firecracker?"

"Arturo?" Sheena said with a grin. "Did Newton like apples? Art's the last one around now, so I've no competition for spares and I've taken options on all the solid booster production of the four satellites. As long as there's someone to sell me fuel, and Arturo holds together, I'll keep him running, you bet."

"It's good to know some things don't change. I bet you're still a walking arsenal, too."

She took off her necklace. "This is the latest." I had thought for a moment she was going to show him her half of our rf generator, but instead she twisted open one of the fat megohm resistors. It came apart and she put half on the table. After four seconds it gave off a flash like a welding arc. When our eyes adjusted again, there was just a blackened shell on the star-flecked glass top. "Useful distraction in emergencies," said Sheena. "Or for signaling—though I don't know where I'd be if I had to use that to call for help. Actually it's just an ordinary photo-detonator for blasting sticks, dolled up in that casing. It's perfectly safe."

Frederika nodded and smiled lazily, drawing the tip of one slim finger down the condensation on her glass.

Victor was examining the necklace. "You always were a witch with those things," he said, handing it back. "A real witch."

Sheena laughed. "No one's called me that for three years. Martin says I'm a lost sea nymph; but then he's just a vampire in disguise."

"Well," said Frederika, leaning towards me and toying with a copper ankh at her throat, "he does look the part."

Victor turned from Sheena to me and then back. "You both seem happy here," he said. "That's good, but have you ever thought of leaving, moving outward?"

Sheena looked at him. "That might be interesting . . ."

"You mean to Titan?" I said. "From what I've heard they don't have B-R generators there at any price. We'd never get back."

"You're right about the generators," said Victor. "But they also don't have trouble—yet."

Frederika nodded and leaned forward to fix me with ultramarine eyes under long blond lashes. "We left ULT because the complex was getting just too dangerous to live in. They had power failures all the time. The computer would crash and cripple the whole station. We'd have to live without the air recyclers for ten hours. And one time all the thermostatting failed for a day."

Victor leaned forward as well. "I tell you, Sheena, it's bad trouble back there, and it's coming from further in."

"Sabotage?" I said for the second time in two hours. "Do you know who's doing it?"

"No, we don't." He turned his eyes on me. "Ah, you have suspicions too. Has it got this far already?"

"Just a few glitches, and some petty vandalism," I said, not too convincingly.

"Perhaps you're still safe then," Victor said. "Let's drink to that."

As we lowered our glasses, Sheena said, to break the mood, "Hey d'you remember that time on Ganymede when all the lights went out on number Eleven—?"

They both started laughing before she had finished the sentence, and then Victor started telling her about that time on Dione when . . . I stopped listening, and had another drink, remembering Dave and his fantasies, and wondering how safe we would all be in another three years.

We ordered more drinks. Frederika started telling me about Ceres, and how they'd spent the long voyage up to Jupiter. On the screen, the fuel-tug rendezvoused with its shuttle. By the time it had exchanged full tanks for empty, and dived back toward Jupiter for another load, Frederika was starting to describe some of the more interesting things she'd found to do in zero-g.

But by then Victor and Sheena were sitting at the same side of the table, and he was handing her a cassette cube, which she placed against the coupler in her temple and replayed. I saw her face change then; I saw the same expression I'd seen when I came in and found her by the wall screen. I wanted to say something, ask what was going on, but she'd turned to Victor with that look still on her face, and he was talking quietly and intensely to her, and she was all attention, and the glass in my hand came up to my mouth without my thinking about it.

Later I noticed they were whispering together the way spacemen did in the pulps when their radios had failed—helmets together to conduct the sound—except that I could see they weren't wearing helmets.

Soon after that I noticed how far Frederika's green jump suit had opened down the front.

We must all have kept drinking for a while, because the next thing I remember, it was dark, and I was upside down, but it didn't matter, because gravity was Europa normal again and I was half floating. Someone giggled, and I found I was struggling with the fastenings of the green jump suit. I realized the reason I was having difficulty was that she kept trying to string an optic cable between our temples, while I kept trying to stop her. She seemed to have her end of it secured, but it came free as she brought the other end towards my head, and then I got the last of the fastenings undone, and the cable went drifting away to a far corner of the room.

Much, much later, I was sprawled across my hammock, with my stomach contents indistinguishable from my brains, and alone. I spent some time trying to understand exactly what had happened, and then some more time wondering if I could move. Finally I pushed myself out of the hammock and found my way to the bathroom. When I came back, slightly more human, I noticed the length of optic cable coiled behind our herbarium. I picked it up. It wasn't a local product. Wincing, I made the implant adjust my eyes to read the maker's name etched onto its coupling boss. Van Strien. The name was vaguely familiar, but there was no reference to it in my hardware. I wrapped the cable around my hand, and closed my fist so that it made a knuckleduster, but I was just procrastinating; I didn't even know what I wanted to hit. So I threw the cable back into the corner and went next door to look for Sheena.

She was there, strapped at her work bench so that she could use both hands without floating away. She didn't speak or look up when I came in. I stood behind her, waiting, and finally muttered, "You've taken up sculpture again." She was bent over a block of brownish plastic, working on it with fast, nervous movements of a scalpel, and she went on as though she hadn't heard me. I was still feeling too sick to get mad, so I swallowed and put my hands on her shoulders. "Sheena. What is it?"

She stopped working abruptly, turned her head, and blinked. "It's going to be a pair of bookends," she said. "A souvenir for Victor. He's leaving, you know."

She turned and bent over the plastic again. "I've got to finish them."

She seemed to have forgotten I was there. I walked out, and heard the door click behind me.

I decided to take Harley his cosmic ray data. He had started going silicon months before; now he was almost incapable of getting outside, and he relied on people like me to supply data for his research projects. I found him curled up in his hammock, sucking synthavite from one of half a dozen squirt bulbs, while an optic cable snaked out of a mass of wiring and microprocessor cubes to his temple. After thirty seconds or so he noticed me.

"Harley," I said, "you look like hell."

His eyes flickered; he lifted one hand, and let it float down. "Yeah, suppose I do. Don't feel like hell, though. *You* look like hell; what's up? Hey—you got the numbers? That why you're here?"

"Right, Harley. But give me a diskpak. No way I'm messing with your synapses, man."

"Do you good," he said, "widen your outlook beyond the sins of the flesh." But he handed over the diskpak.

It's a peculiar, clinical sensation, interfacing with a machine; I still don't understand the attraction. I handed him the loaded cube and watched him devour the data. The change in his expression while he was hooked up made me uncomfortable. There was a kind of hunger in it that looked unpleasantly familiar. I didn't want that sort of need working on me or on anyone I cared about.

He took more than two minutes, and by the end I was looking for something to keep my mind occupied. He came out of it looking drained, and I handed him a coil of optic cable that had been lying beside me.

"Harley, is all this stuff made locally?"

He nodded, his mouth twitching, his eyes blinking independently. I glanced away from his face, and said, "A firm named Van Strien makes some; know anything about them?"

"Van Strien," he muttered, and from the way his eyes steadied, I could tell he was running a memory search. His hands jerked. "Yeah. Van Strien of Olympia—that's Mars, not the Big Tube—they make optical hardware. Stuff's pretty good for the price. Seventy klicks per dB at five hundred nanometers. But it's not worth the import cost if you're thinking of buying, Martin. I'm not paying you that much for mass spec data."

I shrugged. "Just curious. Saw the name on a piece of cable someone was showing me." One or two things were beginning to slot together in my mind, but they weren't making much sense yet.

I left Harley muttering and twitching in his own digitally enhanced universe again, and decided I'd better get hold of Victor and Frederika. I didn't know their address, but Sheena would have to. I found a call box with its *Operational* light still glowing, but when my call had wormed its way through a tangle of static, all I reached was our cyber telling me that Sheena was busy and could not be disturbed. Before I could set about overriding that, the static got worse, and the line died on me.

I thought about it, and decided I wasn't ready to go back and start a fight with Sheena, and that Dave was my next best bet.

I caught the shuttle car to the communications center, and found Dave at his desk, trying to cope with half a dozen crises at once.

"It's spreading," he muttered. "They're really flaying us now."

This time I didn't feel like smiling. "What's happening exactly?"

"Virus programs in half the network. I'm shutting down the sections one by one and sending a team in to clean them out. But it's spreading faster than we can keep up." He pointed to the holo array showing traffic in the parking orbit. "That's the only thing that's a hundred percent right now. If we can't stop the spread before I go off shift, I'm going to quarantine every piece of software in the Base, if it means shutting down the city for a week."

"Do you know where it's coming from?"

"Everywhere, nowhere, I don't know. Haven't you found anything, Mr. Juarez?"

"That's what I've come to see you about. Can you dig into arrival records and tell me where I can find one Victor Sixl, and a woman named Frederika something. Arrived three weeks ago."

He wiped his hair back from his eyes. "Christ, I don't even know if that much is still up." He plugged a cable into his temple, frowned, then shook his head and began keying commands into his desk console. After a few seconds he nodded. "Okay, here we are. Victor Sixl, Frederika von Mannheim"—he paused, staring at the screen—"arrived twenty-seventh from Phobos, with a stopover at Ceres ULT. Moved twice since they got here. Now at three-zero-one theta, sector four. You think they're the ones behind this, Mr. Juarez?"

He sounded anxious. I shook my head. "No, just some people who might give me some more clues. Thanks, Dave."

I caught the next car to sector four. Three-zero-one was closed and, when I used my Militia pass key, empty. They had moved again; I was less surprised than I might have been. I tried calling

Sheena twice, got through for half a minute the second time, and met the same response from our cyber as before.

I had been on the return car for two minutes when it came to a dead stop, with all its cybers inactive, evidently as the result of a crash at the transit control. It took me five hours to work my way out of the transit tunnel, and then through corridors packed with angry steelyarders and closed by emergency doors for half an hour at a time, and get back to the communications center.

Dave had gone off shift two hours earlier, Marcie at the next desk told me. He'd been working for nineteen hours straight, and he'd just quarantined the system when his girlfriend came for him. When I raised my eyebrows, Marcie started to explain about the blond woman in green with the old-fashioned name. I'd hurriedly thanked her, and was turning to go looking for them, when I noticed what was on Dave's desk. Yes, Marcie said, they had been a present from that lady: she'd said he needed something to make the place look more friendly.

The present was a pair of brown plastic bookends, each carved in the shape of an amiable witch with two fat resistors under her arm.

It took me twenty minutes to get to Dave's apartment, and another two to convince myself he wasn't answering, and to use the Militia pass. For a moment I was certain I'd made a fool of myself; then my eyes adjusted to the dark, and I saw the two of them clearly. Dave was sprawled across a couch, bleeding from his face and neck, and he clutched one end of an optic cable in his left hand. Frederika was lying about two meters away from him. The cable was still at her temple, and she twitched when I closed the door.

I slapped skin-seal from the apartment's emergency kit over Dave's wounds, and gave him a transfusion.

As I pulled the needle out, his eyes flickered, then opened. "Worked, Mr. Juarez," he whispered; "my software defenses, they worked." He opened his right hand to show me a diskpak cube, and fainted again.

I hesitated, then took the cube and put it in my pocket and went to look at Frederika. One of her eyes jerked, tracking me; the other hunted at random. Her jaw quivered as I approached. Then her hand twitched, and I saw scalpel tips flicker from under her fingernails. From her lips came a sound like the buzz of an idling machine. I swallowed and backed away.

After I had got medical attention for Dave, I went back to see Harley. He was still curled up in his hammock, wired into his hardware.

"Harley," I said, "I want you to tell me about virus programs. What happened to Amato-Singh's work on Mars? What makes people go silicon?"

"Say, Martin, it's you again, is it?" He returned to my reality slowly. "Ask me one at a time, okay? I can't do more than one at a time, Martin."

"Okay, let's start with virus programs. You feed them into a computer, and they take it over, control its software. They're weapons, right?"

"Now they are; but when they started out, they were just a way of making best use of whatever hardware was free at the moment."

"Okay, but now they're weapons. Who makes them?"

"You want a list? It'll be out of date by the time I give it to you."

"Who makes them on Mars?"

"Lots of people." His eyes flickered, steadied. "You know what happened to Syrtis?"

"No."

"That's right. Nobody does. No one's supposed to know anything happened, but it just vanished off the map for six days as far as communications were concerned. But the word is that someone was developing Amato-Singh's codes into weapons software there."

"Okay. That fits. Now, the other end of the thing. Could there be a program that alters the behavior of our implants, that makes them start to take over the user?"

"Now there's a funny thing. No one here knows what factors make someone like me amenable and you not. Plenty of ideas, but no real data. But I know three groups were doing research on that five years ago; two of them on Mars. So either they've all failed to make one iota of progress since then, or they're not being allowed to publish. I know which one I'd believe."

"Right," I said. "Okay, now put it all together. Could we have a virus program that takes over the implant, and makes that take over the carrier, turns him into an agent—a vector that passes the virus to others and infects any software around? Because if there could be such a thing, Harley, we may have a plague on our hands."

He considered, and was starting to speak when we heard the explosion.

I shoved him back into his hammock and dashed to the communications center; I got there in time to get several lungfuls of smoke helping to get the fire under control and the wounded out. The last part of the center which had been working fully, the orbital traffic monitor, was going to be down for two or three days. It took me a minute to realize what that meant, and then I took the first working car home.

Sheena had gone, of course.

I walked around the apartment cursing my stupidity. I was only reserve Militia, and no one on Europa had any real experience of major crime. But that didn't help.

I looked at her workroom. It was the same room it had always been, and yet it would never be the same again. Tools and ICs were scattered across the workbench. Holos of Vesuvius, Fuji, Olympus on the side wall. Half a dozen music cubes among the tree-fern pots. I picked up one of the cubes. *Four-D Damnation* by Möhwald and the Wolf Pack. It had come out when we were both in the tunneling teams on Ganymede—when we'd met. We still kept playing it, though neither of us liked the piece very much. I opened my fingers and wished there was enough gravity to smash the cube on the edge of the bench; it merely glanced off with a faint click and floated to the floor, and left me still wondering what else I could have done, what I was going to do for the rest of my time in Dawson, and why I had to stand there in that unbearable room.

The cube had landed among some curls of brown plastic from Sheena's carving. I bent and picked one up, touched it to my tongue.

In some sense I'd known what it was ever since I'd smelt the smoke in the communications center, but I'd been ignoring the knowledge, because I hadn't wanted to think about what must have happened to Sheena's mind to make her carve solid booster fuel into a bomb.

Now I realized that was how I'd find her again. I recorded a report for Henriksen of Security, started to feed it to his cyber, then realized what I was doing and made my way to his office. There I eventually found a pen and some paper, and left a longhand summary on his desk. Then I climbed to the departure lock and waited for an orbital shuttle.

Drowned bells and cinnamon gravel. I was looking for something other than cosmic rays this time, and I adjusted the settings of the mass spectrometer. I found the salty drizzle of caesium ions from the thrusters of transfer ships, and then I found what I wanted. Carbon dioxide, metal particles, ice, and soot with absorbed organics: I could track the exhaust from Sheena's boosters, and even estimate the thrust vector from the intensity distribution. I spread my wings and set out after them. For two hours I followed the trail; they seemed to be in a transfer orbit for Ganymede, but were still burning fuel. The radar was a clutter of space junk without an identifiable echo. Finally I detected a burst of power, a course change. I lost the trail for half an hour, burned docking fuel to backtrack, found it again, and twenty minutes later I was sure where they were heading.

I examined Dave's defense cube and made what preparations I could, and five hours later was putting out grapples to dock at the starship bay.

The kliegs and welding arcs were dead; the scaffolding seemed deserted, and most of the personnel craft had gone. I could see Sheena's ship pulled in against the cylindrical service dock. Otherwise there was just the dark lattice of the scaffolding and the cetacean bulk of the starship itself. I guessed that they'd had computer trouble too, and had cleared the site until it was sorted out.

In response to my Militia call sign, a passenger tube was extruded and mated to my air-lock. I checked that I was as ready as I could be and climbed into it.

The official who met me seemed genuine enough. He pointed out that the site was undergoing a Class Three emergency, and while I could not be required to leave since I had Militia authority, I would be there at my own risk. He checked my fiche with a cyber, and then said that as there were not likely to be any more visitors, he would be glad to accompany me in my investigations.

His eyes were moving independently.

"No," I said; "I don't want to put you to any trouble."

He followed me to the exit. "I must insist." When I turned, there was a pistol in his hand.

"Thought you people were strictly software," I said. "You sure you know how to handle that?"

He ignored that and waved me into a storage hold. Victor was there with four others, and a mass of electronics. The five were all enmeshed in wiring. Their eyes were open, but they did not appear to see me. Then Victor stirred; his eyes focused; he stripped the cable from his temple, freed himself of a tangle of wires, and came toward me. "Martin," he said, "I'm glad it was you who came."

I said half-truthfully: "You realize of course that the head of Security knows I'm searching for you. If I don't report back in thirty minutes, the alarm will go out and they'll come looking. They'll have a platoon of riot troops here within twenty-four hours."

"I'm sure you're right," Victor said. "But we won't be here by then. Nor will most of this."

I didn't say anything. I knew what a kilo of rocket fuel could do as an explosive; they had a ton of it in Sheena's ship.

He saw my expression. "You don't understand, Martin. Yes, we destroy, but we are fighting for our existence. We are the hunted; your kind is the hunter. I'm not being figurative: there are men from the inner worlds seeking us now. If we didn't take this course, it would be only a matter of time before we were identified and destroyed. As it is, we have saved ourselves as individuals, and helped preserve our race. If Europa and the other worlds we have seeded do survive, it will be as our colonies. Then, perhaps, we may return."

I said, "You've just explained why we hunt you."

"You find me callous? I find you ridiculous. You and your kind hold the greatest evolutionary advance since the flint hand-axe, literally in your heads, and you treat it as a toy—those of you who aren't too afraid to use it at all. You're still the same death-haunted creatures that daubed the Lascaux caves. Why should I care for such a race, even if it did not hate me? Our survival now depends on abandoning the past. It is regrettable, but you have forced us to it. Instead, we have embraced the future, let it change us. And it has made us immortal."

He gestured to the banks of electronics. "We can inhabit a matrix of semi-conductors as comfortably as that complex of fats and proteins we were born into. In a few hours we shall do so. Yet our perceptions will be wider than any possible for either flesh or machine alone. We are what you have turned back from, Martin, and you are paying a greater price in knowledge and intelligence—in wisdom—than you can hope to comprehend. That shell of a starship is not ready for human occupants, but it is already sufficient for our needs. We will destroy here what we cannot use, but with that ship and its tanks of helium as refrigerant, we will be free to explore our own natures until the solar system is fit to receive us."

"They'll come after you; they'll want that ship."

"They have enough chaos of their own to deal with at the moment," he said. "And besides, you will be here to misdirect and delay them. I assure you, you will be eager to do so."

Now we were getting to the point. "You'll have to damage me beyond repair if you want to get that program into me," I said. "I'll fight anyone who comes near."

Victor nodded, and one of the others freed himself and went behind the array of electronics. He came back leading Sheena.

"You've gone pale, Martin," Victor said. "Are you afraid?"

"No," I said thickly, "not afraid."

"I assure you, she's unharmed. Once she is through the incubation period, she will be fully one of us, and we have enough facilities on the starship to help her through the hardest phase. You yourself will be helping her now. In its early stages, the program demands to be transmitted. Failure to do so becomes quite distressing to the carrier. Or do you intend to fight her too?"

Before I could move, the man who had brought me seized my arms from behind. Victor produced a length of optic cable, and Sheena came toward me. I could still have twisted, bitten and kicked— but not without hurting her.

The connections were made to our temples, and the circuit opened between us. I was aware of darkness, and a threat.

"Sheena," I whispered.

The darkness eddied, thickened. Something was creeping toward me.

"Sheena, it's me."

"Martin." Her voice was thin and remote, like a worn-out recording. "I tried to stop it."

"I know," I said. "It's all right."

The thing in the dark reached out.

"I can't hold it back, Martin. I'm sorry. I'm so sorry."

"It's all right. Just follow me."

As Dave's defense programs met the intruder in a burst of crimson, I twisted the control on my half of our rf generator. Sheena swayed as the counterattack shocked her through the implant, but her fingers went to the silvery capacitor at the center of her necklace. She twisted it and fell forward, and I ripped the cable from her temple and caught her in my arms as the world blew up in rainbow fire.

I held her and shivered and wept, and felt her shivering against me as the modulations passed between us. For a moment I could believe that nothing had changed since the previous evening when I had found her watching the wall screen. Then I became aware of the others, thrown into convulsions by the induction field. I lowered Sheena to the ground and turned to see the official with the gun trying to rise to his knees and make his fingers close on the butt of the weapon. I kicked him under the jaw and took the gun away.

Victor got to his feet, took two steps toward me, and fell again. I went and grabbed him by the hair.

"Victor! Can you hear me?"

"Turn it off."

"Not yet."

"I can't tell you where we came from. None of us can. It's blocked. Turn it off."

"That's not what I want," I said. "How can I

stop what's happening to her? How do I get her back?''

"You can't. She's one of us. The program will destroy her if you try to cancel it. Turn it off. You're too late.''

"Am I?'' I carried Sheena to the door, made sure the rf generators had enough power to run for several hours, and threw them back into the storage bay. Then I ran with her to the airlock.

I got Sheena back to Europa, and Henriksen finally sent over a ship to collect what was left of the saboteurs. But Victor was right. It was too late for her. In the next weeks I watched the program take over the rest of her mind. Dave's software enabled us to clean up the mess in Dawson before it got much worse. Most of the carriers wound up as cybers, but all Security ever extracted from any of them about where the program had come from, or why, was the name Helsing. Henriksen swears he'll track down this Helsing, whoever he is, and make him pay, and I'm sure he will. Unless I find him first.

It needed some wire-pulling, but I got Sheena's brain out of Dawson. I had her cleared for the starship and wired into the sensor bank. Since then the ship had been completed, named the *Gilgamesh*, and fueled for its voyage. Tomorrow its trials will be complete and it goes into transfer orbit, and after that, I'll have no more reason to stay here. I'll terminate my contract and take the next light-clipper to Phobos. But I'll watch until the starship is out of sight, and pray that somewhere behind the crystal eyes and metal nerves, among the semiconductors and the cyberprotein, there is still the ghost of an awareness that once ached for such a journey through night to the infinite stars.

EDITOR'S INTRODUCTION TO:

CHEAP SHOTS

by
G. Harry Stine

I'm writing this on election night, 1984. In less than a month I will chair the fifth meeting of the Citizens Advisory Council on National Space Policy. The Council is a thoroughly unofficial group which has been able to get its policy papers read at rather high levels.

Harry Stine is one of the members of the Council. At its first meeting in 1981, Harry, Gary Hudson, Larry Niven, and Texas space lawyer Art Dula were sent off to prepare a draft of the Council's position on commercialization of space. The resulting paper, "How To Save Civilization And Make A Little Money," has been read at all levels of government from the White House down.

One of that paper's recommendations was that some government agency other than the Department of State be given jurisdiction over private space ventures. I am pleased to say that just after Harry wrote this paper, Gary Hudson was invited to a White House ceremony to witness the signing of an Executive Order doing just that.

If we can loose the engines of free enterprise in the space environment, we need no longer worry about NASA and government appropriations; and we may have our space colonies sooner than you think.

CHEAP SHOTS

G. Harry Stine

So you want to put something in orbit around the Earth? How do you go about it today?

Your first thought might be to give NASA a call and book space on an upcoming Space Shuttle flight. The cost will range from $3,000 for a small "Quick Getaway Special" to $39.7 million for a full dedicated flight. You'll pay in advance and wait an average of 33 months. Better do this soon, however. In 1985, the cost jumps to $71 million.

But NASA is no longer the only game in town. They've got competition. There are at least *two* other organizations who will gladly launch your satellite into orbit right now for a price competitive with the NASA Space Shuttle. Just pick up the telephone and call Arianespace in Paris, or the Soviet Union.

The old space race began in 1957 when the Soviets launched Sputnik-I and ended when Neil Armstrong set foot on the Moon. It was strictly a race for national prestige. The United States won. There's still a space race going on, but it's different. Very different.

Today, it's a race to launch satellites for profit.

Arianespace is a French-based stock company formed to produce and market the European Ariane three-staged expendable rocket. Its stockholders include 36 European aerospace firms, 11 European banks, and the French version of NASA: CNES. It boasts a capital of 120 million French francs subscribed by shareholders in 11 European countries. As of this writing, Ariane has had seven flights, two of which were unsuccessful, from the launch site in Kourou, Guiana on the east coast of South America. Ariane can put 2,200 pounds into geosynchronous earth orbit (GEO) where comsats and metsats must be located. Cost of flying a payload on Ariane is competitive with the Space Shuttle, but bank financing and other incentives are available to customers. Ariane has already taken one Space Shuttle customer: an Intelsat communications satellite previously booked on the Space Shuttle.

The super-secretive Soviet Union also stepped into the marketplace in 1983. They're offering to launch commercial satellites on their SL–12 "Proton" rocket from the Tyuratam launch complex east of the Aral Sea. This is the booster the Soviets use to launch their Salyut space stations. It can put upwards of 6,590 pounds into GEO. The Soviets have never released any data or complete photos of the SL–12, and a user must deliver a payload and let the Soviets launch it secretly. But the price is less than that of Ariane, especially if you pay in hard currency.

Other nations are ready to enter this new space race with low-cost launch vehicles and services. The biggest potential competitor is Japan.

The Japanese space program is little known but extremely advanced and very active. Dr. Hideo Itokawa of the University of Tokyo got started in

1955 by launching little Pencil rockets six inches long and less than an inch in diameter. By February 1970, the Japanese had developed their own solid-fuel Lambda 4S–5 satellite launcher and successfully orbited the Ohsumi satellite from Kagoshima Space Center. Today the Japanese National Space Development Agency (NASDA) has three space launch centers, the Lambda and Mu solid fuel boosters, and the N–1 booster based upon the highly-successful U.S. Delta booster and built in Japan under license from MacDonnell-Douglas. The N-II booster with a hydrogen-fueled upper stage is capable of placing a 772-pound satellite in GEO. In addition, the Japanese are building and orbiting their own communications, weather, and earth resources satellites. They're as potent a potential competitor in space as they've already proven themselves to be in electronics and automobiles.

India has developed a small, inexpensive satellite launcher, the SLV-3, which in its present form can put 35 pounds into low Earth orbit. This may not peg India as a potential competitor in the new space race. But in 1958, the U.S.A strained to launch Explorer-I—which weighed a mere 30.66 pounds. Look how the U.S.A. program forged ahead. India can certainly do it faster, learning from our mistakes.

The case of India is an excellent example of an oft-ignored factor of technological progress: What is impossible for one generation of engineers becomes difficult for the next and commonplace for the third.

It's this principle of "trickle-down technology" that's responsible for a totally new phenomenon in astronautics, yet one in other areas that's as old as the United States itself: *Seven* U.S. entrepreneurial companies are now in the process of designing and building privately funded low-cost satellite launch rockets.

This shouldn't really surprise anyone because, historically, rocketry started out as a privately funded and privately researched activity. In the 1920s, rocketry wasn't even an acceptable program for a government to undertake. Dr. Robert H. Goddard, as well as dozens of German rocket experimenters, worked with their own meager funds or managed to obtain private grants for their work. The Soviets meagerly funded two groups of rocket enthusiasts in Leningrad and Moscow, men who later went on to design and launch the first Earth satellites and provide the foundation for the Soviet Union's present-day space and ballistic missile programs.

The pre-eminence of government in space rocketry can be traced to the Treaty of Versailles which ended World War I and prohibited the Germans from having long-range artillery guns. It said absolutely nothing about long-range rockets. However, Professor (later General) Karl Becker, Captain Ritter von Horstig, and Captain Dpl. Ing. Walter Dornberger of the Waffenprufamt of the Wehrmacht began investigating what German inventors were doing and came upon a group of rocket enthusiasts, the Verein fur Raumschiffarht (Society for Space Travel) working at an old munitions dump in Reinickendorf outside Berlin. They were impressed with what they saw and with a young student named Wernher von Braun.

On October 1, 1933, von Braun became the first rocket engineer employed by a government. He became not only an outstanding engineer and a charisimatic technical team leader, but also a consummate politician. (He was the the *only* man to whom Adolf Hitler publicly apologized; Hitler had

originally opposed von Braun's ballistic missiles.)
During the next 12 years, von Braun learned how
to get a national treasury to pay for research and
development. This had never been done before. It
worked and produced the world's first large rocket,
the German A.4 (V-2), which forms the basis for *all*
of today's government-funded space boosters. When
von Braun brought his rocket team to America in
1945, he added his know-how to the budding field
of government supported R&D that had gotten
started in Britain and America with radar, the
atomic bomb, the jet engine, and other World War
II developments.

Government-supported, military-based space
rocketry is a strange animal. Developments are
carried out to satisfy rather arbitrary government
specifications. Hardware is designed and built to
extremely close tolerances with unimpeachable
quality control and operates with the highest possible technical efficiency. There's no room for error,
no substitute for quality, and no excuse for failure.
Cost and difficulty be damned! Hire another acre
of engineers and print another billion dollars! This
philosophy isn't basically dishonest. A ballistic or
guided missile is very much like a 16-inch naval
shell that must be able to sit in storage for years
and be absolutely dependable when it's finally shot
from that expensive gun mounted on that expensive battleship by men who've been expensively
trained for years.

But recently a group of young entrepreneurial
engineers, encouraged by a rocket pioneer who
was a contemporary of Goddard and himself is
deeply involved in private launch vehicle development, began to sense there was another way to
build space boosters: cheap and dirty.

Robert C. Truax has always been an enthusiastic

advocate of rocket power. During his midshipman days at the U.S. Naval Academy in Annapolis between 1936 and 1939, he designed and built liquid rocket motors in his spare time, usually scrounging old parts, materials, and machinist's help. In 1941, he was assigned the duty of forming a companion rocket team to that of Dr. Goddard at Annapolis for the purpose of developing liquid rockets to assist the takeoffs of heavily-loaded naval seaplanes. He was a member of the 1955 Project Orbiter Committee that recommended the U.S. use the Redstone military rocket to place the first Earth satellite in orbit. (The recommendations of the Committee were ignored, with the result that the USSR beat the U.S. into orbit.) He headed up the study team that recommended the development of the Thor IRBM (the core of the current Delta launch vehicle) using ICBM components then under development. He was instrumental in the development of the submarine-launched Polaris ballistic missile and the Titan-III space launcher.

Although a retired naval officer now, Bob Truax has long been an ardent believer in private enterprise. He got a great deal of publicity from his almost tongue-in-cheek "Project Private Enterprise," a single-staged man-carrying suborbital liquid rocket put together from surplus Atlas ICBM parts. This was an early attempt to show that formerly difficult technological feats could not be carried out in an inexpensive manner. Truax was also one of the first to consider the concept of the "big dumb booster," a cheap and simple no-frills space launch rocket. Naturally, the idea of a big dumb booster didn't and still doesn't sit well with many aerospace companies whose expertise has been built on years of designing big, smart, complex, and expensive boosters.

Truax Engineering of Saratoga, California is now in the process of designing and building a big dumb booster. As a naval officer, Truax knows that the easiest way to handle very large objects is on and in the water, not on a huge and expensive land crawler. His new "Sea-Dragon" will be launched while floating in the ocean off Cape Canaveral. It has a payload capability of 100,000 pounds to low-Earth orbit. Truax is aiming for a launch cost of $100 per pound and expects to offer launch services by 1990.

One might be tempted to consider the Sea Dragon as another case of "born thirty years too soon" but for the fact that Truax is no longer alone in the field of private enterprise space launch vehicles.

As it was back in 1939 when Truax was experimenting with rockets at Annapolis and the Germans were actually flying rockets over the Baltic, a West German firm called OTRAG (Orbital Transport-und-Raketen Aktiengesellschaft) pioneered the field of private launch vehicles in the 1970s. The OTRAG rockets were simple, inexpensive modular liquid propellant units. Each module consisted of tanks made from standard oil field pipes. The propellant valves were off-the-shelf units actuated by Volkswagen windshield wiper motors. Launch vehicles of increasing payload capability were to be made up of clusters of basic modules stacked in various arrangements. Three test flights were made in 1977 and 1978 from a leased test range in equatorial Zaire. An inflammatory and generally incorrect magazine article by Tad Szulc in the March 1978 issue of *Penthouse* magazine claimed OTRAG was a cover for a Bonn government attempt to develop a West German cruise missile. The resultant political flap caused the Zaire government to cancel its contract for the launch site and "throw the rascal Germans out."

A subsequent series of negotiations resulted in a new OTRAG launch site at an oasis some 373 miles south of Tripoli in Libya. But the possibility that OTRAG might be developing ballistic missiles for Omar Kaddafy created another political furor. When the dust settled, it turned out that OTRAG was, in essence, a neat tax shelter for West German investors because of peculiarities in the tax laws of the Bonn government. As a result, OTRAG today is no longer considered to be the leader or the prime contender for top dog in the private enterprise space race.

Back in 1980, a young man who'd been dreaming about space all his life—and who, like many other youngsters, had made thousands of sketches of futuristic space rockets in the margins of school notebooks—decided to turn those dream drawings into hardware. Gary C. Hudson decided to build a big dumb booster. In a light industrial complex in Sunnyvale, California, Hudson put together a group of about a half-dozen young engineers to design and build a modular space launch vehicle that would serve as a work horse. Hence its name, "Percheron." Hudson found backing from a Houston real estate developer and born-again Christian, David G. Hannah, who set up a company called Space Services, Inc. (SSI) to provide satellite payload marketing and launch services with Percheron rockets purchased from Hudson's GCH, Inc.'

Percheron-I was a development test version of a more complex modular launch vehicle. It had welded aluminum tanks to hold its propellants—liquid oxygen (LOX) and kerosene—while future versions would use lightweight tanks made from filament-wound fiberglass. There were no propellant pumps; the liquids simply fell into the combustion chamber under the force of gravity and vehicle acceleration, assisted slightly by pressurization provided by LOX vaporization. The simple combustion chamber was a one-shot unit made from composite plastics that would ablate; the well-proven TRW pintle-type propellant injector would be used. Propellants would be let into this simple chamber by two surplus ICBM propellant valves.

It was a big bird—4 feet in diameter and more than 52 feet long—*larger* than the German V-2 or the U.S. Navy's "Viking" research rocket of 1952–57. With a lift-off weight of 20,000 pounds and a thrust of 60,000 pounds (equal to that of the V-2) for 60 seconds, Percheron would have climbed to a calculated altitude of more than 70 miles. That's all Percheron-I was designed to do: Get hardware on the pad and into the air to prove it could be done.

The launch site was Matagorda Island on the Gulf coast of Texas southwest of Houston, an absolutely flat, uninhabited, isolated, steamy, swampy barrier island, the site of a World War II air base (now grown to weeds) and a wildlife preserve. Cattle graze on it. Rocket tests have always required isolated tracts of land—the Baltic coast of Germany, the deserts of Kazakhstan and New Mexico, and the swamp land of Cape Canaveral and the Texas Gulf coast.

Getting the Percheron-I to Matagorda Island in July 1981 was a logistics problem of military proportions. (In fact, transporting the Percheron by truck from Sunnyvale to Texas was a feat, too, because some state police officers were highly suspicious of a private company hauling a 53-foot rocket along their highways.) The only way to get the large components to the island was by ferry barge. Hudson and his cohorts flew people and small parts back and forth in a Cessna, landing on a dirt road next to the launch pad. And, once on the island, the launch team had trouble with the local fauna. Cattle would come to gaze curiously at the goings-on. Anne Roebke was given the task of feeding the alligator that resided in the nearby pond which held the cooling water for the launch pad's flame deflector. The whole affair took on the frontier aspects of Dr. Goddard's Roswell site during the 1930s or White Sands in 1950. Private rocketry was being re-born in America.

NASA and the aerospace companies looked on with more than a modicum of quietly critical skepticism and perhaps a few snickers at these wet-behind-the-ears young rocket engineers who were trying to do in a simple and inexpensive manner something the "pros" *knew* couldn't be done. But suddenly, there was hardware on the pad. The people at nearby NASA's Johnson Space Center sat up and took notice.

But rocket development has never been known for its smooth road to success. And Percheron repeated history. On August 5, 1981, the GCH crew loaded Percheron with enough LOX and kerosene for a 5-second "burp test" of the ignition sequence. "No need to run the nitrogen purge of the propellant valves. There isn't enough propellant there," Gary Hudson decided. But condensation moisture had frozen on the liquid oxygen valve, rendering it inoperative (as later analysis determined). When the ignition command was given, the pyrotechnic igniter fired and the kerosene value (not frozen) opened; the LOX valve didn't. The sooty yellow flame of a fuel-rich mixture erupted from the base of the rocket. After 1.5 seconds, kerosene-rich vapors and flame from the chamber backed up through the injector to the LOX valve and unfroze it. Lots of LOX entered the picture. The result was what is known in the rocket business as a "catastrophic disassembly" or a "hard start." Percheron's nose cone went an estimated 250 feet in the air, not quite high enough to beat the altitude record for a static test set by Viking #8, which broke loose and climbed at an estimated 4 miles on June 6, 1952.

The crew recovered from the shock, shook their ringing ears, and proceeded to pick up pieces and douse the largest cow-chip fire of the year around the unharmed launch pad. A quick look indicated that the alligator in the cooling pond had survived.

The news media had a field day (as they always do) with the "explosion and failure" of the Percheron. Here was a return to the good old days of 1957 when "all rockets blew up," as Tom Wolfe pointed out in *The Right Stuff.*

But some people at NASA's Johnson Space Center nearly came unglued. These bleedin' amateurs had not only put hardware on the pad but had gotten a fire started under it! If it hadn't been for a mistake similar to one all of them had made during their careers at one time or another, that supersimple big dumb booster would have flown! Actually gotten into the air!

A very large divot had suddenly been put in the sacred turf of the professional space engineers. The very foundations of their expertise had been challenged. What they managed to do with a great deal of complexity, redundancy, high technology, and money had been done by a bunch of people who weren't members of the Club. And for less than a million dollars in the bargain.

Suddenly, the NASA people were all over the Percheron people like a rug, offering their expert help in determining the cause of the hard start. Sure it was help! The NASA people had to find out what these amateurs had done, then cut them off at the pass.

It should be well understood here that not all NASA people are bureaucrats willing to kill to protect their sacred turf. NASA is one of the finest R&D outfits in the world, and they've proved it time and time again. But there are always some people in every organization who . . .

Less than 60 days after Percheron blew up on Matagorda Island, Dave Hannah and his attorney were in Sunnyvale at GCH, Inc. with a check and a contract cancellation.

It took a while for the story to come out, but it seems that some NASA people at Johnson Space Center got to Dave Hannah and convinced him to get rid of GCH, Inc. and go instead with a proven aerospace outfit. The following things then occurred:

Maxime Faget, the man responsible for the Mercury program, retired from NASA; he eventually went to work for Dave Hannah's Space Services, Inc. In Alamogordo, New Mexico on October 3, 1981, I asked him about what had happened following Matagorda Island, and he told me, "There's no room for amateurs in this game, and we had to get rid of them."

In addition to Faget, a number of others resigned from NASA: astronaut Donald K. "Deke" Slayton, Christopher C. Kraft, Jr., and Les Scherer (former director of Johnson Space Center). Some of them turned up on the payroll of SSI and another company, Eagle Engineering.

Eagle Engineering was retained by SSI to put together the Conestoga launch vehicle.

The Conestoga rocket's contractor was Space

Vector, Inc., an old hand in the rocket business because Conestoga-I turned out to be an Aries-1 sounding rocket designed and assembled by Space Vector. The U.S. Air Force and NASA had bought lots of Aries-1 rockets from Space Vector. Aries-1 consists of a surplus M56A-1 "Minuteman" solid-propellant second-stage rocket motor plus fins, payload section, nose, and simple guidance system.

Now comes the incredible story of the "first commercial space rocket." Conestoga-1 turned out to be a "borrowed rocket."

SSI and Eagle Engineering went to their friends at NASA to arrange for the purchase of the Conestoga/Aires rocket. But it turned out they couldn't. In order for NASA to sell the M56A-1 rocket motor to SSI, it would have to be declared surplus by NASA, which meant that the USAF would want it back for use with their own Aries rocketsondes. So NASA "loaned" the M56A-1 rocket to SSI, who put down a $300,000 deposit which would be cheerfully refunded if SSI returned the rocket in good condition before November 1, 1982.

Amid much publicity, hoopla, and media hype, Deke Slayton of SSI supervised the people of Space Vector launching the Conestoga-1 from Matagorda Island at 10 AM on the morning of September 9, 1982. Not only were 130 media people on hand to record the event, but a lavish party was laid on for an equal number of potential SSI investors.

Conestoga-1 flew perfectly. It should have. It was a reliable, previously-tested NASA/USAF rocket based on the Minuteman ICBM. It climbed to 196.9 miles and dumped a payload of 40 pounds of water. Ten minutes and 40 seconds after launch, the remains splashed into the Gulf of Mexico 326 miles southeast of the launch site.

On November 1, 1982, SSI informed NASA that

the $300,000 deposit would be forfeited because they couldn't recover the expended and well-used rocket from the Gulf.

There are other strange stories connected with the Percheron and Conestoga launches. The Federal Aviation Administration had to give a waiver for the flight under the provisions of Part 101 of the Federal Air Regulations, but both the Percheron and Conestoga people anticipated this. What they *didn't* anticipate was the fight for turf that occurred in other federal bureaucracies. NASA had no authority over private launches at that time. Neither did the Department of Defense. But because of the UN treaty on liability for damage caused by space vehicles, the Department of State became involved. If the rocket landed outside the 3-mile limit, it was also considered to have been "exported," and the Munitions Control Board got interested. In the bureaucratic fracas that ensued, the State Department managed to beat down all the other government agencies because nobody else had any clearcut authority. By virtue of the UN treaty and the "munitions export" aspect of space launches, the State Department did. That is why, at this time, the official United States policy on private space launch vehicles announced by the White House on May 16, 1983 is being administered jointly by NASA and the Department of State!

SSI is no longer alone, however. Gary Hudson wasn't about to be left in the lurch, so he's working on the totally reuseable, manned Phoenix rocket that—investors willing—will be flying by 1987. Transspace, Inc. and Space Transport, Inc. both have reuseable vehicles on the drawing boards. By 1988, Phoenix Engineering, Inc. of Redwood City, California, will offer a four-stage expendable rocket capable of putting 5,000 pounds in GEO. Starstruck,

Inc., also in Redwood City, is testing a "hybrid" rocket (liquid oxidizer and solid fuel). Stennon Partners of Sunnyvale is trying to organize to build an expendable rocket to carry 1000 pounds to 500 miles. And SSI talks about the multi-staged Conestoga they intend to launch in 1984 or 1985; it's made up of various solid-fuel rockets derived from military missiles and manufactured primarily by Morton-Thiokol, the same people who make the big solid rocket boosters for the NASA Space Shuttle.

Some existing launch vehicles have gone private, too. Operating as Fedex Spacetrans, Federal Express will launch your satellite on Martin-Marietta's proven Air Force rocket, the Titan-III. General Dynamics offers its NASA-proven Atlas-Centaur, an ICBM with a hydrogen upper stage. The former NASA project managers of the highly successful Delta launch vehicle resigned and have set up TransSpace Carriers, Inc. in Greenbelt, Maryland to sell launch services on civilian Delta rockets built by MacDonnell-Douglas and capable of delivering 2,800 pounds to GEO.

Everyone is offering "attractive packages" and "innovative financing" arrangements.

Competition has arrived in the space business in spite of turf protecting, inside deals, and questionable activities on the part of many. Some of the companies with big plans and ideas today probably won't make it; others will, and their founders and investors will become the first space millionaires. The big question, of course, is *who*. In any horse race, some horses run faster than others . . . but which ones?

You may not be able to buy a ticket to space in the 1980s. But because space travel is being tackled by American free enterprise in response both to international competitive pressures and "trickle down" technology, we're now in a totally new space race.

Cheap shot, anyone?

EDITOR'S INTRODUCTION TO:

AVENGING ANGEL

by
Eric Davin

Are alternate time track stories "really" science fiction? The question is sometimes debated at conventions. Fortunately we need not answer it here.

Stories of a particular alternate time track which change the outcome of what is known in the U.S.A. as "The War between the States," "The Civil War," or, in a few areas, "The war of the slaveholders' rebellion," have long been popular. Probably the best known was Ward Moore's *Bring The Jubilee*, but there are plenty of others.

Eric Leif Davin has studied his period well. Most of the people in this story are real—and most of the events could very well have happened, with what ultimate effect on history we can only guess.

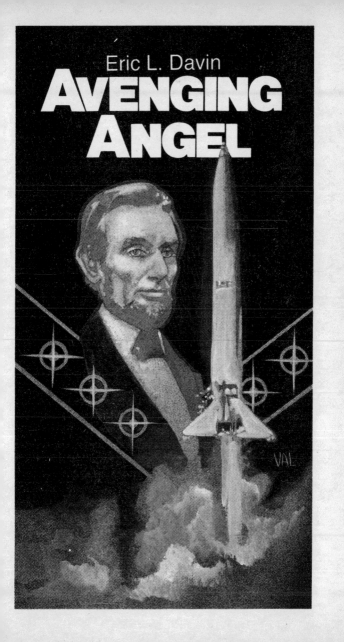

Eric L. Davin

AVENGING ANGEL

Being an Account of
The Confederacy's Last Offensive
from the Memoirs of
Colonel Cyrus H. Mandeville, CSA
as edited by
Eric Leif Davin

London, March 4, 1908.

I am reluctant to begin. For many years I and the other major participants in our enterprise felt that only great harm to the Southern cause could result from committing our memories to paper. Possible harm to our own persons was, if present at all, a secondary consideration. Our great desire was to serve—even at a late date—the interests of the Confederacy by maintaining silence.

Yet, it is March 4th. Every March I am haunted still by the great terror we unleashed now 43 years past.

And, with the passing of time, perhaps there has come that cooling of passions and the mutual forgiveness so fervently desired by Mr. Lincoln before his death.

In any case, with the recent death of Lord Kelvin, all the principal figures in our enterprise—excepting myself—no longer dwell in this vale of tears. They, at least, are beyond the reach of any possible retribution.

As for my own person, I feel the obligation to record the events for posterity to be far more important than my personal safety. In any event, I fear little as I am now an old man, nearly blind, with few years left to my earthly tenure.

And, I have General Lee's example before me. Much as we all desired to have the General's own account of his part in the War for Southern Independence, he kept putting aside the task for "a convenient season"—till, at last, there were no seasons.

I do not wish that for myself.

Therefore, it seems incumbent upon me to reveal, at last, my own part in the most audacious operation of the great War Between the States.

But, a prefatory comment: It is not my intention herein to glorify or enlarge my own contribution to the war effort. Rather, it is my purpose to record, to the best of my ability, events as I witnessed them, events which—had they transpired as planned—might have changed momentously the history of the North American peoples.

Unfortunately, all our official records were destroyed in the Fall of Richmond when the Confederate government archives were burned. Therefore, I have had to rely upon my own recollections and the meager notes I surreptitiously made at the time—a practice expressly forbidden by my superiors, but difficult to comply with for a journalist.

Additionally, being no scientist, it is possible there may be errors of omission or miscalculation in my account. Let these errors, then, be attributed to my own technical ignorance rather than to any lack of historical veracity on my part.

I was a newspaper journalist in Richmond when the South Carolina government signed the Ordinance of Secession. Sentiment in Virginia was overwhelmingly against the secessionists and we heartily desired to stay out of the impending conflict.

Mr. Lincoln, however, forced us to do otherwise. While still part of the Union, the coasts of both Virginia and North Carolina were ordered blockaded by the President. In addition, we were informed by him that we could not remain neutral.

We must either fight with the seceding states—or fight against them.

Reluctantly, we cast our lot with the new-born Confederacy. I, too, offered my services to the new Confederate government.

Shortly after his inauguration as President of the Confederacy, Jefferson Davis appointed that brilliant Jew, Judah Benjamin, as Secretary of State. Secretary Benjamin was a type of man desperately needed by the South: urbane, cosmopolitan, learned.

In turn, Secretary Benjamin desperately needed men like himself as Confederate representatives in Europe, men who could be entrusted with our cause before the courts of the Old World. While Southern independence might have been won on the field of battle, it could also have been won in the drawing rooms of the Continent if Lord Palmerston's government, or that of the Emperor Louis Napoleon, could have been persuaded to recognize the legitimacy of the Confederate government.

Unfortunately, able representatives were difficult to discover. Even before the war, the United States had not been well represented abroad. Having absolutely no governmental structure at the beginning of the conflict, the Confederacy was even less prepared for international diplomacy.

Thus, I was such a man as Secretary Benjamin sought. My father, Francois Mandeville, was Parisian, while my mother was of German origin, born in Trier. I was therefore raised speaking not only my native English, but Parisian French and German as well—the latter with the accent of Alsace-Lorraine and the German provinces along the Moselle.

In addition, I was educated and had already begun to establish a promising reputation in journalistic circles as a reporter for the *Richmond Examiner*.

I was immediately dispatched by Secretary Benjamin to England to work on the London *Index* under the editorship of that extraordinary Confederate publicist, Henry Hotze.

Although subsidized by the Confederate government, the *Index* was not a vulgar propaganda sheet. Mr. Benjamin recognized that the Southern cause could best be served in European eyes by a reputable and trusted forum, which we labored mightily to create.

Thus, the *Index* offered sound journalism and the best European coverage of the war's progress. Of a certainty we trumpeted every Southern triumph—but we also reported every Southern setback.

In this manner, we came to win the trust and respect of the major European intellectual circles and established invaluable contacts with men of learning throughout the Continent.

Perhaps, "at a convenient season," I shall write a formal history of Southern diplomatic efforts in Europe during the war. However, this is not the place for such a work. Suffice to say that as the war progressed badly at home, our economic and diplomatic position in Europe deteriorated apace.

As the summer of 1864 came to a close, it became evident to everyone that the Confederacy, valiant though it was, could not compete with the manpower, industrial capacity, and financial resources of the North. All the North needed was to remain steadfast, for, without a miracle, the South would be slowly ground into the dust.

It was then that General Josiah Gorgas, Confederate Chief of Ordnance, initiated his program of "secret weapons" development. Its purpose was to utilize the last resources of the Confederacy to win in the laboratory what was being lost on the battlefield.

One such "secret weapon" was a bomb manufactured to resemble a lump of coal. A notable victim of this "coal bomb" was the Southern blockade runner *Greyhound*, which had been captured by the Federals and was in operation against us on the James River.

Confederate agents infiltrated the *Greyhound* disguised as roughly dressed stowaways, planted the bombs in the coal bunker, and fled. As the steamer plied the James, the bombs were fed into its boilers as coal. The *Greyhound* exploded and sank, almost taking Admiral Porter and the despicable General Butler to a watery tomb.

In late October, shortly after Sheridan decisively cleared the Shenendoah Valley of Confederate units in anticipation of a final drive upon Richmond, Secretary Benjamin introduced me to General Gorgas' most audacious "secret weapon"—the Avenging Angel endeavor.

Conceived by Gorgas, this fantastic scheme called for nothing less than a gigantic aerial bomb to be manufactured in the huge Tredegar Iron Works in Richmond.

It was believed that if such an aerial bomb could be, by some means, exploded in Washington, and if the North could be convinced the Confederacy had an arsenal of such weapons, victory might yet be snatched from defeat.

Initially, Gorgas met with stiff opposition until he carried the day by reminding his incredulous superiors that the concept was no more preposterous than the "sub-marine" *H. L. Hunley* which sank the *U.S.S. Housatonic* in Charleston harbor earlier that year.

In addition, he pointed to those singular steel ships, the "ironclads," which were revolutionizing both Southern and Northern navies. Using these arguments, General Gorgas received permission to proceed.

Because of my linguistic background and my contacts with some of Europe's foremost scientists, established through my journalistic efforts on the *Index*, I was assigned the task of securing the necessary cooperation of certain eminent men.

By then, Confederate brown paper was virtually worthless. However, our agent in Paris, the very able John Slidell, had procured the needed funds for our enterprise. Slidell's daughter had married into the French banking firm of Emile Erlanger & Company. In March of 1863, Erlanger & Co. made a loan to the Confederate government of $15,000,000, to be secured by cotton bonds.

By late '64, over $5,000,000 yet remained in the Erlanger loan account. Through the War Department's Bureau of Foreign Supplies, Colin McRae, agent in charge of the account, was instructed to make all remaining funds available to me for the Avenging Angel endeavor.

Also residing in London at this time was another agent of the Confederate government, Matthew Fontaine Maury, later to be known as "the father of modern navigation." Maury, a native of Fredericksburg, Virginia, served for twenty years as Superintendent of the U.S. Naval Observatory. After the war, Maury would teach as a Professor of Meteorology at the Virginia Military Institute until his death in 1873.

When Virginia joined the Confederacy in 1861, Maury, like myself, joined it as well. He resigned as Superintendent of the Naval Observatory and, in 1862, Secretary Benjamin sent him to London to represent the Confederacy.

Maury and I journeyed to Glasgow to discuss the project with the Baron William Kelvin, the noted mathematician and physicist. Through the personal intercession of William Gladstone, then Chancellor of the Exchequer, and Lord Russell, then the Foreign Secretary—both of whom were champions in Parliament of Southern independence—Lord Kelvin was persuaded to abandon his teaching for the nonce and devote himself entirely to our endeavor.

Lord Kelvin and Maury realized at once that known propellants would be pitifully inadequate. The Avenging Angel endeavor called for an aerial bomb to be flown, somehow, from Richmond to the newly completed Capitol Dome in Washington—a distance of some one hundred miles.

However, making the European funds of the Confederacy available to the Baron enabled Lord Kelvin to complete experiments he had been engaged upon privately for some time—the perfection of a process for liquifying oxygen. When mixed with the proper propellants, Lord Kelvin's experiments proved that liquid oxygen would produce a faster burning of fuel—and thus, greater thrust.

Utmost secrecy was the order of the day and, true to his word of honor as a gentleman, Lord Kelvin never revealed the results of his experiments—even though his impressive accomplishment in perfecting this new propellant catalyst, long in advance of its accepted date of development, would have added immeasurably to his reputation.

Leaving Maury in Glasgow to complete the work with Lord Kelvin, I continued on to Vienna with coffers bulging with the last gold of the Confederacy.

I had previously met the renowned German physicist Dr. Ernst Mach when writing a column on him for the *Index*. This time, however, I came to offer something more than mere publicity. What sympathy to the Southern cause could not obtain, the remains of the Erlanger loan did. By the time I left Vienna, Dr. Mach had contributed a turbine engine and a gyroscopic stabilizer for the Avenging Angel.

In the meantime, time was running out for the Confederacy. On November 16, Sherman burned Atlanta and began his long March to the Sea. If the Avenging Angel were to be of any use, it had to be in place before the Confederacy was cut off from the outside world.

Thus, on December 19, 1864, we set sail for St. George, Bermuda, on a British Royal Mail steamer.

Our one remaining route into the Confederacy was Wilmington, North Carolina. Already blockaded by a Federal fleet under Admiral Porter and beseiged by a Federal army under General Butler, Wilmington was yet protected by Fort Fisher on the Cape Fear River. As long as Fort Fisher held, we had a chance of running the Federal blockade and reaching Richmond.

In St. George, Maury and I learned of Sherman's occupation of Savannah, which occurred on Christmas Eve while we were in transit. The Southland was effectively cut in twain.

Maury and I quickly transferred our entourage of Scottish workmen, Mach's turbine engine and stabilizer, and British-built machinery for liquefying oxygen onto the blockade runner *Don*, under the command of a "Captain Roberts."

On December 29, Captain Roberts set out for the Cape Fear River and the blockading Federal gunboats.

Wilmington was an ideal harbor for blockade

runners as the Federal gunboats could not effectively block the mouth of the Cape Fear River. The
river itself was divided by an island and barri-
caded by a shallow bar. In addition, the big guns
of Fort Fisher dominated the mouth of the river.

The black painted blockade runners slipped in
and out of this river in the night time mist, invisible more than a hundred yards away and their
engines lost in the roar of the breakers.

Nevertheless, it was dangerous. The unceasing
increase in Federal gunboats resulted in the capture of one out of every two runners at this time.
What is more, over thirty blockade runners had
already been lost on the treacherous twelve-mile
stretch of beach above Cape Fear.

Either the blockading Federal navy or the natural dangers of Cape Fear could have doomed our
efforts, but Captain Roberts brought us safely into
Wilmington harbor on New Year's Day, 1865.

Shortly after our arrival, on January 15, a new
Federal offensive under General Terry renewed the
assault on Fort Fisher and carried it. With this
loss, the South was sealed off from the outside
world. Indeed, the Confederacy itself was now es-
sentially reduced to the Carolinas and the southern strip of Virginia.

But our expedition had already reached Richmond.

While Maury completed his calculations on the
trajectory, workmen prepared a deep launching
hole in the banks of the James River outside
Richmond. Most of their labor consisted of fitting
a tube composed of dismantled naval gun barrels
into the river bank launching site.

On February 3, our last hope for a negotiated
peace was shattered. Vice President Alexander
Stephens, President Pro Tem of the Senate Robert

Hunter, and Assistant Secretary of War John Campbell met on a Federal steamer in Hampton Roads with President Lincoln and Secretary of State William Seward to discuss surrender terms.

Lincoln demanded unconditional surrender.

On February 6, President Davis delivered a most eloquent and impassioned speech to a patriotic mass rally in Richmond's African Church. President Davis made it clear in his speech, the notes of which I have before me, that our only hope now lay in fighting to our last breath.

Or, it was secretly hoped, in the Avenging Angel.

It was now obvious to us all that any chance for the Confederacy's survival lay in this, our last and greatest secret weapon. If the Avenging Angel aerial bomb could be dropped on Washington at a propitious moment—and if the North could be persuaded we had a stockpile of such weapons with which to devastate Baltimore, Philadelphia, and other Northern cities—a negotiated peace respecting Southern rights might yet be forced.

March 4th was selected as the launch date. On the morning of March 4th, Mr. Lincoln would celebrate his Second Inauguration with a speech in Washington, at a site known in advance to us. If the Avenging Angel aerial bomb were big enough and accurate enough, we would not only be able to destroy the newly completed U. S. Capitol Dome—a symbolic blow—but insure Mr. Lincoln's death as well.

In the resulting chaos and confusion, President Davis would let it be known that other such infernal devices were held in restraint, ready to be hurled like veritable avenging angels from the skies. Only an immediately negotiated peace treaty would stay their deadly flight.

On March 1, the Avenging Angel aerial bomb

was carted through the streets of Richmond from the Tredegar Iron Works to its launching site on the James River. Workmen from the Torpedo Bureau there labored unceasingly to complete final preparations.

The Avenging Angel aerial bomb was a rocket composed of three separate, but attached, sections. The entire rocket was to obtain its launching thrust from a huge quantity of guncotton at the base of the tube, to be ignited by an electrical switch. Steam pipes led into the launching tube to provide power for the stabilizing vanes.

After launching, small timed fuses would explode, separating the initial section of the rocket from the remainder just as its inertia was spent. The next section would immediately ignite its liquid oxygen fuel and propel the rocket upward on its way to Washington, being similarly jettisoned when it became useless. If all went as planned, the third and final section would expend its own liquid oxygen fuel supply shortly before the fall upon Washington.

A rough and ready network of lookouts equipped with telescopes was in place in the countryside between Richmond and Washington and the final impact would be instantly relayed to us.

All was in place in the rainy predawn hours of March 4th. The words "Confederate States of America" and the date had already been cut into the forward section of the aerial bomb. President Davis himself cut his name into the bomb shortly before launching.

Then, in the cold and drizzly morning light, President Davis closed the switch, thus firing the Avenging Angel aerial bomb toward Mr. Lincoln's Inauguration ceremonies.

A pillar of flame belched out of the launching

tube and we followed the rocket skyward with our telescopes. I witnessed the first section separate from the rest of the missile and fall back to earth. It was later retrieved by workmen from the Torpedo Bureau and returned to the Tredegar Iron Works. The rocket itself continued towards Washington until lost from sight in the overcast sky.

The rest is well known.

The Avenging Angel aerial bomb dropped upon the U.S. Capitol Dome and exploded. Mr. Lincoln, Vice President Johnson, the Speaker of the U.S. House, and most of Mr. Lincoln's Cabinet and the U.S. Supreme Court perished in the Avenging Angel detonation.

President Davis released a prepared statement to the *Richmond Examiner* revealing the existence of the Avenging Angel aerial bomb and exulting in what was perceived as the salvation of our fortunes. He also caused a message to be delivered to the encircling Federal army of General Grant to the effect that a similar fate awaited other Northern cities if hostile actions against Richmond did not cease immediately pending anticipated truce talks.

In the North, chaos reigned. Panic seized Washington and other Northern cities when President Davis' message to Grant was made known. Crazed mobs of refugees in Baltimore and Philadelphia battled small Federal troop garrisons as they stampeded into the surrounding countryside.

Chicago, Boston, New York, and a dozen other Northern cities were convulsed as mobs rioted in fear of an unknown death dropping from the skies.

This had been anticipated by us and events proceeded as expected. General Grant ceased operations around Richmond and awaited further orders.

It was unclear, however, who would issue those

orders. Almost the entire leadership of the U.S. government had been exterminated.

Then, the unanticipated took control of our destinies. To our great misfortune, Secretary of War Stanton had been ill on March 4th and had absented himself from the Inauguration ceremonies. Thus, he escaped the dreadful fate of his colleagues—and sealed ours.

Stanton rose from his sick bed and, amid the chaos and disorder that was Washington, seized control of the Federal government. He suspended the Constitution and quickly clamped order upon the tumultuous Northern cities by imposing martial law throughout the country. Under his dictatorial fist, Northern fear subsided—to be replaced with anger.

Always a rabid bitter-ender, Stanton never considered negotiations with the Confederacy a possibility. His ad hoc government immediately left Washington and went into hiding to escape the threatened rain of Southern terror from the skies. Meanwhile, he ordered the capture of Richmond, regardless of the cost.

General Lee's pitiful defending forces crumpled under Grant's bloody assault, and a fire storm of Federal anger swept over Richmond. It was now our turn for fear and hysteria as the avenging Federal troops pillaged and looted freely. Homes were put to the torch, civilians were indiscriminantly shot, and Southern women were violated in the burning streets.

On express orders of Stanton, members of the Confederate government, then in fugitive flight, were hunted down and brutally executed. I, myself, saw the body of Vice President Stephens, blackened and bloated, hanging from a telegraph pole.

President Davis and his family were captured

while trying to flee the flames of Richmond hidden in an ice wagon. Grant swiftly ordered him to Washington where he was hastily condemned in a mad mockery of a trial as a traitor and a murderer. On Good Friday, April 14, he was hanged on the very spot where Mr. Lincoln met his death from the Avenging Angel.

Meanwhile, on March 15, General Lee surrendered the gallant Army of Northern Virginia—or what remained of it—to Grant at Harper's Ferry. Thus, the War Between the States ended where it had begun.

The South was prostrate before a vengeful occupation army which proceeded to enforce the harsh rule of the exploiting carpetbagger and Stanton's unforgiving Radical Republicans.

Of course, no more Avenging Angels fell from the skies to lay waste Northern cities. Stanton had called our bluff, and the game was his.

We had horribly misjudged what the Northern temper would be in the aftermath of Avenging Angel and I realized how misconceived the Confederacy's last offensive had been from the beginning. In the frantic haste of our efforts to stave off defeat, our passion ruled. It had been a final, insane effort to bring the Temple down on top of ourselves—and we paid the price in blood.

Instead of Northern fear, we created fury. Instead of a call for a negotiated truce, we engendered a crazed clamoring for retribution.

The balm of peace had no chance to heal the wounds of war.

But, despite vigilant efforts on the part of Stanton's government to root out the particulars of our enterprise and bring us to trial, nothing but the public facts were discovered. The official records were gone in the destruction of Richmond and we who participated in the creation of the Avenging Angel—out of mingled fear and partriotism—kept our silence.

Until now.

Thus, at last I, the sole survivor of this baleful endeavor, set down a true account of Avenging Angel, the last offensive of the Confederacy.

May the Lord God have mercy upon my soul.

EDITOR'S INTRODUCTION TO:

HOUSE OF WEAPONS

by
Gordon R. Dickson

Gordon Dickson was Guest of Honor at the 1984 World Science Fiction Convention held in Los Angeles—well, really in Anaheim because the Worldcon has gotten too big for any hotel or convention center in Los Angeles—but the Convention Committee all lived in Los Angeles. As Master of Ceremonies for the Convention, it was my privilege to organize a "roast." This was ostensibly a benefit for the Science Fiction Writers of America, and did indeed raise enough money to pay off the lingering indebtedness caused by former SFWA President Dickson's addiction to the telephone—but mostly it was just plain fun.

It did present a problem. How can you properly roast someone whose worst crime is that he doesn't get hangovers? Gordie was suffering from an asthma attack while in Anaheim; at least that's what he said. Robert Silverberg's opinion is that he was suffering from a hangover earned in 1956.

Booksellers at the Worldcon sold just-off-the-press copies of *The Final Encyclopedia*, part of Dickson's great series which he calls "the Childe Cycle."

Fans have long awaited the next installment in the Cycle. Not so many know about Gordy's other big novel: the Pilgrim series, about the invasion of Earth. Dickson's invaders—the Aalaag—are frighteningly competent, and their race has the benefit of experience: this isn't the first civilized world they have seized and not merely held, but governed. Aalaag history teaches that the native inhabitants of conquered worlds learn, sooner or later, to love their captors; and it is then well for the Aalaag and their descendants.

The first two stories of the Pilgrim appeared in a rival magazine. *Far Frontiers* is proud to present the next installment of what many believe is Dickson's finest work.

HOUSE
OF WEAPONS

Gordon R. Dickson

The dumbbell shape of the two-place Aalaag courier ship in which Shane Everts was being transported dropped like a meteorite slung from the altitude of its extra-orbital journey.

Shane felt his body temporarily weightless, held in place only by the restraining arms of the seat in which he sat. A meter and a half before his nose, his November view of the Twin Cities of Minneapolis and St. Paul, below, was all but hidden by the massive, white-uniformed shoulders of the eight-foot Aalaag female, who was his pilot.

In summer these cities, chief population centers of what had once been Minnesota, one of the former United States of America, would have been only partly visible from this angle above them. Thick-treed avenues and streets would then have given the illusion of nothing more than two small, separate downtown business centers surrounded by heavy forest. But now, in the final months of the dying year, the full extent of both cities and their suburbs lay revealed among the leaves stripped from tree limbs by the winds of early winter.

No snow was yet on the ground to soften what the fallen leaves had uncovered. Shane looked around the pilot and down into the empty-seeming thoroughfares. Under Aalaag rule they would be as clean as those of Milan in northern Italy. He had just left that city to be carried here to the Headquarters of all the alien power on Earth. Its building was placed about the headwaters of navigation on the Mississippi River. To this place Shane now, his nerves on edge, returned.

The body odor of his pilot forced itself once more on his attention. It was inescapable in the close confines of the small vessel—as no doubt his human smell was to her. Though as an Aalaag she would never have lowered herself to admit noticing such a fact. The scent of her in his nostrils was hardly agreeable, but not specifically disagreeable, either.

It was the smell of a different animal, only. Something like the reek of a horse or cow barn, only with that slightly acid tinge which identifies a meat-eater. For the Aalaag (though they required that Earthly foodstuffs be reconstituted for their different digestive systems) were like humanity, omnivores who made a certain portion of their diet out of flesh—though of earthly creatures other than human.

That exception of human flesh from the Aalaag diet might be merely policy on the part of the Aliens. Or it might not, thought Shane. Even after two years of living here at the very heart and center of the Aalaag Command on Earth, in many cases like this he had no way of knowing what their real reasons were, or whether what he believed might be merely an assumption on his part. . . .

He forced his mind to stop playing with the question of the aliens' diet. It was unimportant, as unimportant as the differences in appearance of the Twin Cities between June and November. Both thoughts were only straw men thrown up by his subconscious as excuses to avoid thinking of the situation which would be facing him momentarily.

In only a few minutes he would be once more in the House of his master, reporting to him—to Lyt Ahn, First Captain and Commander of all the Aalaag on this captive and subject Earth. And this time, for the first time, he would face that ruler, knowing himself guilty of what to these Aalaag were two capital crimes, for themselves, or any one of their servants. Chief of these was not merely the violation of an order, but the violation of it while he was on duty, as a translator and courier for the First Captain.

It was ironic. He had clung to the thought of himself as someone well able to endure existence under the domination of the alien rulers. This belief had persisted in him until just a few hours ago. But now he had to face the fact that even though he had been among the most favored of humans, there was one vital area in which he was no less vulnerable than any of the rest of his race.

As a courier translator for Lyt Ahn, he was well fed, well housed, well paid—tremendously so in comparison with the overwhelming mass of his fellow humans. He had therefore believed in his own ability to avoid trouble with the overlords. But in spite of all this, twice now, the insanity which the Aalaag called *yowaragh*—a sudden overwhelming urge to revolt against the conquerors, regardless of personal consequences—had overtaken him, just as if he had been one of the ordinary, starving mass of Earth's population.

The first explosion of that suicidal emotion had come on him two years ago in a square of the city of Aalborg, in Denmark, when he had been an involuntary witness to a man being executed by the Aalaag; and—to his own later shock—in a half-drunken reaction of defiance had secretly drawn on the wall under the executed man the stick figure of a pilgrim with a staff. The act had had unexpected consequences. To his astonishment, that figure had since been picked up by other humans and spread over the world as the particular symbol of covert opposition to the alien rulers. Its authorship had never been traced back to him, even by those humans who had come to use it.

Nonetheless, for a moment there, he had blindly courted execution, himself. Even though neither alien nor human knew it, he had defied the all-powerful masters.

Then, once again in the grip of yowaragh, in the hours just past in Milan, he had risked himself to rescue a woman called only Maria, whom he had never seen before; and this had revealed his existence, if not his identity, to the human Resistance group there, of which she was one.

It was only now, on the return trip to his master's Headquarters, aboard an Aalaag special courier ship, that he had finally admitted to himself that he, like all the rest of his race, walked a razor's edge between the absolute power of his rulers—and a possibility, which he now recognized starkly, that at any moment an uncontrollable inner explosion might drive him to do something that would bring his hatred of the Aalaag to their attention.

It was strange, he thought now, that this should only be striking home to him at this time, three years after the aliens had landed and taken over Earth in one swift and effortless moment. Squarely, he faced the fact that he was terrified of the consequences of another such bout of madness in him. He had seen Aalaag interrogation and discipline at work. He knew, as the underground Resistance people did not, that there was literally no hope of a successful revolt against the overwhelming military power of their alien masters. Anyone attempting to act against the Aalaag was courting not only certain eventual discovery, but equally certain, and painful, death—as an object lesson to other humans who might also be tempted to revolt.

And this would be as true for him as for any other human, in spite of the value of his work to the aliens and the kindness with which his own master had always seemed to regard him.

At the same time the logical front of his mind was reading him this lesson, the back of it was playing with the notion of finding ways around his situation and avoiding any such future risks of triggering off the *yowaragh* reaction in him. He remembered how simple it would be to contact the Resistance people again. All he had to do was buy himself a used pilgrim's gown of two different colors, one inside and one outside—and pay for the purchase with the gold that only an alien-employed human like himself would be carrying. The dream of revolt was an unbelievably seductive one—in the years before the coming of the Aalaag, he could never have imagined how seductive—but at the same time he must never forget how hopeless and false it was. He must always remember to hold himself under tight control and continue to chart his way cool-headedly in the Aalaag Headquarters and under the Aalaag eyes that were always upon him.

His problem was twofold, he reminded himself as he flew toward his destination. He must cover up any dangerous results that might come from his previous attacks of yowaragh; and he must make sure that he never, never, fell into the trap of that dangerous emotional explosion again.

To begin with, as soon as he got the ear of Lyt Ahn, he must set up excuses against the two crimes he had just committed in Milan. The lie to Laa Ehon must be covered; and there was still deep danger in the fact that he had helped to rescue Maria. The Aalaag, if they should ever actually come to suspect him, had devices which like bloodhounds could sniff out his having slipped away from the Milanese Headquarters without orders,

to confront and confuse the Alien guard who had
originally arrested Maria—all this while he had
supposedly been given time off to rest in a human
dormitory in the building.

That was the most dangerous of the two crimes
he had just committed in Aalaag terms—crimes,
as they would be seen by Aalaag eyes. The lesser
crime, but one sufficient enough for his execution,
was that he had lied to Laa Ehon, the Commander
of the Milanese District, when that Aalaag had asked
him what the price was Lyt Ahn had placed upon
him—obviously with an eye to buying Shane from
the First Captain. Shane had claimed a price that
Lyt Ahn had never mentioned, gambling that his
master would not remember never having set such
a price and that the price was one that Lyt Ahn
would have set, if he had indeed ever gotten around
to doing so.

A lying beast, in Aalaag eyes, was an untrustworthy beast; and should therefore be destroyed.
Somehow, this statement of his to Laa Ehon must
be handled—but at the moment he had no idea
how to do it. Perhaps, if he simply relaxed and put
it deliberately out of his mind once more, a solution would come to him naturally. . . .

He made a conscious effort to relax; and instinctively his released mind drifted off into its favorite
fantasy—of an individual called The Pilgrim, who
was at the same time himself, under the cover of
being a translator-courier for Lyt Ahn; and who
was also superior to all Aalaag, as they were superior to all ordinary humans. It was this familiar
daydream that had caused him to choose the pilgrim image for the stick-figure he had drawn under the executed man.

The Pilgrim, he luxuriated in his dream, would
wear the same anonymous garb in which Shane

himself came and went among his fellow humans who, otherwise, catching him alone and away from Aalaags or the Interior Guard who policed them, would have torn him apart if they had known that he was one of those favored and employed by their masters.

The Pilgrim would be uncatchable and uncontrollable by the Aalaag. He would set their laws and their might at defiance. He would succor humans who had fallen afoul of those same alien rules and laws—as Shane had, by sheer luck more than anything else, managed to get Maria out of the clutches of the Milanese garrison.

Above all, the Pilgrim would bring home to the aliens the fact that they were not the masters of Earth that they thought themselves to be. . . .

For a little while, as the courier ship dipped down toward its destination, he let himself indulge in that fantasy, seeing himself as The Pilgrim with a power that put him above even Lyt Ahn, and all those other alien masters who made his insides go hollow every time they so much as looked at him.

Then he roused himself and shook it off. It was all right as a means to keep him sane; but it was dangerous, indulged in when he was actually under alien observation, as he was about to be within seconds. Besides, he could afford to put it aside for the moment. Five minutes from now he would be in the small cubicle that was his living quarters and he could think what he liked, including how to protect himself against Lyt Ahn's discovery of either of his recent crimes.

The courier ship was now right over its destination. The landing spot to which it dropped was only a couple of hundred meters below, the rooftop of an enormous construction with only some twenty stories or so above ground but as many below, and covering several acres in area. Like all structures now taken over or built by the Aalaag, it gleamed; in this chill, thin November sunlight looking as if liquid mercury had been poured over it. That shining surface was a defensive screen or coating—Shane had never been able to discover which, since the Aalaag took it so for granted that they never spoke of it. Once in place, apparently, it needed neither renewal nor maintenance.

Just as it seemed their ship must crash into the rooftop, a space of the silver surface vanished. Revealed were a flat landing area, and a platoon of the oversized humans recruited as Interior Guards to the aliens. These stood, fully armed, under the command of an Aalaag officer who towered in full, white armor above the tallest of them. The officer was a male, Shane saw, the fact betrayed by the narrowness of his lower-body armor.

As the ship touched down, its port opened and Shane's pilot stepped out. The Ordinary Guards at once fell back, leaving the Aalaag to come forward alone and meet the pilot. Shane, lost behind her powerful shape, had followed her out.

"Am Mehon, twenty-eighth rank," the pilot introduced herself. "I return one of the First Captain's cattle, at his orders—"

She half-turned to indicate, with the massive thumb of her left hand, Shane, who was standing a respectful two paces behind her and to her left.

"Aral Te Kinn," the Aalaag on guard introduced himself. "Thirty-second rank. . . ."

His armored head bent slightly, acknowledging the fact that the courier pilot outranked him by four degrees. But it would have bent no further for the First Captain, himself.

Theoretically all Aalaag were equal; and the lowest of them, when on duty, could give orders to the highest, if the other was not. Here, on the roof landing space of the House of Weapons, as the First Captain's residence and headquarters were always called, the officer on guard, being in control of the area, was therefore in authority. Only courtesy dictated the slight inclination of his head.

"This beast is to report itself to the First Captain immediately," he went on now. His helmet turned slightly, bringing its viewing slit to focus on Shane. "You heard me, beast?"

Shane felt a sudden, sickening emptiness in his stomach. Surely it was impossible that what he had done in Milan could have been found out and reported to his master this quickly? He shook off the sudden weakness. Of course it was impossible. But even with the sudden fear gone, he felt robbed of the anticipated peace and quiet of his cubicle, the chance to think and plan, he had been looking forward to. But there was no gainsaying the order.

"I heard and I obey, untarnished sir," answered Shane in Aalaag, bending his own head in a considerably deeper bow.

He walked past the pilot and Aral Te Kinn toward the shed-like structure containing the drop pad that would lower him to his meeting with the alien overlord of all Earth. The tall humans who were the Ordinary Guards gazed down at him with faint contempt as their ranks parted to let him through. But Shane was by now so used to their attitudes to such as himself that he hardly noticed.

". . . I had heard there were a rare few among these cattle who could speak the actual language as a real person does," he could hear the pilot saying to Aral Te Kinn behind him, "but I'd never believed it until now. If it were not for the squeakiness of its high voice—"

Shane shut the door to the shed alike on the rest

of her words and the scene behind him, as he entered the structure. He stepped on to the round green disk of the drop pad.

"Subfloor twenty," he told it, and the alien-built elevator obeyed, dropping him swiftly toward his destination, twenty floors beneath the surface of the surrounding city.

Its fall stopped with equal suddenness; and his knees bent under a deceleration that would not have been noticed by an Aalaag. He stepped forward into a wide corridor with black and white tiles on its polished floor, with walls and ceiling of a hard, uniformly gray material.

A male Aalaag officer sat at the duty desk opposite the elevator, engaged in conversation with someone in the communication screen set in the surface of the desk before him. Shane had halted at once after his first step out of the dropshoot and stood motionless, until the talk was ended and the Aalaag cut the connection, looking up at him.

"I am Shane Evert, translator-courier for the First Captain, untarnished sir," said Shane as the pale, heavy-boned and expressionless human-like face, under its mane of pure white hair, considered him. This particular alien had seen him at least a couple of hundred of times previously; but most Aalaag were not good at distinguishing one human from another, even if the two were of opposite sexes.

The Aalaag continued to stare, waiting.

"I have returned from a courier run," Shane went on, "and the untarnished sir on duty at the roof parking area said I was ordered to report myself immediately to the First Captain." The desk officer looked down and spoke again into his communications screen—checking, of course, on what Shane had said. Ordinarily, the movements of a single human would be of little concern to any

Aalaag, but entrance to the apartments of the First Captain, along the corridor to Shane's right, was a matter of unique security. Shane glanced briefly and longingly along the corridor in the opposite direction toward his left and his own distant quarters, with those of the other translators, and such other private servants of Lyt Ahn, or his mate-consort, the female Adtha Or Ain.

Shane had been continuously on duty and in the presence of Aalaag for three days, culminating in that disasterous, if still secret, act of insanity he had given way to in Milan. His desire to return to his own quarters, to be alone, was like a living hunger in him, a desperate hunger to lock himself away in a place that for a moment would be closed off, away from all the daily terrors and orders; a place where he could at last put aside his constant fears and lick his wounds in peace.

"You may report as instructed."

The voice of the Aalaag on duty behind the desk cut across his thoughts.

"I obey, untarnished sir," he answered.

He turned to his right and went away down the long hall, hearing the clicking of his heels on the hard tiles underfoot echoing back from the unyielding walls. Along those walls at intervals of what would be not more than half a dozen strides for an Aalaag, hung long-weapons—equivalents of human rifles—armed and ready for use. But for all their real deadliness, they were there for show only, a part of the militaristic Aalaag culture pattern that justified the name of House of Weapons for this abode of Lyt Ahn.

A house of weapons it was indeed; but its military potency lay not in the awesomely destructive, by human standards, devices on its walls. Behind the silver protective screen that covered the building were larger mounted devices capable of leveling to slagged ruin the earth surrounding, to and beyond the horizon in all directions. For a moment Shane was reminded of what he had not thought of for years, of those human military units that, in the first few days of the Aalaag landing on Earth, had been foolish enough to try resisting the alien invasion. They had been destroyed almost without thought on the invaders' part, like tiny hills of ants trodden underfoot by giants.

To any engine of destruction known to human science and technology, including the nuclear ones, even a single Aalaag in full battle armor was invulnerable. Against the least weapon carried by an individual Aalaag, no human army could, in the end, survive. Nor would an Aalaag weapon work in the hands of any but one of the aliens. It was not merely a matter of humans understanding how to activate it. There was also some built-in recognition by the weapon itself that it was not in alien hands, which in others turned it into no more than a dead piece of heavy material; at most, a weighty club.

Walking down the wide, high-ceilinged, solitary corridor where no other figures, human or alien, were to be seen, Shane felt coming over him once again a sensation he hated, but which he never seemed to be able to escape from here, the sense of shrinking that always took him over in this place.

It was a feeling like that which Swift's hero, Lemuel Gulliver, had described in Gulliver's Travels, as happening when he had found himself in the land of the giant Brobdingnagians. Like Gulliver, then, each time Shane found himself in this place, a time would come when he would begin to feel that it was the Aalaag and all their artifacts which were normal in size; while he, like all other humans and human creations, were shrunken to the scale of pygmies. Shrunken, not only in a physical sense but in all other senses as well; in mind and spirit and courage and wisdom, in all those things that could make one race into something more than mere "cattle" to another.

He checked abruptly, passing a door that was uncharacteristically human-sized in one wall of that overlarge hall; and turned in through it to one of the few rooms on this corridor equipped to dispose of human waste. There would be no telling how long he might be in the presence of Lyt Ahn, and there would be no excusing himself then for physical or personal needs. No Aalaag would have dreamed of so excusing himself while on duty, and therefore no human servant might.

He stood before a urinal, emptying his bladder with a momentary sense of stolen freedom, only secondary to that which he yearned for in his own quarters. Here, too, for the moment, in theory he was free of Aalaag observation and rules, and the Gulliver-like sensation lifted, briefly.

But the moment passed. A minute later he was toy-sized again, back outside in the corridor, walking ever nearer to the entrance of Lyt Ahn's private office.

He stopped at last before great double doors of bronze-colored material. With the tip of the index figure of his right hand, he lightly touched the smooth surface of the panel closest to him.

There was a pause. He could not hear, but he knew, that within the office a sensor had recorded his touch as being that of a human and a mechanical voice was announcing that "a beast desires admittance."

"Who?" came an Aalaag voice from the ceiling.

Unusually, it was not that of an Aalaag secretary or aide but of Lyt Ahn himself.

"One of your cattle, most immaculate sir," answered Shane. "Shane Evert, reporting as ordered, following a courier run to the immaculate sir in command at Milan, Italy."

The right hand door swung open and Shane walked through it, into the office. Under a white ceiling as lofty as that of the hall, and large enough for a small ballroom by human standards, the gray-colored desk, the chairs, the couches standing on the rugless floor wearing the same black-and-white tiles, were all almost human in their design. Only the fact that they were all built to the scale of the eight-foot aliens made them different. That, and the fact that there was no padding or upholstery on any of them.

Lyt Ahn was indeed alone, seated, looming behind his desk; which held in its surface a screen like that in the desk of the officer in the corridor, plus a scattering of some small artifacts, each tiny enough to be encompassed in Shane's merely human hand, but showing no recognizable shapes or purposes. In a like situation, on a human desk, they might have been miniature sculptures. But the Aalaag owned no art, nor showed interest in any. What they really were, and their purpose in being there, still puzzled him. On the wall to his right was a larger screen, now unlit, some three by two meters in area. In the left wall was an Aalaag-sized single door that led to Lyt Ahn's private apartments.

Lyt Ahn raised his head to look at Shane as the human stepped through the doorway, taking one pace and then halting.

"Come here," the alien commander said; and, both permitted and ordered—the words were one word in Aalaag—Shane came up to the far side of the desk.

The First Captain of all Earth gazed at him. Just as Aalaag had difficulty distinguishing between individual humans, so most humans, aside from the fact that they saw their overlords most commonly in armor and therefore faceless, were not adept at telling one Aalaag from another. Shane gazed back. He had been in close contact with the alien commander since Lyt Ahn had formed his corps of human interpreters, nearly three years before. Shane not only recognized the First Captain, he had become expert at studying the other for small clues to his master's momentary mood. Like all subjects he was dependent, in this case dependent upon the First Captain not only for food and shelter, but for a continuance of life itself. He studied the First Captain daily, as a lamb might study the lion with which it was required to lie down each night; and just at the moment, he thought now that he read fatigue and a deep-seated worry, plus something else he could not identify, in the visage of the towering individual before him.

"Laa Ehon, of the fifth rank and Commander of the Milan garrison has received your sending, most immaculate sir, and sends his courtesies to the First Captain," said Shane. "He returned no message by me."

"Did he not, little Shane-beast?" said Lyt Ahn. Shane's name was uttered in as close to an affectionate diminutive as the alien language allowed; but the words were obviously spoken more to himself than the human.

Shane's heart took an upward leap. Lyt Ahn was clearly in as warm and confidential a mood as it was possible for an Aalaag to be—and more so than Shane had ever seen any other alien permit himself. Nonetheless, there was also that impression of worry and some concern for an unknown source that he had noted on first entering the room; and he continued covertly to study the heavy-boned face opposite. There was a greater impression of age about his master than he had ever seen before, although the face was barely lined, as always; and there was no way that age could have made the hair of the Earth's supreme commander any whiter than that of any other adult Aalaag—it would have been yellowish at birth, but purely snow-colored by puberty, which in the aliens seemed to come about the age of eighteen to twenty-five Earthly years.

Nor was there anything else different about the grayish eyes in the pale Aalaag skin that never appeared to tan. With its great, sharp bones and pale color it gave the impression of being carved out of a soft, gray-white stone. But still, somehow it also managed to give Shane not only the impression of great age, but of that same weariness and emotion that currently seemed to be at work in the First Captain.

As Shane watched, the massive figure got slowly to its feet, walked around from behind its desk and sat down on one of the couches. The change of position was a signal that the meeting had now become informal. Lyt Ahn was dressed in black boots and a white, single-piece suit, like any other alien on duty. Shane turned as the other moved, in order to keep facing his master; and, after a moment, saw the eyes that had been more looking through him than otherwise, focus once more directly upon him.

"Come here, Shane-beast," said Lyt Ahn.

Shane moved forward until he stood one step

from the seated alien. Lyt Ahn studied him for a long moment. Their heads were on a level. Then, reaching out, he cupped an enormous hand gently, for a moment, over Shane's head.

Shane checked his body from tensing just in time. Physical contact was almost unknown amongst the Aalaag themselves, and unheard of between Aalaag and human; but Shane had learned over the last two years that Lyt Ahn permitted himself freedoms beyond those generally used by those lesser in rank than himself. The large hand that could easily have crushed the bones of Shane's skull rested lightly for a moment on Shane's head and then was withdrawn.

"Little Shane-beast," said Lyt Ahn—and unless it was his imagination it seemed to Shane that he heard in the Aalaag voice the same tiredness he had suspected in the First Captain's face— "are you contented?"

There was no word in the Aalaag language for "happy." "Contented" was the closest possible expression to it. Shane felt a sudden fear of an unknown trap in the question; and for a second he debated telling Lyt Ahn that he was, indeed, contented. But the Aalaag could accept nothing but truth; and the First Captain had always allowed his human interpreters a freedom of opinion no other Aalaag permitted.

"No, most immaculate sir," Shane answered. "I would be contented only if this world was as it was before the untarnished race came among us."

Lyt Ahn did not sigh. But Shane, used to the First Captain, and having studied him as only children, animals and slaves have always studied those who hold their life and every freedom in their hands, received the clear impression that the other would have sighed if he had only been physiologically and psychologically capable of doing so.

"Yes," said the First Captain, absently looking through him once more, "your race makes unhappy cattle, true enough."

Fear came back to Shane and chilled him to the bone. He told himself that Lyt Ahn could by no means have discovered this soon what he had done illegally in Milan; but the words the alien supreme commander had just now used came too close to his knowledge of guilt not to cause him to stiffen internally.

For a second he debated trying to entice Lyt Ahn to be more explicit about whatever had caused him to make such a remark. Ordinarily, a human did not speak unless ordered to do so. But the First Captain had always allowed Shane and the other translators unusual freedom in that respect. Shane checked, however, at the thought for two reasons. One, his uncertainty of how such a question could be phrased without offense; and two, a fear that if Lyt Ahn did indeed suspect him of some violation of proper conduct, any such asking would only confirm the suspicion.

He stood silent, therefore, and simply waited, in the helplessness of the totally dependent. Either Lyt Ahn would speak further, or the First Captain would dismiss him; and neither of these things could Shane control.

"Do you find your fellow cattle in any way different these days, Shane-beast?" asked Lyt Ahn.

Shane thought involuntarily of the small tenement room in Milan to which he had been kidnapped; and in which he had been held and questioned by those human revolutionaries who had innocently adopted as their symbol the rude sketch he had himself conceived of a year earlier, in a

moment of drunken desperation—though that was
not something they or any other, human or alien,
could have known.

"No, most immaculate sir," he answered; and
felt the danger of his lie like a heavy weight in his
chest.

There was another pause that could have been a
sigh from Lyt Ahn.

"No," said the alien commander, "perhaps . . .
perhaps even if there were, it would not be such as
you they would admit their feelings to. Your fellow cattle do not love those who work for us, do
they, little Shane-beast?"

"No," said Shane, truthfully and bitterly.

It was that very fact that required him to wear
the pilgrim's cloak and carry the pilgrim's staff
when he moved about the Earth on Lyt Ahn's
business. Among so many true wearers of that
costume, it became a cloak of protective anonymity,
particularly with the hood of the cloak pulled up
over his head and shadowing his features. If he
had betrayed the fact that he was actually a servant of the aliens his life would literally have been
in danger from his fellow humans, from the moment he was out of sight of an Aalaag, or one of
the armed human Interior Guards—who themselves
did not dare go among the mass of ordinary humans without their uniforms and unarmed. Lyt
Ahn was in a strange mood, with his mind off on
some problem which at this moment was still unclear to Shane; but which had plainly directed his
attention elsewhere than at Shane himself. It occurred to Shane suddenly that now might be an
opportunity to cover his tracks in regard to the
lesser matter of his having lied to Laa Ehon, the
Aalaag commanding the Milan area, when that

alien had asked him what price Lyt Ahn might put upon him.

"If the most immaculate sir pleases," Shane said, "this beast was asked a question by the sir who is called Laa Ehon. The question was what price my master might put upon me."

"So," replied Lyt Ahn, his thoughts clearly still occupied with that primary concern Shane had noted in him. The First Captain's response was in fact no response at all, merely an acknowledgement of the fact that he had heard what Shane had said. Shane allowed himself to hope.

"I answered," said Shane, "that to the best of my knowledge, the most immaculate sir had valued all of his translator-beasts at half a possession of land—" Shane tried to keep his voice unchanged but for a fraction of a second his breath caught in his throat—"and the favor of my master."

"So," said Lyt Ahn, still in the same tone of voice.

He had heard, but clearly he had not heard. Internally, Shane felt the weakness of relief. The truth was that Lyt Ahn had never, to Shane's knowledge, put any kind of price on Shane or any of the other humans in the translator section. Shane had gambled in answering Laa Ehon that the First Captain would not remember whether he had or not—and the gamble had now paid off. The half a possession of land, in what it represented in terms of Earthly territory according to Aalaag measurements, was a princely enough price for any single human beast. But the favor which Shane had mentioned meant far more. Effectively, its meaning was that in addition to any other price, the buyer could be called upon at any time in the future to return an as-yet-unnamed favor to the buyer, with a worth in direct proportion as the buyer envisaged its value. In theory, at least, the cost of buying Shane might include Lyt Ahn's calling upon Laa Ehon sometime in the future for anything the other owned, up to and including his life.

A single musical note from the door leading to the private apartments of the First Captain interrupted the thoughts of both Shane and Lyt Ahn.

The door swung open to let in a second Aalaag. But this one was a female—and Shane recognized her with something close to panic. She was Adtha Or Ain, the consort of Lyt Ahn; and the panic arose from the fact that Shane was, for the first time in a long time, encountering a situation involving Aalaag mores with which he was not familiar. When, on rare occasions before this, he had to do with the consort of the First Captain, it had been with her alone; when he had been sent about the planet with one of her private messages.

His encounters with her had been purely formal and entirely conducted within the known code of behavior between Aalaag and human beast. On the other hand his private meetings with Lyt Ahn had largely come to be informal. There was no way of telling now how she would react to the informality he was used to being permitted by Lyt Ahn. On the other hand, it would raise the question of his disobeying Lyt Ahn's authority if he suddenly reverted to the formal mode, after Lyt Ahn, by sitting down on the couch, had, in effect, ordered him to abandon it. There was no way for him to tell whether, if either should address him, he should respond in the formal or the informal mode. Either mode could be a response that would offend either Lyt Ahn or Adtha Or Ain.

Shane stood motionless and silent, praying that he would be ignored by both aliens. He studied Adtha Or Ain as he had studied Lyt Ahn earlier—

and for the same reasons. There was something like a bitterness that he had always noted in her, but it had always seemed to be hard held under control. In this moment, however, that control seemed to have loosened.

For the moment, his luck seemed to be holding. Lyt Ahn had risen from the couch and gone to meet Adtha Or Ain. They stopped, facing each other, an Aalaag arm's length apart, looking into each other's faces.

Adtha Or Ain was slightly the taller of the two; but, aside from that, if Shane had not come to recognize the sexual differences in Aalaag bodies, it would have been hard to tell the two apart. Their dress was identical. Only the slight individuality of their features, that individuality which Shane had finally taught himself to look for over these past years, and the difference in their voices, marked them apart. Adult Aalaag females, like human ones, tended to speak in somewhat higher voices than the males of their race—although the difference was nowhere near as marked as in humans—particularly in the case of an older Aalaag female like Adtha Or Ain, whose voice had deepened with age.

Now, the two stood facing each other. There was a tension between them that Shane sensed strongly, and with that sensing came another wave of relief. If these two would just stay completely concerned with each other, he would in effect be invisible—of no more importance to them than the furniture in the room; and the chances of either requiring an answer from him were almost nil. For the first time, Shane dared to look on them as an observer might, rather than as a potential victim of their meeting.

They did not touch. Nonetheless, Shane's experience with the Aalaag, and elsewhere, let him read into their confrontation a closeness—"love" was a word that did not exist in the Aalaag language—which implied that, had they been humans, they might have touched. At the same time, however, Shane felt a sadness and an anger in Adtha Or Ain and a sort of helpless pity in Lyt Ahn.

The two ignored him.

"Perhaps," said Lyt Ahn, "you should rest."

"No," said Adtha Or Ain. "Rest is no rest to me, at times like this."

"You make yourself suffer unnecessarily."

She turned aside and walked around the First Captain. He turned also to look after her. She went to the wall bearing the large screen; and although Shane could not see her make any motion to turn it on, it woke to light and image before her, the starkness of what it showed dominating the room.

The three-dimensional shape on it was the last that Shane could have imagined. It was of an adult male Aalaag, without armor, but carrying all personal weapons and encased in a block of something brownishly transparent, like a fly in amber.

It was only after he got past his first shock of seeing it and began to examine it in detail, that he noticed two unusual things. One was that there was a faintish yellow tinge to the roots of the white hair on the head of the encased Aalaag, and the second—it was unbelievable, but the Aalaag shown was alive, if completely helpless.

He could see the pupils of gray eyes move minutely, as he watched. They were focused on something that seemed to be outside the scene imaged on the screen. Other expression there was none—nor could be any, since the face, like all the rest of the body, was imprisoned and held immobile by the enclosing material.

"No," said Lyt Ahn behind him.

Shane's ears, sharpened by over two years of servitude, heard that rare thing, a note of emotion in an Aalaag voice; and, faint as it was, he read it clearly as a note of pain. Those years of attuning himself to the moods of the First Captain had finally created a bond that was all but empathic between them; and his own emotions felt Lyt Ahn's in this moment without uncertainty.

"I must look at it," said Adtha Or Ain, standing before the screen.

Lyt Ahn took three steps forward, moving up behind her. His two great hands reached out part way toward her shoulders and then fell back to his sides.

"It's only a conception," he said. "A mock-up. You've no reason for assuming it represents reality. Almost certainly no such thing has happened. Undoubtedly he and his team are dead, destroyed utterly."

"But perhaps he is like this," said Adtha Or Ain, without turning her head from the screen. "Maybe they have him so, and will keep him so for thousands of lifetimes. I will have no more children. I had only this one, and perhaps this is how he is now."

Lyt Ahn stood, saying nothing. She turned to face him.

"You let him go," she said.

"You know—as I know," he answered. "Some of us must keep watch on the Inner Race who stole our homes, in case they move again and the movement is in this direction. He was my son—my son as well as yours—and he wanted to be one of those to go and check."

"You could have denied him. I asked you to order him to stay. You did not."

"How could I?"

"By speaking."

Shane had never before seen emotion at this level between two of the normally expressionless Aalaagi and he felt like someone tossed about in a hurricane. He could not leave; but to stay and listen was all but unbearable. Against his will, the empathic response he had so painstakingly developed to the feelings of Lyt Ahn was at him now with a pain he felt at second hand, pain he could not understand or do anything about.

"In a thousand lifetimes," she said, "a thousand lifetimes and more, they made no sign of moving again. They only wanted our worlds, our homes; and once they had them they were content enough. We all know that. Why send our children back to what's theirs now—so that they can catch them and make toys for themselves of our flesh and blood—make a toy and a thing of my son?"

"There was no choice," said Lyt Ahn. "Could I protect my son before others—when he'd asked to go?"

"He was a child. He didn't know."

"It was his duty. It was my duty—and your duty—to let him go. So the Aalaag survive. You know your duty. And I tell you again, you've no way of knowing he's not at peace, safely dead and destroyed. You make yourself a nightmare of the one most unlikely thing that could happen."

"Prove it to me," Adtha Or Ain said. "Send an expedition to find out."

"You know I can't. Not yet. We've only held this world three of its years. It's not properly tamed, yet. The crew, the needs for the expedition you want aren't to spare."

"You promised me."

"I promised to send an expedition as soon as team and materials were to spare."

"And it's been three years, and still you say there're none."

"None for only a possibility—none for what may be nothing more than a nightmare grown in your own mind. As soon as I can in duty and honor spare people for something of that level, the expedition will go. I promise you. It will bring back the truth of what happened to our son. But not yet."

She turned from him.

"Three years," she said.

"These beasts are not like some on other worlds we've taken. I've done with this planet as much as I might, given the force I had to work with. No one could do more. You are unfair, Adtha Or Ain."

Silently, she turned, crossed the room once more and passed back through the doorway by which she had entered. Its doors closed behind her.

Lyt Ahn stood for a moment, then looked at the screen. It went blank and gray once more. He turned and went to sit down again at his desk, touching the smaller screen inset in it and apparently returning to the work he had been doing when Shane had come in.

Shane continued to stand, unmoving. He stood, and the minutes went by. It was not unusual that a human should have to hold his place indefinitely, waiting for the attention of an Aalaag; and Shane was trained to it. But this time his mind was a seething, bewildered mass. He longed for the First Captain to remember he was there and do something about him.

A very long time later, it seemed, Lyt Ahn did lift his head from his screen and his eyes took notice of Shane's presence.

"You may go," he said. His gaze was back on the desk screen before the words had left his lips.

Shane turned and left.

He went back down the long corridor, past the Aalaag officer still on duty at the desk and after some distance, to the door of his own cubicle. Opening that door at last, he saw, seated in the room's single armchair by the narrow bed, a human figure. It was one of the other translators, a brown-haired young woman named Sylvia Onjin.

"I heard you were back," she told him.

He made himself smile at her. How she had heard did not matter. There was an informational grapevine among all humans in the House of Weapons, that operated entirely without reference to whether the giver and receiver of information were personally on good terms. It was to the benefit of all humans in the House that as much as possible be known about the activities of both Aalaag and humans there.

Probably, word of his return had been passed through the ranks of the Interior Guards, either directly to the corps of translators, or by way of one of the other groups of human specialists personally owned and used by The First Captain.

What did matter was that now, of all times, was not a moment in which he wanted to see her—or anyone. The need for privacy was so strong in him that he felt ready to break down emotionally and mentally if he did not have it. But he could not easily tell her to go.

The humans owned by Lyt Ahn, being picked beasts and therefore of good quality, were encouraged to intermingle; and even to mate and have young if they wished, although Aalaag mores stood in the way of the aliens making any specific command or order that they do so. Only the Interior

Guard welcomed the idea of being parents under these conditions. None of those in the translator ranks had any desire to perpetuate their kind as slaves of the aliens. But still, sheer physical and emotional hungers drew individuals together.

Sylvia Onjin and Shane had been two so drawn. They had no real lust or love for each other, in the ordinary senses of those words. Only, they found each other slightly more compatible than either found others of the human opposite sex in the House of Weapons. In the world as it had been before the Aalaag came, Shane thought now, if they two had met they would almost undoubtedly have parted again immediately with no great desire to see more of each other. But in this place they clung instinctively together.

But the thought of Sylvia's company, now, when his mind was in turmoil and his emotions had just been stretched to a breaking-point, was more than Shane could face. At best, it was only an act he and she played together, a pretense that erected a small, flimsy and temporary private existence for them both; away from the alien-dominated world that held their lives and daily actions in its indifferent hand. Also, now, after Shane's encounter with the other young woman, the one called Maria, whom he had saved from questioning by the Aalaag, and who had been a member of the Milanese resistance group that had later kidnapped him, there was something about Sylvia that almost repelled him, the way a tamed animal might suffer in comparison with one still wild and free.

But the narrow face of Sylvia smiled confidently back up at him. Her smile was her best feature; and in the days before the Aalaag she might have emphasized her other good features with makeup to the point where she could have been considered

attractive, if not seductive. But the aliens classed
lipstick and all such other beauty aids with that
uncleanliness they were so adamant in erasing from
any world they owned. To an Aalaag, a woman
with makeup on had merely dirtied her face. Ordinary humans, in private, might indulge in such
actions, but not those human servants which the
Aalaag saw daily.

So Sylvia's face was starkly clean, pale-looking
under her close-cropped, ordinary brown hair. It
was a small-boned face. She was a woman of one
hundred and thirty-four centimeters in height—
barely over five feet, a corner of Shane's western
mind automatically calculated—and narrow-bodied
even for that height. Her figure was unremarkable,
but not bad for a woman in her early twenties.
Like Shane himself she had been a graduate student when the Aalaag landed.

She sat now with her legs crossed, the skirt of
the black taffeta cocktail dress she had put on
lifted by the action to reveal her knees. In her lap
was a heavy-looking, cylindrical object about ten
inches long wrapped in white documentary paper,
held in place by a narrow strip of such paper
wrapped around its neck, formed into a bow and
colored red, apparently by some homemade substance, since such a thing as red tape—let alone the
red ribbon the paper strip was evidently intended
to mimic—was not something which the Aalaag
would find any reason for allowing.

"Happy homecoming!" She held it out to him.

He stepped forward automatically and took it,
making himself smile back at her. He could feel
through the paper that it was obviously a full
bottle of something. He hardly drank, as she knew—
there was too much danger of making some mistake in front of their owners if some unexpected

call to duty should come—but it was about the only gift available for any of them to give each other. He held it, feeling how obvious the falseness of his smile must be. The image of Maria was still between them—but then suddenly it cleared and it was as if he saw Sylvia unexpectedly wiped clean of all artifice, naked in her hopes and fears as in the pretentions with which she strove to battle those fears.

His heart turned suddenly within him. It was a physical feeling like a palpable lurch in his chest. He saw Sylvia clearly for the first time and understood that he could never betray her, could never deny help to her in this or any like moment. For all that, there was not even the shadow of real love between them. He felt his smile become genuine and tender as he looked down at her; and he felt— not the actual love for which she yearned, or even the pretense of it, for which she was willing to settle—but a literal affection that was based in the fact that they were simply two humans together in this alien house.

Not understanding the reasons for it, but instinctively recognizing the emotion that had come into him, she rose suddenly and came into his arms; and he felt a strong gush of tenderness, such as he had never felt before in his long months in this place of weapons, that made him hold her tightly to him.

Later, lying on his back in the darkness, the slight body of Sylvia sleeping contentedly beside him, he was assaulted by an unexpected tidal wave of self-pity that washed over him and threatened to drown him. He fought it off; and after a while he, too, slept.

He was roused from deep slumber by the burring of his bedside phone. He reached out toward it and the action triggered to life the light over the nightstand where the square screen of the phone sat. He touched the screen and the face of an Aalaag above the collar of a duty officer appeared on it.

"You are ordered to attend the First Captain, beast," said the officer's deep, remote voice. "Report to him in the Council Conference Room."

"I hear and obey, untarnished sir," Shane heard his own voice, still thick with sleep, answering.

The screen went blank, leaving a silvery gray, opaque surface. Shane rose and dressed. Sylvia was already gone and the chronometer by his bed showed that the hour was barely past dawn.

Twenty minutes later, shaven, clean and dressed, he touched the bronze surface of the door to the Council Conference Room.

"Come," said the voice of Lyt Ahn.

The door opened itself and he entered to find twelve Aalaag, five males and seven females, seated around the floating, shimmering surface that served them as a conference table. Lyt Ahn sat at the far end. On his right was Laa Ehon, the Commander for the area capitaled in Milan, Italy; and for a second a dryness tightened Shane's throat as he remembered his secret crimes against that officer and his Command. But then common sense reasserted itself. No such august assemblage would be convened only to deal with the criminal acts of a simple beast; and his tension slackened. He looked down the table surface toward the First Captain and waited for orders. He had halted instinctively, from custom, two paces inside the opened door; and the twelve powerful alien faces were studying him as just-fed lions might study some small animal that had wandered into the midst of their pride.

"This is the one you spoke of?" asked the female

Aalaag closest on Lyt Ahn's left and second down the table from him.

Her voice had the depth of age and it came to Shane that she—in fact, all the aliens here—would be officers of no lower than the fifth rank. Otherwise they would not have been called into a Council such as this. He wondered what District the speaker commanded. She was no alien he recognized.

"It is one of the cattle I call Shane-beast," said Lyt Ahn. "It is the one I sent only the day before yesterday to Laa Ehon with communications."

He turned to look at the Commander of the Milanese area.

"I'm still uncertain as to how you think his presence here can contribute to the discussion," he went on to Laa Ehon.

"Order it to speak," replied Laa Ehon.

"Identify yourself and your work," Lyt Ahn said to Shane.

"By your command, immaculate sir," said Shane clearly, "I am a translator and courier of your staff and have been so for nearly three of our planet's years."

There was a moment's silence around the table.

"Remarkable," said the female Aalaag on Lyt Ahn's right, who had spoken earlier.

"Exactly," put in Laa Ehon. "Notice how perfectly it speaks the true language—all of you who are so used to the limited mouthings of your beasts, when they can be brought to attempt to communicate in real speech at all."

"It's one of a special, limited corps of the creatures, all of whom have been selected for special ability in this regard," said Lyt Ahn. "I'm still waiting to hear how you think, Laa Ehon, that its presence here can contribute to our discussion."

" *'Special,'* " echoed Laa Ehon. The single sound of the word in the Aalaag Tongue was completely without emphasis.

"As I said," replied Lyt Ahn.

Laa Ehon turned his head to the First Captain, inclined it in a brief gesture of respect, and then turned back to look around the table at the others there.

"Let's return to the matter in hand, then," Laa Ehon said. "I asked for this meeting because it's been three local years approximately since our Expedition to this world first set down upon it. That length of time has now passed and certain signs of adjustments to our presence here, in the attitudes of the local dominant race, that should by now be showing themselves, have not done so—"

"The incidence of *yowaragh* among the beasts," interrupted the female who had spoken before, "isn't that much above the norm for such a period. Granted, no two situations on any two acquired worlds are ever the same—"

"Granted exactly that," Laa Ehon reinterrupted in his turn, "it is not *yowaragh* with which I am primarily concerned, but a general failure on the part of the cattle to keep production levels as expected. Past Expeditions on other worlds have found such a slump in production in their early years, but always it's turned out in the end to be caused by depression in the beasts at finding themselves governed—even though that governing has resulted for them in a safer, cleaner world—as it has here. On this world, however, it is something much more like silent defiance than depression with which we seem to be dealing. I repeat, it is this, not incidents of *yowaragh*, with which I am concerned."

A cold shiver threatened to emerge from its hiding place in the center of Shane's body and betray itself as a visible tremor. With a great effort, he held it under control, reminding himself that the aliens here were not watching him. For the moment, once more, he had become invisible, in the same sense that the furniture and the walls of the room about them were invisible.

". . . It is," Laa Ehon's voice drew his attention back to what the Milanese Commander was saying to the rest of the table, "a matter of hard statistics. May I remind the untarnished and immaculate officers here assembled that the preliminary survey of this world, carried on over several decades of the planet's time, gave no intimation of such an attitude or such a potential falling off of production. The projection gave us instead every reason to believe that the local dominant race should be tameable and useful in a high degree; especially when faced with the alternative of giving up the level of civilization they had so far achieved; and on which, in so many ways, they had become dependent. Remember, they were given a free choice and they chose the merciful alternative."

"I've never been quite sure, Laa Ehon," put in Lyt Ahn from the head of the table, "about the accuracy of that adjective for the alternative. It doesn't seem to me that I can bring to mind a single incident in which a race of conquered cattle believed the alternative they had chosen to be one deserving of the word 'merciful.' "

"It was clear they understood at the time of takeover, First Captain," said Laa Ehon, "even if your corps of translators had not yet been established. I remember there was no doubt that they understood that their choice was between accepting the true race as their masters, or having all their cities and technology reduced to rubble, leaving them at their original level of stone-chipping savages. How can that alternative not have been merciful when they also clearly understood that we also had the power to eradicate each and every one of them from the face of their planet, but chose not to use it?"

"Well, well," said Lyt Ahn, "perhaps you're right. In any case, let's avoid side issues. Please get to whatever point you were going to make."

"Of course, First Captain," said Laa Ehon.

The words were said mildly enough; but for the first time it exploded in Shane's mind what he suddenly realized he should have sensed from the first: and that was that there was a power struggle going on in this room, at this table.

And the antagonists were Laa Ehon and Lyt Ahn.

Immediately the realization was born in him, his mind was ready with excuses for its not being obvious to him minutes before. Even six weeks ago, he told himself, he would not have recognized the subtle signals of such a conflict, blinded by an unquestioning assumption that his master's supreme position among the Aalaag was unquestioned and unassailable. But now those same signals leaped out at him. They were everywhere, in the tone of the voices of those speaking, in the attitudes with which the various officers sat in their places about the table—in the very fact Laa Ehon could request that Lyt Ahn have Shane himself brought here; and then delay this long in giving his full reasons why he had requested it.

Shane had not read those signals more swiftly because he had been too secure in his belief in Lyt Ahn's authority. Only now, the curious small freedoms allowed him by the First Captain, as well as the momentary Aalaag-uncharacteristic confidences and transient betrayals of emotion on the part of the ruling officer should have prepared him for this moment of understanding, but had not.

Lyt Ahn, he suddenly realized, was vulnerable. The First Captain had to be vulnerable in this sense. Shane had come to understand how the Aalaag lived by tradition and the mores developed by that tradition. Tradition and those mores could not have failed to provide means for removing a supreme commander who became incapable or proved himself inept. Just how such a procedure would work, Shane as yet had no idea. But of this he was suddenly, utterly convinced. Lyt Ahn was under attack here and now; and Laa Ehon was either the attacker or the spearhead of that attack.

As for the others present . . . Shane was reminded of the social patterns of a wolf pack. All those there would follow unquestioningly the Alpha leader—who was Lyt Ahn—right up until the moment when his leadership was seriously brought into question. Then, if that question was not effectively answered, they would turn to follow the questioner and aid him in rending their former leader. But if it was effectively answered, then the questioner would lose all support from them—until the next time of questioning. It was that moment of doubt in which the majority would swing behind the questioner that Lyt Ahn must foresee and avoid.

". . . I have requested this meeting," Laa Ehon was saying, "primarily because of my own difficulties in meeting production estimates with the cattle of my area; and hoping that my fellow senior officers could suggest ways by which I might improve the situation. I must admit, however, that it begins to appear to me lately that the problems I notice are not restricted to my district alone, but reflect a general problem of attitude which is world-wide—and may even be growing—among the subject beasts."

"It seems to me," broke in a thick-chested male Aalaag halfway down the table on Lyt Ahn's right, "that what you say almost approaches insult to the rest of us. Laa Ehon, are you saying we others have failed to notice something that you've clearly seen?"

"I did not say, or imply, that I had seen anything with particular clearness," said Laa Ehon. "I'm only attempting to point to the importance of something you must all have already noticed— the discrepancy between the original estimates of beast-adjustment to our presence in the time since our landing, and the actuality of that adjustment. I believe there's cause for concern in that discrepancy."

"We've been following the patterns established by successful subjugations on other worlds in the past," said another of the female Aalaag, one whose face showed the hollowness of age beneath her cheekbones. "It is true, as Maa Alyn just said, that each world is different, each race of beasts different—"

"And some, a rare few such races, have even turned out to be failures," said Laa Ehon.

A feeling of shock permeated the conference, perceptible to Shane where it might not have been to any other human, even another one of the special handful of humans employed by Lyt Ahn; the expressions of the Aalaag officers there had not changed at Laa Ehon's last words. There had been only an unnaturally prolonged moment of unnatural silence; but Shane was sure he had read it correctly.

"It seems to me, Laa Ehon," said Lyt Ahn, finally breaking that silence, his heavy voice sounding strangely loud in the room, "that you're holding back something it's in your mind to tell us. Did you ask for this conference merely to air a concern, or have you some special suggestion for us?"

"I have a suggestion," said Laa Ehon.

He turned to look again at Shane, and the eyes of the others at the table followed the changed angle of his gaze.

"I suggest that the situation here—insofar as it reflects a delay in beast-adjustment to our presence—calls for some actions which must necessarily break to some small extent with the patterns of successful subjugation mentioned by Maa Alyn—"

He glanced toward and inclined his head slightly toward the elderly Aalaag female who had recently spoken.

"I suggest," he went on, "that we vary that pattern—oh, in no large way, but experimentally, by attempting to counter this marking on walls we've all been seeing in our districts, this evidence of some rebellious feeling among a few of these beasts—"

—A chill passed through Shane. Clearly now, Laa Ehon was talking of the activities of foolish and doomed underground groups like Maria's in Milan; and the marking was equally clearly his sketch of the pilgrim figure.

"Such things," said the thick-chested Aalaag, "are familiar, expected, during the early years of the subjugation of any race of beasts. Such defacements cease as succeeding generations adapt to serving our purposes, and forget the resentments of their forebearers. This is far too soon to see a problem in a few rogue creatures."

"I beg to disagree," said Laa Ehon. "We know

that of course the beasts communicate among themselves. This one standing before us now may be aware of more discontent among its race than we suspect—"

"You suggest we put it to the question?" inquired the female Aalaag called Maa Alyn, who had been the first to reply to Laa Ehon; and the chill within Shane became a solid iciness of fear.

"If I may interrupt," said the heavy voice of Lyt Ahn, almost sardonically, "the beast in question is my property. Moreover, it is an extremely valuable beast, as are all the talented small handful like it that I keep and use. I would not agree to its being questioned to destruction, without adequate proof of need."

"Of course I don't suggest the damaging of such a valuable beast, particularly one which is the property of the First Captain, and which I myself have seen to be so useful." Laa Ehon turned back to face Lyt Ahn. "In fact, quite the contrary. I only asked the beast be produced in order to illustrate a point I think is important to us all. With all due respect, First Captain, I've yet to be convinced that what this beast does can't also be done by at least a large number of its fellow beasts, if not most of them. Certainly, if they have the physical vocal apparatus which can correctly approximate the sounds of the true speech—or even approach those sounds understandably—and their minds have the ability to organize that speech in coherent and usable fashion, one almost has to assume this to be a property common to their species as a whole."

"I can only assure you," said Lyt Ahn, with a touch of formality in his voice, "that this isn't the case. There seems to be something more necessary— a conceptual ability, rare among them. At my orders many such cattle were tested and only the few I use here were found capable on a level with this one you see before you. In fact, this particular beast is the most capable of all those I own. None speaks as accentlessly as this one."

"Far be it from me to differ with you, First Captain and immaculate sir," said Laa Ehon. "You are informed on this subject and I'm not. Nevertheless, as I have pointed out, faced as we are with a problem of adjustment on the part of this species—"

"—As you have continued to point out to us, untarnished sir," said the thick-chested Aalaag, "almost to the point of weariness since we first sat down together here."

"If I have overemphasized the point," said Laa Ehon, "I apologize for that to the immaculate and untarnished persons here assembled. It merely seemed to me that enunciating the point is necessary as a preamble to stating my personal belief; and that is that under the circumstances it's worth exploring even some unorthodox solutions to the problem, since it threatens to diminish world-wide production by these beasts. A production, which I don't need remind any of us, that is important, not merely to us on this planet, but to all our true people on all the worlds we have taken over; not only for our present survival, but for the protection of the immaculate people as a whole in case the inner race that stole our home worlds originally should make another move, this time in this direction."

"As you say," murmured the voice of Lyt Ahn, "you don't need to remind us of that. What exactly is this suggestion of yours, then?"

"Simply," said Laa Ehon, "I propose we depart from standard procedure and set up specific beasts as governors in our respective districts, holding them responsible for the production of the cattle in their districts; and allowing them to use other cattle as subsidiary officers to set up their own structures of authority to guarantee such production."

"Absolutely against standard procedure," said the thick-chested officer, promptly.

"Indeed," said Maa Alyn, leaning her body slightly forward to stare down the tabletop directly at Laa Ehon, "those who've gone before us have found by hard experience that the best way to handle native cattle is to give them all possible freedoms of custom and society according to what they have been used to, but never to allow individuals among them power as intermediaries between ourselves and the rest of the beasts. Whenever we've set up intermediaries of their own race like that, between us and them, corruption on the part of their officials has almost invariably occurred. Moreover, resentment is born among the general mass of the cattle; and this, in the end, costs us more than the original gains achieved by using intermediaries."

"I seem to remember something just said, however," answered Laa Ehon, "about each world and each race upon it being a different and unique problem. The recalcitrance shown by the local cattle as a whole on this particular world of ours, as shown by the statistics, are of an order above those shown on any previous world we have taken over. It's true there's been no show of overt antagonism on the part of the general mass of cattle—yet, at least. But on the other hand, it would be hard to show any except our directly used beasts, such as those in the Interior Guard, or this translator-courier corps of the First Captain, who can be said sincerely to have made a full and proper adaptation to us, as their owners and rulers."

"That doesn't mean your proposal is the correct solution to the problem," put in a male Aalaag who had not spoken before. He sat little more than a meter from Shane's right hand, at the extreme far end of the table from Lyt Ahn.

"Of course," answered Laa Ehon. "I recognize the danger of making any large changes—let alone ones that go against established procedure—without having adequate data first. Therefore, what I'm actually suggesting is that certain measures be put into effect on a trial basis."

He tapped the tabletop before him and screens alit with data in the Aalaag script appeared in it before each alien there.

"I've had surveys made," he went on, "and you see the results of them on the screens before you. I've also had hard copies delivered to your offices by available underofficers of mine. You'll note my survey turned up three districts best suited to the putting into effect of temporary test procedures to see if my estimations are correct. Two were island areas; one being what the cattle formerly called the Japanese Islands, the other called the British Islands. There are advantages of homogeneity and diversity in each case. Of these two, the British Islands seems the better prospect—"

"These islands, of course, are within my district," said Maa Alyn, stiffly. "But you also mentioned, I think, three—not two—areas as being possibly suitable as testing areas?"

"I did," said Laa Ehon. "However, the third area, according to my surveys, would be this one surrounding the House of Weapons; and I didn't think we'd want to make any experiments that close to our prime seat of authority, even if the

First Captain would give permission ... as, of course, I would expect to wait upon your permission, Maa Alyn, before proposing to experiment in the area of the British Isles."

There was a murmur around the table that seemed to Shane to express diverse opinions.

"So," went on Laa Ehon, ignoring the sound, "what I would like to suggest, with the concurrence of this Council and everyone concerned, is to set up a temporary governing structure such as I described earlier; monitored directly by us, with an officer of the true race supervising and working in parallel with each individual beast who is in a position of intermediate authority as governor."

There was a moment's silence.

"I see a great many difficulties ..." began Maa Alyn.

"Frankly, I do myself," said Laa Ehon. "This is unknown territory to all of us. For one thing, as has been pointed out, any tendencies for the beast-governor and his staff to take advantage of their positions over their fellow cattle would be difficult for us to see and check promptly. This, however—it has recently occurred to me and this was why I asked our First Captain to send for the beast who stands before us now—could be greatly helped by requiring all beast-governor staff to have contact with their supervisory numbers of the true race in the real language."

"But such a condition would need that the beast-governor, to say nothing of his staff, be not merely adequate, but fluent, in the true language—" the thick-chested Aalaag broke off suddenly. "Are you proposing that the First Captain lend his corps of translators to this task? If so, that immaculate sir would of course have to volunteer them for the duty. There is no way in honor this Council could suggest—"

"Not at all—not at all," said Laa Ehon. "I was merely about to suggest that the beasts chosen to be governor and staff be put first through an intensive course of teaching, to make them fluent in the true language, using as teachers—if the First Captain agrees—some of his translators such as the beast before us—and, of course, provided that my overall suggestion meets with the approval of the Council. The intent would be to produce cattle who'd be able to explain themselves clearly to their own kind while still being clear and understandable in their reports to ourselves, thereby making for a strong, plain link of understanding between us and the mass of cattle in general."

"I have already said," put in Lyt Ahn, "that it is only the rare beast that can be taught to speak with such adequate clearness. The evidence for this is in the efforts I mentioned, to which I was put in staffing this particular corps of beast-translators and couriers, to which you refer and of which the beast now present is an example."

"It seems to me we lose nothing by trying," said Laa Ehon.

"We stand to lose something by trying," said Lyt Ahn, "if what we are trying is foredoomed to a failure that may make us look ridiculous in the eyes of our beasts."

"Of course," said Laa Ehon, "but at the same time I find it hard to believe that what this handful you use as translators can do, others of their kind can't also be brought to do. The idea flies in the face of logic and reason. What is hypothesized to be missing from those who, according to your experience, are incapable of being taught to use the true language clearly?"

"Exactly what the blocking factor is, we've never been able to discover," answered Lyt Ahn. "Would you care to question the beast we have present?"

"Ask a beast?" said Laa Ehon; and experience made Shane perceptive enough to catch the evidence of shock and surprise, not only in Laa Ehon, but in the others about the table.

"As you have said," replied Lyt Ahn, "it'll do no harm to explore any and all possibilities; and this beast might, indeed, be able to provide you with some information or insight."

"The suggestion is a—" Laa Ehon hesitated, obviously searching for a way of putting what he wanted to say in words that would not fall into the category of insult to his First Captain, but would still express his reaction to such a suggestion, "—far-fetched idea."

"What have you to lose?" said Lyt Ahn; and a murmur of agreement ran around the table. Laa Ehon's expression showed no change, but Shane guessed that the Milanese Commander was seething with anger, within. He turned and his eyes met Shane's.

"Beast," he said, "can you offer any information as to why a majority of your species cannot be taught to speak the true language as well as you, yourself, have come to?"

"Immaculate sirs and dames—" Shane's voice sounded high-pitched and strange in his own ears after the deep tones of those around the table, "it is a characteristic of our species that during our first few years of life at a time when our pups are learning how to speak, that their capability for so learning is very great. In the years just before the untarnished race came among us, it had been established that our young could learn as many as four or five different variants of our tongue, simultaneously; but that this facility was lost for most beasts by the time these young were five to eight years of age. Only a fortunate few of us keep that ability; and it's been from such fortunate few that the First Captain's corps of translator-couriers has been drawn."

There was a moment of silence—a long moment.

"I don't think I'm completely ready to believe this without independent substantiation," said Laa Ehon. "It's well known that, unlike ourselves, these subject races use the lie quite commonly. Moreover, even when they do not consciously lie, they can be ignorant or subject to superstitions. The point this beast has just made, that the language learning ability of his race is largely lost after the first five to eight years of their life may be a lie, the result of ignorance, or simply belief in a superstition that has no real basis in fact."

"I," said Lyt Ahn from the far end of the table, heavily, "am inclined to believe this Shane-beast— such being its name. I've had much contact with it over the last two years and always found it truthful, as well as remarkably lacking in ignorance for one of its species, and not superstitious . . . even in the meaning of that term as understood by our own race."

"If what the beast says is true, however," put in Maa Alyn, "there'd be no point in trying your experiment, Laa Ehon."

Laa Ehon turned toward her.

"When were the plans of the untarnished race ever made or changed upon the basis of input from one of the subject species?" he said. "I mean no disrespect to the First Captain; but the fact remains the beast here may be mistaken, or may not know what we or it are talking about. We should hardly make any decision here on an unsupported faith in its possible correctness."

"True enough," murmured another female, who had not spoken before. "True enough."

"What's been said here does suggest one thing, however," said Laa Ehon, "and that's that we should begin immediately, on the chance that the beast is correct, to put some of the young beasts to exposure to the true language. Then, if this one is correct, we may breed up a generation which takes advantage of this early language ability of theirs, if such actually exists. Certainly, nothing can be lost by trying."

A mutter of agreement sounded around the table, interrupted once more by the heavy voice of Lyt Ahn.

"Am I correct then?" the First Captain said, looking around the table. "At least a number of you are agreeable to taking young beasts into your households and keeping them more or less continuously with you?"

There was a silence.

"A nurse-beast, of course," said Laa Ehon, "could be detailed to take care of each young creature. The young one would no more be in the way, then, under such circumstances, than the adult beasts are when we use them for various duties. The only requirement would be that the nurse-beast keep the infant creature in position to overhear as much of our speech as possible."

"I think Laa Ehon may have the answer," Maa Alyn said. "I can't see any flaws in his reasoning."

"Nor can I—but I am a member of the true race," said Lyt Ahn. "However, perhaps it would be wise for the untarnished and immaculate individuals here assembled to check first with the representative of the beasts we have with us at the moment—

in case there might be some unseen flaw in this
course? It's always possible that there are pitfalls
in it perceptible to one of the species, but which
none of us have observed."

Once more, Shane found the eyes of all the Aalaag
there turned upon him.

"Beast," said Maa Alyn, "we have been discuss-
ing the possibilities of raising some of your young
with early exposure to true language, assuming
this theory of yours for early aptitude for the learning of it is a fact—"

"You need not recap, Maa Alyn," interrupted
Lyt Ahn. "I can assure you that this Shane-beast
has overheard and understood all we've been
saying."

There was a strange, almost startled silence
around the table. Almost as if it had been suggested that there was a spy in their midst. Shane
realized that, with the exception of Lyt Ahn, all
those there had until that moment not really made
the connection between his knowledge of their language and the fact he would be able not only to
follow but to understand all that they had been
saying to each other. Comprehension of that fact
clashed violently with their habit of ignoring the
underraces.

"Well then, Shane-beast, since the First Captain
assures us that's your name," said Laa Ehon after
a second. "Have you any comment on our plan to
raise some young of your species when they can
overhear the true language being spoken, during
their receptive years of growth?"

"Only," answered Shane, "if the immaculate sir
pleases, that I believe if you follow the plan as you
have outlined it, the result will be that these young
of my species will understand Aalaag, but not necessarily be able to speak it."

He hesitated. He had been given no order to volunteer information. To do so would be greatly daring. But that lack was almost immediately remedied.

"Go on, Shane-beast," said Lyt Ahn from the head of the table. "If you have any suggestions to make, make them."

"Yes, make them," said Laa Ehon, his black eyes glittering on Shane. "The most immaculate First Captain seems to feel there may be a flaw in our reasoning which you might have discerned."

"I might merely suggest," said Shane, picking his way as carefully through the alien vocabulary as through a mine field, in search of words which would at once be absolutely truthful but at the same time carry his meaning without implying any pretence to equality, or possible offense, "a danger could lie in the fact that you have the young of my species merely listening to the true language as it's correctly spoken. As I say, there might be a danger that the young referred to might only learn to understand, but not to speak, the true language; since they are given no opportunity to speak it."

He hesitated. There was a dangerous silence around the table.

"What I am trying to say," he said, "is that perhaps the untarnished or immaculate individuals dealing with these young beasts should consider speaking to and allowing themselves to be answered by these young ones in the true tongue. It would have to be understood that, being so young still, the small beasts would not yet have acquired a knowledge of polite response; and might inadvertently fail to show the proper respect. . . ."

The shock around the table this time was a palpable thing; and the pause was longer than at any time since Shane had entered the room.

"You are suggesting," said Maa Alyn, "almost that we treat these young of your species as if they were young of the true race."

"I am afraid that is my meaning, immaculate dame," said Shane.

There was a further silence, broken at last by Maa Alyn.

"The suggestiong is disgusting," she said. "Moreover, even more than any other suggestion put forward here today, this flies in the face of all the rules evolved from the experience of the true race with their underspecies over many worlds and many centuries. There must be some other way. . . ."

There was a general noise of concurrence from those gathered around the table. For a moment, Shane was sure that while Laa Ehon had lost his point about introducing humans into Aalaag inner households, he had come dangerously close to gathering the leadership of the Council to him. He saw that all eyes had now turned sharply to Lyt Ahn, as if awaiting some magical alternate solution from him. Then the First Captain spoke; and with the first words, Shane realized his master had seized the most propitious moment for forestalling Laa Ehon's bid for power and regaining his own position of Alpha Leader in the Council. To the clear surprise of those around the table, he not only overrode Maa Alyn by endorsing the Milanese Commander's suggestion; but went beyond it, in part assuming authorship and control of the plan.

"I fully realize the distastefulness of the suggestion. Nonetheless," said Lyt Ahn, "I'm going to ask all those around this table to take this matter of bringing human young into their households into consideration, and think about it seriously between now and our next meeting. It is true that we're at variance with the prognosis and the estimates originally made for our settling of this particular world; and recently there has been an outbreak of what can only be regarded as an attitude inimical to the true race in these drawings that appear in the cities from time to time—and, I believe, more frequently lately."

"Clearly they are of a human wearing what they call 'pilgrim' clothing," said Maa Alyn. "Has the First Captain considered ordering that no such clothing be worn in the future?"

"It's hard to see what that would accomplish at this date, untarnished dame," answered Lyt Ahn. "The symbol has already been established. In fact, we would be dignifying it by paying that much attention to it. The beasts might consider that we actually saw the drawing as a threat—which is what those who put them up undoubtedly want.

"True enough," Maa Alyn nodded.

"On the other hand, something undoubtedly must be done; and the untarnished sir who is our Commander in Milan has at least come up with a proposal, which is more than anyone else has done. I suggest in addition to considering the taking of beast children into our households, we put Laa Ehon's other suggestion to trial. I therefore authorize him—hopefully, Maa Alyn will not object—to set up a trial beast as governor in the British Isles area, with whatever staff is necessary; and I will temporarily lend the project one of my translators to ensure communication between governor and the true race to commence with."

"I do not object." It was very nearly a growl from Maa Alyn.

"If I might have this Shane beast as translator,

then—" Laa Ehon was beginning, and Shane chilled. But Lyt Ahn interrupted the other.

"Shane-beast, I have special uses of my own for," said the First Captain. "I will, however, provide you with a beast adequate to your needs. I will permit this much—that Shane-beast be available to you as liaison on this project to keep me informed of its progress and such special advice as you wish to pass on to me by courier."

"If you wish, and as you wish, of course, First Captain," said Laa Ehon, smoothly; but his eyes flashed for a moment on Shane with something of cold calculation in them. Shane chilled again.

"That being settled," said Lyt Ahn, "shall we close this meeting?"

There were sounds of agreement in which the Milanese Commander joined. A moment later, Shane found himself outside the room, in the corridor, hurrying to match Lyt Ahn's long-legged strides back toward the First Captain's private offices. Shane had been given no orders to follow. On the other hand he had not been dismissed, so he hurried along, half a pace behind his master, waiting for orders.

These were not forthcoming even after they had reached and passed into the office. Perhaps they would have been, but when they stepped inside the heavy doors, they found Adtha Or Ain. She was standing once more before the large screen, which was again showing the figure of their son in whatever it was that encased him. She turned as they entered; and spoke to Lyt Ahn.

"It went well—the meeting?"

The First Captain looked at her soberly.

"Not well," he said, "I have broken slightly with custom to allow Laa Ehon to make a trial of interposing native governors between ourselves and the cattle, using the British Isles as an experimental area."

He turned to Shane.

"I will lend him a translator to help. Shane-beast here, however, will act as my liaison with the project, and as my own private eyes and ears upon its progress."

His eyes were steady on Shane.

"You understand, Shane-beast?" he said. "You will observe everything carefully, and I will question you equally carefully each time you return from there."

"So, it did not go well," repeated Adtha Or Ain, as much to herself as to the First Captain.

"No, how could you expect it to?" said Lyt Ahn. He seemed to become suddenly conscious of the image in the large screen. "Put that away."

"I need to look at it," responded Adtha Or Ain.

"You mean you need it to use as a club against me," said Lyt Ahn. He made no visible gesture that Shane could see, except a small jerk of the head; but the image disappeared from the screen, leaving it pearly gray and blank.

"It doesn't matter if you take it from me," said Adtha Or Ain. "I can see it just as well with the screen off. I see it night and day. Now, more than ever."

"Why, now more than ever?"

"Because I can't avoid seeing what's coming."

Adtha Or Ain turned from the empty screen to face Lyt Ahn.

"What do you mean?" There was a note of demand in Lyt Ahn's voice.

"No expedition will go to look for my son."

"Why do you say that? I've promised you—" began Lyt Ahn.

"Your promise is only as good as your authority," said Adtha Or Ain, "and your authority. . . ."

She did not finish.

"I was elected by the senior officers of this Expedition. I hold my rank by that authority, which remains with me," answered Lyt Ahn, in a steady voice, "and the rank can only be taken from me by popular vote of these same officers—which will never happen."

"No," said Adtha Or Ain. "But you could resign it on your own decision, as other First Captains on other New World Expeditions have occasionally done before you."

"I have no intention of resigning."

"What does that matter? You will resign," said Adtha Or Ain. "It's as much a certainty as that screen on the wall before us—the screen you do not want me to use; and once you are no longer First Captain, whoever holds that rank will have no interest in sending an expedition to find out what happened to my son."

"You talk in impossibilities," said Lyt Ahn. "Even if I could spare the officers and material for such an expedition now, who would lead it?"

"I would, of course," said Adtha Or Ain. "I'm of fourth rank—or had you forgotten that?"

"I can't spare you," retorted Lyt Ahn. "The Consort of the First Captain belongs with the First Captain."

"Particularly when the position of that First Captain may become questionable," said Adtha Or Ain.

"There is no 'may.' My position is not questionable; and it is not going to become questionable."

The attitude of Adtha Or Ain changed subtly, although the signs of that change were so slight that only Shane's long experience with her allowed him to note them. But some of the tension went out of her. She seemed to soften and went to Lyt Ahn, close enough to touch him, standing to one side of him and looking very slightly down into his eyes.

"In all things I am your Consort," she said, in a lower voice. "Also, in all things I am the mother of the son you had. I must see clearly, even if you refuse to. Laa Ehon intends to replace you as First Captain. Let that, at least, be out in the open between us."

"I have no intention," said Lyt Ahn, "of abandoning the First Captaincy to Laa Ehon, or anyone else."

"Consider the situation honestly," said Adtha Or Ain. "The possibility is there. The possibility means that no expedition would ever be sent to find my son; and not only that, it means I would lose you as well, since I think you would not merely accept duties under another's command."

"That much is true," said Lyt Ahn. "If it was shown to me that I was no longer worthy of the post of First Captain, I would consider myself excess of our effort here and make sure that the Expedition was no longer burdened by my presence."

Shane felt a new sense of shock. This was the first intimation he had had that some sort of honorable suicide was practiced among the Aalaag. But the fact that there was such a practice made sense. It made very good sense for this race of male and female warriors. He thought of Laa Ehon in the post of First Captain of Earth and, if anything, his inner fears increased.

His own life was just barely endurable now under Lyt Ahn. It could become literally unbearable under Laa Ehon; and if it became literally unbearable, sooner rather than later a fit of *yowaragh* would take him again and he would do something that would lead to his own end. The best he could hope for under those circumstances would be that it would lead him to a quick and relatively painless end.

"You may go, Shane-beast," said Lyt Ahn.

Shane went. The next two days were a blur of duties in attendance on Lyt Ahn, during one of the periodic twice-yearly internal inspections of all services housed within the House of Weapons. On the third day, however, he was summoned back to Lyt Ahn's office, where an assistant Aalaag officer handed him a hard copy message to be hand-delivered to Laa Ehon. Laa Ehon, he was told by Lyt Ahn, had already set himself up in London with the staff of the Project he had described to the Council.

". . . I deduce from this, small Shane-beast," said Lyt Ahn, once the underofficer had left and they two were alone in the office together, "that the immaculate Commander of Milan had already picked and trained the individuals he would need for his Project before mentioning his plan to the Council. You will find his offices already in place and staffed. I would desire you to take particular notice of what kind of humans he uses. You will be in a better position to judge this than myself or any of the true race. Also, report to me anything else you think I might find of interest. I'll want to know, of course, about the general arrangement. I have the plans on record, of course, but that's not the same thing as receiving a direct observation report from a trustworthy pair of eyes."

"I will do as the First Captain orders," said Shane.

"You may go."

"I thank the immaculate sir."

Two hours later, once more in a courier ship and headed toward London, Shane watched from the window beside his seat as the vessel lifted until the world's horizon was a perceptible curve and the sky overhead was black with the airlessness of space. Curiously, now that he was on his way, for the first time he had a moment in which to think, and to his surprise, he found himself strangely clearheaded.

It was remarkable—remarkable almost to the point of being funny. After the episode in Milan, when he had first seen and saved Maria, then later when he had been kidnapped, he had yearned for the sanctuary of his small cubicle in the House Of Weapons, as a retreat where he could sit down and take stock of what had happened, and was happening, to him. Then that imagined oasis of peace had ceased to be an oasis, when he found Sylvia Onjin waiting there for him.

In the end, in the House Of Weapons, he had found no time—no moment of personal freedom at all in which to try and think of some way of avoiding what seemed to be a greased slide to inevitable self-destruction. Now, here, in the last place he would have looked for it, he had found it. He was on duty. Therefore the eyes of the Aalaag were momentarily off him, and he was free at last to stand back and consider his position, to think his own thoughts for a small while before they touched down in the British Isles.

It was freedom-on-duty. There was no human word for it, but there was an Aalaag one, *alleinen*. It meant the supreme authority and freedom of being under orders—one's own master or mistress within strictly specified limits.

He pronounced it now, silently in his mind— *alleinen*—and smiled slightly to himself. For of course he did not pronounce it correctly, in the strict sense. The truth was he did not speak Aalaag as well as even his masters gave him credit for doing. Certain sounds were physical impossibilities to his human throat and tongue.

The truth, in fact, was that he cheated in all his Aalaag-speaking. The alien word that had just come to his mind should properly be pronounced with something like a deep bass cough in the middle syllable; and that deep bass cough, which was so much a part of many Aalaag words, was simply beyond his capabilities. He had always got away with pronouncing it without the cough, however, because he was able to hide behind the fact that his voice was too high-pitched to manage the sound. He had learned to pronounce words containing such a sound as the equally high voice of an very young Aalaag child would say them; and while the ears of such as Lyt Ahn and even of Laa Ehon and others consciously noted the lack, they unconsciously excused him for not making it, because of the otherwise excellence of his pronunciation and because the word as heard resembled what they had heard so many times from the high voices of their own children.

So, in just such a manner, had humans always excused (and with familiarity, become deaf to) the accents of their own children and foreign-born friends. The Aalaag, he thought now, were indeed humanoid (or humans were Aalaagoid?). Similar physical environments on similar worlds during the emergence of both races had shaped them, not only physically, but psychologically and emotionally, in similar ways. Yet they were not really like humans in the fine points—any more than, for example, the average human was eight feet tall. In the fine points, they differed. They had to differ.

One race could not catch the other race's diseases, for example.

There had been a time when he had dreamed of a plague on Earth that would decimate the aliens but leave the humans untouched—a sudden plague that would wipe out the conquerors before those conquerors had time to pass, to their own kind on other worlds, the word that they were dying. Of course, such a plague had never come; and probably, long ago, the Aalaag had devised medical protections against any such happening. He pulled his mind away from such wool-gathering. The important problem was a solution to his own situation. In the silence of the hurtling courier ship, caught between the green of Earth below and the black of space above, he forced himself to face that question squarely, now, while there was a chance.

Leaving Milan, several days earlier, headed back to the House Of Weapons, he had faced the fact that *yowaragh* had twice driven him to do foolishly desperate things against the Aalaag regime; and that therefore, it was only a matter of time until he would be drawn back—for powerful emotional reasons with which the last words of Maria had been connected—into contact with this human Resistance, this Resistance that he knew, if those in it did not, was doomed to certain discovery and destruction at Aalaag hands.

He had faced the fact then that, given sufficient provocation, he would not be able to help himself; as he had not been able to help himself the year before, when an uncontrollable burst of rage had driven him to draw the first pilgrim-symbol on the wall under the executed man in Aalborg, Denmark—as he had not been able to stop himself from acting, a week since, when he had seen through the one-way glass the captive woman who was Maria awaiting questioning by the Aalaag.

Human cattle, according to the way the Aalaag thought, were not supposed to have such reactions as *yowaragh*. It was not their deliberate fault, only a weakness in them. But those who showed it were obviously untrustworthy and sick, and must be disposed of.

Even when they were as valuable as Shane-beast.

Therefore, leaving Milan, he had finally faced the fact that what had happened twice must happen again. Eventually, a third attack of *yowaragh* would catch him in a visible situation where either he had no choice but to appear openly as one of the Resistance people and share their fate, or else he would simply make some wild, personal attack upon one of the aliens which would result in his death. He did not want either of those fates. But there had seemed no way of avoiding one or the other; and it was this dilemma he had carried back with him to the House of Weapons, with a desperate desire to study the situation for some kind of solution.

But now, out of nowhere, events pushed by Laa Ehon's ambition seemed to have offered him a possible way out. The basic situation had not changed; but just now, sitting here in his first moment of *alleinen* peace, for the first time, unexpectedly, he saw the glimmer of a hope he might have something with which he could bargain for his own life and possibly that of Maria as well. It was a wild hope, a crazy hope, but it was nonetheless a hope where before there had been none.

As he considered it, the small glimmer suddenly expanded into a glare like that from a doorway suddenly opened to outer sunlight. It would be a matter of setting two dragons to destroy each other, of using one evil to eat the other up—like the Gingham Dog and the Calico Cat of the children's poem.

The operative factor behind it all was the fact that even after three years together the two races did not understand each other. Humans did not understand Aalaag and the Aalaag did not understand humans.

Basically, the solution to his problem was no less than the fact that he should destroy Laa Ehon. It was a far-fetched thought, like that of a mouse deciding to destroy a giant. On the face of it the notion seemed ridiculous; but he had one advantage which even Lyt Ahn—who was even larger as a giant than Laa Ehon—did not have. He, Shane, was not restricted by the Aalaag mores. In fact, he was restricted by no mores at all, alien or human; but only by his own need to survive and, if possible, save Maria.

The operative factor was that the two races did not really understand each other. He repeated that to himself. Humans did not understand the Aalaag, with whom they had never had any real chance to have contact on what might be called a person-to-person basis; and the Aalaag could not understand humans, walled in as they were by the armor of their own alien attitudes and traditions.

It was because of this that what had been planned at the Council table would not work. The theory of bringing up the children in the Aalaag households would never turn out as Laa Ehon and the others hoped. Shane thought of the human babies to be used this way and shuddered—out of his knowledge of the difference in human and alien responses.

The bitter part of it would be that the scheme would actually seem to work at first as the human youngsters began to pick up the Aalaag tongue and get responses that would seem at least friendly, if not loving, from these large creatures looming over them. The children would respond automatically with affection, which would last up until that devastating moment when they were reminded clearly by the large figures that they were only humans—only beasts. In that discovery, as the children matured and began to have minds of their own, was more fertile ground for *yowaragh* than in anything else the aliens had done on Earth since their arrival; and it would be *yowaragh* by humans who knew their overlords, and the weaknesses of those overlords, better than these had ever been known before by any of the underraces.

For the same reason of racial misunderstanding, Laa Ehon's plan to set up human governors would not work. The Aalaag who lived under unquestioned authority among themselves could not really appreciate that a human governor would be no more palatable to most other humans than an alien would—perhaps even less so. The governor would simply be included in the detestation in which the mass of humanity already held all servants of the Aalaag, such as the Interior Guards and the translators like Shane, himself. Noncooperation would be the order of the day, automatically. Unless . . .

It was in exactly this area that his own scheme might work. He owed nothing to the Resistance groups, he told himself, once more. They had no hope of success—no hope at all, though it would be impossible to tell them that. Inevitably they would be caught, found out and executed by the Aalaag. He shuddered again, thinking of what would happen to them. But he reminded himself that that happening was unavoidable, no matter what he might do or not do. Meanwhile, they could be the instrument which would save him; and, possibly even more important, aid him in destroying Laa Ehon at one and the same time.

He looked more closely at the plan that had just been born in him.

It would be risky. He would have to appear to lend his aid to the Resistance groups; and without letting Lyt Ahn know. For Lyt Ahn would never countenance what Shane was planning, although he might well concur with what Shane had done once Laa Ehon had been destroyed as a result of the translator's efforts.

It would be necessary for Shane to keep his identity as secret as possible from the Resistance people themselves. Those few who had captured him in Milan already had some idea of who he was —but if it could be done, they should remain the only ones. That would be difficult because he would have to do more than just join them; he would have to effectively take charge of their movement.

This was possible, since he knew more about their enemy than they did themselves. His scheme itself was simple in the extreme. It would merely be a matter of coordinating the Resistance groups —and there must be some in at least every large city and they must know each other, already, even if they were not already part of one overall organization. With their help he could cause an apparent cooperation to take place with the governorship organizations Laa Ehon had in mind; so that these seemed to be an unqualified success. While, at the same time, the organization of the Resistances into a single coordinating unit could make possible a plan for a world-wide uprising against the aliens everywhere. That would attract the revolutionaries. Only he would know that such a revolt would stand no chance of success. In fact, it would almost certainly never reach the point of taking place. Long before it was ready to explode, he would have pulled the plug of the cooperation that had been given the governors; and Laa Ehon's plan—in which by this time the Aalaag would have invested deeply—would reveal itself as a total failure. For which Laa Ehon could only take the blame.

And, if some sort of honorable suicide was indeed part of the Aalaag tradition, Laa Ehon might thereupon remove himself. Even if he did not, his power within the Council and his presence as a threat to succeed Lyt Ahn would be destroyed.

Meanwhile, of course, the Resistance members, who by this time would have exposed themselves, or become easily identifiable, would be rounded up and disposed of by the aliens. Shane set his teeth against the mental picture of what that would mean, reminding himself fiercely that he had a right to think of his own survival first; and again, that there had never been any hope for them in any case.

It was a cruel and bitter plan. It had no justification beyond the fact that its fall-out would save him—and possibly Maria as well. He might be able to rescue her in the process. Just at the moment he was not sure how he might do that; but the beginnings of some ideas were tickling at the back of his mind, all of them dependent upon the claim he would have on Lyt Ahn's good graces after Laa Ehon was taken care of.

One necessary matter would be to get the Resistance's agreement to Maria's helping him personally. Later on, therefore, to Lyt Ahn, he could credit part of his success to her association with him, which he would make appear to be a willing and informed one.

The strange thing, he found himself thinking, was that he should be contemplating doing what he had earlier been deathly afraid of doing—associating with those who were subversive to the aliens. The equation of life and death for him in any association like that had not changed; and yet he found himself now feeling good, almost buoyant, about the plans he had just considered. He felt in fact more alive than he had felt since word had first come of the Aalaag landings on Earth.

A sense of something almost like triumph possessed him. So engrossed was he in his thoughts that he hardly noticed when the courier ship set down at last with a slight jolt in the main terminal area which had been blasted out of the center of London. As a member of Lyt Ahn's special corps, he was allowed a special consideration in choosing where he might be let off. He preferred that this be at terminals where he could mingle with the ordinary human traffic and be lost to the sight of anyone who might otherwise identify him as one who worked for the aliens.

He took the subway into the city and registered at a small, middle-class hotel. His destination was Laa Ehon's Project, but they were not expecting him there at any particular time. He was beneath contempt and therefore, happily, beneath suspicion; and meanwhile, there was time for the things he had to do.

He sought out a shop selling second hand clothing, and bought himself a two-color robe—blue on its outer side, brown when turned inside out. It was a common enough purchase, but the gold oblongs he threw down in payment were not. He saw the eyes of the lean but pot-bellied, middle-aged shopkeeper flash as the man picked them up and ducked into a back room to make change in the ordinary base-metal currency of ordinary human commerce. Such gold tabs, in which Shane and the other translators were ordinarily paid, saw their way into ordinary human monetary channels only through the hands of those who worked for the aliens or those who dealt in the black market that sold special luxuries to those who so worked. The word of his purchase would reach local Resistance headquarters quickly.

"Deliver this robe to room 421, the Sheldon Arms Hotel," Shane said to the proprietor. "Can you do that for me?"

"Of course sir, of course," said the proprietor, making a note on a piece of unbleached wrapping paper.

Scooping up his change, Shane returned to his room in the hotel. He ordered up a meal, ate, and then lay on the bed, thinking and waiting.

It was only a little over two hours before there was a knock at the door of his room.

"Delivery for you, sir," said a voice beyond the door.

He was on his feet instantly and as silently as he was able to move. He stepped across to the darkest corner of the room and stood there with his back to the window. He pulled up his pilgrim's hood over his head, drawing the sides of the hood in, so that his face was hidden in deep shadow. He said nothing.

He had expected at least one more knock at the door; but there was a sudden splintering crash as the lock gave and two very large men erupted into the room. They stared at the empty bed and around them, for a moment plainly not identifying him as a human figure in his stillness and the shadow of the corner. In that moment a third man moved into the room from behind them. It was the man called Peter who spoke Italian with an English accent and had been in charge of the group that had kidnapped Shane in Milan.

"I thought this was your home ground," Shane said to him.

At the sound of Shane's voice they saw him. Before they could move, he went on. "I am the Pilgrim. I'll talk to you, Peter, and you only. Get the others out."

There was a moment in which it seemed anything might happen. The two large men glanced back at Peter.

"All right," said Peter, after a moment's hesitation. "Outside, both of you, and put the door back in place. But wait right outside it, there."

He looked directly at Shane.

"But what you've got to say better be worthwhile," he added.

"It is," said Shane. "I'm going to help you. I know the Aalaag and what their weaknesses are. I can tell you how to fight them." Having said this much, the rest came easily to his lips. "I may even be able to tell you how to get rid of them, altogether. But you're the only one who ought to hear what I've got to say, or know who I am."

Peter stared at him for a long, blank-faced moment. Then he turned to the two men, who were lifting the door back into place in its opening.

"On second thought, wait down the hall," he said. "That's an order."

He turned back and smiled at Shane. It was a smile of pure relief.

"It's good to have you with us," he said. "You don't know how good it is."

EDITOR'S INTRODUCTION TO:

THE LEADING EDGE

Book Reviews by
Richard E. Geis

Richard Geis, Hugo Winner, is author and publisher of the fan magazine *Science Fiction Review* (PO Box 11408, Portland, Oregon 97211). It was once called "The Alien Critic" until a somewhat obscure Chicago-based magazine called "The Critic" claimed they had exclusive right to use the word "critic" in magazine titles. While it's unlikely they could have won a lawsuit, it's very likely they had more money than Dick Geis and could have caused him quite a lot of trouble.

There are times when I think it would be a lot cheaper if the United States simply subsidized lawyers directly; it might save no end of mischief. There is another alternative: the Constitution of one of the tiny mountain nations of Europe states that "those black-robed ones, whose profession is to stir hatred among our people, shall be forever banned from this land on pain of instant hanging."

THE LEADING EDGE

BOOK REVIEWS

Richard E. Geis

JOB: A COMEDY OF JUSTICE by Robert A. Heinlein
Del Rey, $16.95, 1984

Yes, it's a good, enjoyable novel, with a hell of a narrative hook and a series of intrigues and intriguing questions presented to the reader as the story progresses.

I liked it. There are a few problems. . . .

But, first—what's it all about?

Alex Hergensheimer, a likeable bigot who is a well-paid fundraiser for a politically powerful fundamentalist church in an America which is not in our timeline, is on a many-stops cruise in Polynesia when he bets some fellow cruise ship passengers that he can follow a small group of natives across a long bed of red hot coals and burning ash.

Incredibly, he accomplished the feat, but faints at the finish. When he awakens a few minutes later he discovers himself to be in an alternate Earth, a slightly different time line, and further that he now has the identity of Alec Graham, a man of apparently questionable morals and possible underworld crime connections.

In addition, and to his discomfiture, a Danish shipboard maid named Margrethe is in love with him—and everyone accepts him as Graham. Further, the cruise ship is now of a different national registry and has a different name.

The men he bet with in the previous world now pay him off in this world, for they remember Alec Graham walking the bed of coals a few hours previous.

These radical, inexplicable changes have Alex/Alec mightily puzzled and anguished, especially when he, a married man (though alone on this trip) finds himself falling deeply in love with Margrethe. And when he has an ominous encounter with two thug-like agents who are after the one million dollars in cash he had discovered in one of Alec Graham's suitcases.

Alex/Alec succumbs to his love, and one night at sea while he and Margrethe are making love the cruise ship strikes an iceberg (yes, an iceberg in the South Pacific!) and he and Margrethe are washed out of the ship, naked, into yet another alternate Earth.

They survive on a raft, are picked up by a Mexican seaplane (and Alex had never seen an airplane before—in his original world dirigibles were the air-travel vehicles and church/religious strictures on science had prevented the development of heavier-than-air craft) and taken to nearby Mazatlan.

No sooner do he and Margrethe—more deeply in love than ever—manage to cope with this radical shift in culture and technology and begin to accumulate some money for a journey to his home in the United States, than another violent Shift occurs.

These world changes occur in the blink of an eye, and usually when he and she are asleep.

Doggedly, resolutely, Alex/Alec never wavers in his faith in God nor in his love for Margrethe, though he does have some bad moments, especially when remembering his shrewish wife and his marriage vows, and also in regard to the terrible injustices and suffering he sees around him as he and Margrethe pass from one alternate Earth to another. He cannot help but ask himself what in hell is going on? What kind of game is being played with him? What forces are responsible? Is God testing him as Job was tested? Is Satan the manipulator? Or is his feeling that all these world-shifts are aimed at him and Margrethe only paranoia and solipsism?

Believe me, the reader is wondering, too. Heinlein grips the reader with an iron hand—around the neck. You can't stop reading.

Finally, after how many—a dozen?—jolting shifts to different worlds and cultures, Alec (he now has accepted this identity, since Margrethe *insists* he is Alec Graham) concludes that all these disasters and tests of his faith and character are a prelude to Judgement Day, and he begins telling friends that the end of the world is nigh.

And, by God, it is! The Last Trumpet sounds and the destruction of the world is total.

Incredibly to Alec, he is sorted out after death and passed on to Heaven . . . and he cannot find Margrethe!

Here we enter into a kind of rigorous science fantasy, for Heinlein's Heaven (and later, Hell) seem illogical in many ways . . . bound by difficult logistics and mean-minded angels and assistants coping with billions of souls suddenly thrust upon them by an apparently capricious God . . . with computers on the one hand and slow-moving mechanical transport on the other, a class system in place and restaurants available for enjoyment of food and sociability if so desired.

To his amazement, Alec is designated a saint and given special privileges. But he still cannot find Margrethe, whom he loves beyond life, beyond sainthood itself. Has she been sent to Hell? Is she in Limbo?

Desperately, against all advice, he makes the endless fall into Hell and is surprised to discover that Hell isn't all that bad! And Satan is sympathetic and helpful in his search for Margrethe.

As a matter of fact, the final, vast cosmology revealed to Alec by Satan is probably going to jolt religionists to their cores and make non-believers smile.

In the sense that the afterlife described by Heinlein and the landscapes of Heaven and Hell and the still greater reality beyond are rational and coherent and consistent, this novel is science fiction. But it's old hat.

God is revealed to be less than nice. Satan, God's brother, is competent, of good will, good judgement, good intentions, a fair entity. God and Satan are in competition to run our part of this multileveled universe, and plainly Satan if in control would do a better job than God has done.

But God and Satan are lesser gods in this revealed greater hierarchy, and it turns out that the top Creator is rather pissed off at God for mismanagement, capriciousness, and malicious injustice.

The novel does have a happy ending—at least for Alec and Margrethe. Nothing is said of the billions of people killed when God ordered the Last Trump sounded.

There is a curious old-fashioned quality to this novel, a kind of nostalgia permeates it, a strong feel of Heinlein yearning for a long-gone America. The world of his youth, perhaps, of old-fashioned virtues rewarded.

I did not like the pure, ever-present, gooey-sweet love that exists between Alec and Margrethe, the always-rational conversation. When they disagree they disagree calmly, logically, maturely.

Other characters exhibit emotional problems, tantrums, flaws. Never Alec. Never Margrethe. Heinlein's heroes and heroines—in his past few novels, at least—are always sweetly reasonable and superior.

I resent that. It isn't true to life. It's impossible characterization.

And then there are the odd inserts of first-person present-tense narrative which appear in the usual first-person past-tense storytelling. I wonder if Heinlein was aware of them?

In any event this latest Robert A. Heinlein theology-involved novel effectively destroys Christian religion for anyone who has any niggling doubts about the fundamentals of his beliefs before reading *Job—A Comedy of Justice*. Simply using the old copout, "God works in mysterious ways," will not be an effective counter to what Heinlein says and shows in this book. Heinlein displays a thorough knowledge of the Bible, and in the process of having God test Alec's faith, destroys everyone else's.

Science fiction, as I have said many times before, is a very subversive literature, dangerous to preconceptions. Read it at your own risk.

GREEN EYES by Lucius Shepard
Ace Special, $2.95, 1984

A secret government research project has found that a special bacteria found in graveyard earth, when permitted to grow in a newly-dead corpse, reanimates the corpse to a new life.

It is a short-lived life, however, and there are complications: the corpses do not awaken with the same persona or memories from before they died. They "emerge" as extraordinarily gifted scientists, writers . . . genuinely new people.

But the swiftly spreading, multiplying bacteria which gives them life increases in their brains so quickly that it eventually kills them again for lack of control or natural bodily enemies.

The formerly dead develop a strange, frightening green glow in their eyes as the unrestrained bacterial growth continues, and they are imbued with madness and a sad, last-minute lust for sex.

There are normal humans in the project who act as counselors, friends . . . who are employed to develop a close personal relationship with these brilliant "zombies" and help them adjust to their weird new life.

There are also "slow-burners"—zombies who last far longer than the usual run of reanimated corpses, and who use their extended time to seek solutions to their problem, to seek longer, stabilized life for themselves by limiting the extraordinary bacteria which rages in their brains.

This fine novel is primarily about one such slow-burning zombie, Donnell Harrison, who had been an alcoholic drifter in his former life, and who now is a poet, a faith healer, a seeker for answers in a fantastic "other" world in another dimension, alternate Earth, in his altered brain ... he isn't sure.

He and his personal therapist, a girl named Jocunda Verret, develop a kind of love, and with the help of other brilliant scientist zombies he and she and one other zombie escape the isolated government project. They evade capture while they make their way into Louisiana Cajun country to a shanty in the swamps where they live and where Harrison discovers he can cure diseases in normal humans. He has subtle psi powers. His spreading fame attracts an immensely powerful, wealthy, genetically-haunted woman whose old, warped mansion is filled with her twisted retinue and strange hangers-on.

This woman can provide Harrison with the three tons of cast copper he needs as a focal point (shaped in a giant replica of a voodoo symbol) for a critical experiment in the other-world landscape he has discovered in his altered, psi-powered mind.

The strength and beauty of this novel springs from its realistic, sensual writing. Detail is layered like an endless cake, like a series of dots which are eventually perceived as a picture. Thus Shepard is able to make real inherently fantastic situations. His "zombies" are solid and distinct persons. Shepard forces the reader to accept anything by showing it in utterly believable, colorful, vivid detail. His phrasing hits like an elegant sledgehammer.

And in *Green Eyes* the reader is never sure what the next page will bring. There are surprises, shocks, revelations ... There are beautifully written descriptions, touches of direct and indirect characterization, acute dialog which tells more than expected ... *Green Eyes* is a novel to experience on many levels.

STAR REBEL by F.M. Busby
Bantam, $2.50, 1984

At thirteen years of age, Bran Tregare is sent by his embattled family (the Hulzein clan) to the very brutal Earth empire space academy known as the Slaughterhouse. It was supposed to be a brief hiding place for him until his elders managed to survive a life-and-death power struggle with their arch rival, United Energy and Transport, which controls the government.

Bran Tregare is his assumed name. And the Slaughterhouse is aptly named, as regular "weeding-out" no-holds-barred fighting matches are forced upon selected cadets. Vicious hazing, ambushes, etc. further diminish the ranks until surviving seniors are finally given space training where sadistic ship captains have life-and-death power over the trainees . . . and use it.

Bran is changed, toughened, hardened by these experiences, and develops into a superior space pilot and leader. And he is now secretly a rebel, only waiting for the right moment to join the whispered-about rebels somewhere in deep space.

That moment comes and Bran and his like-minded crewmates take over an armed Earth military spaceship and become renegades, mutineers.

In the following months Bran and his ship survive encounters with empire ships and empire-controlled colonies, and by alliances with other rebel ships and conquest of empire ships he becomes a force in space and conceives a plan to eventually overthrow the empire.

He has become, through the years, selectively ruthless, a man with a terrible goal, a man with enemies he has sworn to kill. He is twenty years old now, and as the novel ends he is the empire's most dangerous enemy.

There are sequels to follow, obviously, and they should be as good or better than this opening novel in this saga. Busby writes well, and there are many gripping fighting, near-death, space battle scenes. Tensions mount to riveting intensity as the book progresses.

BLANK SLATE by Mark J. McGarry
Signet, $2.95, 1984

This is near-perfect hardcore science fiction from a young writer who has the tools and style and talent to be a bestselling sf writer for the rest of his life.

This is taut, exquisitely detailed, utterly convincing future secret agent intrigue involving an alien invasion of Earth via instantaneous-travel portals, multiple identity changes, lost colonies, mixed loyalties, murder, double-crosses, a nearly total authoritarian all-Earth government, a cunning secret society, the likelihood of another attempt at taking Earth by the aliens, horrendous human crimes involving the mass murder of millions of the poor and under-privileged . . .

Mark McGarry writes about the weary, ambiguous life of Kearin Seacord, who is used again and again by a future security officer as an agent, action which requires radical plastic surgery and identity changes, in a complicated game of manipulation and sleight of hand with other major elements of this paranoid, computerized government.

Finally rebelling, Seacord unravels the secrets and motivations which have used him as a pawn and is forced to make decisions which affect mankind's fate.

What most impresses about this novel is the fine characterization and the detailed realism of this oppressive future culture and technology. It all tracks, and the people who inhabit it are convincing, shaped by this warped Earth of massive, elitist citadels and outcast masses who live in the ruins of past, dead cities.

McGarry is a fine writer who is willing to put enormous skill and time and effort into his characters and their lives. He has a superb sense of storytelling, in knowing what to reveal when, and how.

I suspect there will be at least one following novel using Kearin Seacord and this intriguing, depressing future Earth (and isolated colonies); the aliens are coming again and he must somehow find a way to stop them or defeat them, while at the same time covering his back from inter-governmental power struggles, plots, betrayals.

I'm looking forward to those adventures.